The Yellow Diamond

Also by Andrew Martin

Bilton
The Bobby Dazzlers

The Jim Stringer novels:

The Necropolis Railway
The Blackpool Highflyer
The Lost Luggage Porter
Murder at Deviation Junction
Death on a Branch Line
The Last Train to Scarborough
The Somme Stations
The Baghdad Railway Club
Night Train to Jamalpur

The Yellow Diamond

Andrew Martin

FABER & FABER

First published in 2015
by Faber & Faber Ltd
Bloomsbury House
74-77 Great Russell Street
London WC1B 3DA

Typeset by Faber & Faber Ltd
Printed and bound by CPI Group (UK) Ltd, Croydon, CR0 4YY

A CIP record for this book
is available from the British Library

ISBN 978-0-571-28820-5

2 4 6 8 10 9 7 5 3 1

John-Paul had begun to think he could actually *live* in the Coburg Bar of the Connaught Hotel. His friends would be the doorman who gave him an umbrella when he went outside in the rain to smoke, the man in the gents who handed out the linen towels, and the barman who provided the glasses of twenty-five-year Chivas Regal. It would be a male-only set-up. John-Paul had had enough of women for the time being.

From his leather seat by the fireplace, the Coburg was looking so deeply golden: Christmassy, he decided – and that would intensify over the next three months, as actual Christmas approached, not that John-Paul could risk thinking that far ahead. Unfortunately, there was really no excuse to stay, since he had downed the fifth Regal, the bill had come and he had laid out the cash on the silver plate. He checked his phone: nothing from any of the important people. Not that he *wanted* to hear from the important people. He stood, and met his own reflection in the mysterious antique mirror above the fireplace. He saw a distant, handsome – almost pretty – twenty-eight-year-old man in a coat with a velvet collar. A *weak* man, he thought, so he was glad of the mirror's cloudiness.

He looked down at the notes on the table. He added another twenty to the pile, by way of boosting the tip. John-Paul was cash-rich at the moment, having realised a number of assets, and he reasoned that by acts of generosity he might, according to some karmic system, alter his likely fate.

Outside in the rain, his friend the doorman proffered an umbrella. Without a word the doorman made clear that whatever John-Paul planned to do – smoke another cigarette, request a taxi, or just stand watching the silvery haze the rain made above the fountain in Carlos Place – would be fine by him. The fountain was modernistic, a type of infinity pool. It looked always on the brink of overflowing, but it never could overflow, as was being proved in the heavy rain of this Friday evening.

Two minutes later, John-Paul was in a moving taxi, with the driver looking quizzically at him in the rear-view. He was saying, 'Any idea where you want to go, pal?'

They were in Grosvenor Square. You more or less *had* to go into Grosvenor Square from Carlos Place, and for all John-Paul knew they might have driven around it three times, the driver adopting a holding pattern while waiting for his passenger to speak.

'So sorry,' John-Paul said, 'Hampstead please.'

He had been absorbed in the disasters besetting him. Broadly speaking they were either women-related or money-related, although a couple might prove to be both. He sometimes felt that his life might be under threat as a result of recent events. Certainly his freedom was threatened, and when the driver had spoken, John-Paul had been thinking about prison.

Exactly one week ago, on Friday 19 September, he had reported himself for insider dealing, which compliance officer Bennett, at Rolling River Capital, had specifically ordered him not to do. John-Paul had left a message on the Market Abuse Hotline of the Financial Conduct Authority.

A man with the horribly businesslike name of Ross had called him straight back, which John-Paul had not bargained for, and which had unnerved him, but he held firm to his intention of confessing, offering Ross the top-line details of the trade in question. Ross had then suggested he come in for an interview, and the date for that was set for the coming Tuesday.

John-Paul looked out of the window. Already, they were approaching Camden. There were more English people in Camden than in Mayfair. Of late, the women in John-Paul's life had been foreign, one of them especially so. He had considered himself a forward-thinking, cosmopolitan person, yet he had been defeated by this foreignness, couldn't bridge the gap . . .

'Anywhere specifically in Hampstead?' asked the driver.

'East Heath Road please,' said John-Paul. 'Do you know it?'

The driver, it seemed, would not deign to answer such a question. 'Top or bottom end?' he said.

'Top end, please.'

The disastrous trade had originated in the Coburg, which made John-Paul think his affection for the place might be misplaced. He'd gone there with Jack Hayward, so that Hayward could boast about how he'd shown a rough cut of his low-budget horror film at some American film festival, on the strength of which he had secured not only an American distribution deal but also a substantial cash advance. Apparently, most film producers have to beg distributors for a deal, but this one was paying for the privilege. Hayward stressed that there could be no greater endorsement for a film at such an early stage.

Hayward had taken out his laptop and forwarded to

3

John-Paul an online screener. To watch this, he would need a password. John-Paul had feebly said, 'I can never remember passwords,' because he knew what was coming, and he'd thought even then that he ought not to be doing business with a garrulous old friend from university like Jack.

Hayward was from a theatrical family, in every sense of the word. At Cambridge, he had been known as Jack Wayward. He would sing opera while punting, or while sitting alone on the top deck of a bus for that matter. But the password was the name of the film and John-Paul could remember that: *The Masters*. It concerned a chess game between two Grandmasters who were also astronomically rich, and real people corresponded to their pieces. For instance, when White took Black's bishop, a churchgoer nominated by the millionaire playing as White was killed by a team of assassins retained jointly by the two players. As the endgame approached, you were meant to have sympathy for the two women designated as queens, which John-Paul, when he finally watched the entire film, did not. (He'd lost interest during the interminable killing of all the pawns.) But this was all irrelevant because Hayward had talked John-Paul into buying a hundred thousand shares in Wayward Films before he'd seen a minute of *The Masters*.

They were in Hampstead now. All the big houses seemed to be hiding behind the big trees, and all the people hiding inside the houses. The world was retreating from John-Paul.

And yet the car behind was too *close*. A BMW 4 Series, as far as John-Paul could tell, in the dark and the rain. He tried to ignore it in favour of a thought experiment he'd conducted many times in recent days.

John-Paul set before himself an imaginary barrister. Had

he known that Wayward Films was a publicly quoted company, listed on the Alternative Investment Market? Yes. Had he known that the distribution deal was the 'game changer' for the company? That was self-evidently the case. Had he known the deal had not yet been publicly announced? At this, he would beg the court's indulgence: 'I am trying my best to recollect, but on that point I'm a little hazy.' He did feel that deniability was available to him here, whereas compliance officer Bennett had urged him to deny something more fundamental, namely the entire meeting with Hayward at the Connaught. Having learnt that John-Paul had paid for the drinks in cash, Bennett had informed him point-blank that the meeting had not occurred. That's what Bennett sought in place of morality: deniability. Why else were traders advised to use disposable mobiles when seeking out 'intelligence'? But John-Paul had ignored Bennett and contacted the FCA – possibly too late. If he'd called as soon as the news of the distribution deal had come through on the RNS news feed, he would have a stronger case. But he had waited another week after that.

The 4 Series was still close behind. John-Paul would have been reassured to see women and children in there, but it wasn't that kind of car, and two men in suits sat on the front seats. They came and went behind the swishing of the wipers and tinted glass. Neither was compliance officer Bennett, and he had not seen either man at Rolling River. John-Paul noticed that the taxi driver was looking at him in the rear-view. In glancing that way, John-Paul had caught sight of his own reflection.

He looked haggard. But what would he look like after seven years in prison? That was the maximum sentence for insider trading, and the fines could run into millions. But surely it wouldn't come to that. He had turned himself in. Ross of the FCA would protect him as long as he came clean. But there would be trouble either way for Rolling River . . . withdrawal of accreditations if not prosecutions.

'Do you think that car behind is following us?' John-Paul asked the taxi driver.

'It's following us,' he said. 'But that doesn't mean it's *tailing* us.'

The taxi driver spoke like a man who had a lot of experience of being both followed and tailed; and he was now looking at John-Paul with curiosity.

On graduating, John-Paul had gone into private equity, which is where he should have stayed. For a while in that job, he had felt like what is commonly called a 'people person', building bridges between the partners of Relay Management and one firm in particular they'd acquired: a confectioners' in Manchester. He had been the desk officer in London, fielding the monitoring reports from Manchester, where the targets were not being hit. He'd asked to be sent north, and he'd clicked with everyone up there, turned the whole takeover around. He'd brought the last members of the old chocolate-making dynasty – two antiquated brothers called Drummond – on side, making them non-executive directors, and he had often strolled with them in the beautifully laid-out grounds of their factory, which had been built for the benefit of the workers. There were rather fewer of those workers by the time Relay had sold up. But the gardens, the business and the Drummond name had been saved, with most of the production kept in the UK . . . and a £200,000 'carry' for John-Paul.

He looked behind: BMW still there.

Having made a lot of money, John-Paul naturally wanted to make even more money, which could be done in a hedge fund, hence the role as analyst at Rolling River Capital. It was the standard progression. Up or out. But – and let nobody say he was in denial about *this* – John-Paul wasn't suited to the work. He was alone with a trading screen. His people skills were not brought into play, and his trades lacked flare. He heard himself piping up in the Friday brainstorms: 'Inflation's coming back; we should go long on gilts.' He could see Eugene Crawford, the Texan senior partner, looking at him with contempt, hands behind the back of his head, cowboy-booted feet up on his desk. Once, when Crawford had been walking past John-Paul's desk with an unlit cigar in his mouth, he'd drawled out, 'Mornin',' and John-Paul had realised only belatedly that he was being addressed. 'Don't go glazed on me, boy,' Crawford had said, without taking the cigar out of his mouth. If anyone was to blame for the fatal trade with Hayward, it was Eugene Crawford. John-Paul had been trying to impress him by going long on an obscure piece of art.

The taxi driver half-turned towards John-Paul: 'Are you a marked man, or something?' One of the two BMW men was now speaking into a phone. They were on Rosslyn Hill.

Were the BMW men police? Fraud squad? They would be in plain clothes, and possibly in a BMW. But it was surely too late in the day for the police, and too early in the *case*. He hadn't yet told his story to Ross of the FCA.

'Want me to lose it?' said the driver.

John-Paul looked behind. 'You could try,' he said, and he was nearly thrown off the seat as the taxi swerved right.

They were now going fast along Downshire Hill – as was the BMW.

'Interesting,' said the taxi driver.

John-Paul thought: I have become a target. Last night someone had 'keyed' the Audi, scratched a line right down the flank.

They stopped at the junction with East Heath Road. The BMW pulled up behind.

'Top end . . . so left?' asked the driver.

John-Paul nodded into the rear-view.

The driver turned left, and the BMW turned right.

'Panic over,' said the driver.

So there had been nothing in it after all, the apparent pursuit a function of his paranoia. John-Paul was beginning to agree with some recent suggestions that he might need therapy. Certainly he was depressed, and he should go to his doctor.

John-Paul asked the driver to stop on the junction of East Heath Road and Well Walk.

'Good luck, mate,' the driver said, immediately before departing.

John-Paul turned into Well Walk, and there was the Audi, with the scratch along the flank . . . but at least no new scratch on the other flank. It could easily have been a random attack. A lot of people would be jealous of any car parked on Well Walk. The houses were pretty Georgian villas set back from the road by long, dreamy gardens. John-Paul's aim had been to upgrade from his flat into one of these.

Well Walk was deserted. It always seemed to be deserted. John-Paul lit a cigarette, and began walking back towards East Heath Road, and East Heath Mansions, which comprised three blocks. John-Paul's was called Fitzroy. The front door faced onto East Heath Street, while the back door overlooked the garden and the Heath. John-Paul's flat was on the ground floor at the back, so he would usually skirt around the building on the muddy track that cut through nettles and brambles. He would unlock the back gate, which was set into a brick arch of the wall bounding the garden; then he would unlock the back door of Fitzroy. He waited on the road for any sign of the returning BMW. He stood in the light spilling from the front door of the block, because he wanted to be *in* the light if it did come back. But the BMW had gone for good, so he turned towards the darkness of the Heath.

The Heath smelt of mouldering leaves and wood smoke. The rain clattered noisily on the treetops. The entrance to the block was by key card, so John-Paul threw down his cigarette, and took out his wallet. You had to watch out for dog dirt on this track, especially if you were walking over it in brand-new Church's loafers. Looking up, he saw a figure in the gloom by the gate – a figure like a small concierge, somehow caped. But the back gate was not supposed to be attended; there wasn't even a porter in the block. The figure approached John-Paul too rapidly; and then something impossible happened to his eye.

2

The detective who took down Hayley's statement about what she had seen in St James's Park on Thursday 4 December had of course given his name when he arrived at her flat. He'd also given it *before*, when he'd called to say that a female liaison officer could be present if Hayley liked, and when he'd suggested that she might feel more relaxed if the interview took place at her flat rather than in the police station at Charing Cross.

'Do you like coffee?' he'd asked.

'Yes.'

'Well you wouldn't like ours.'

He was trying to put her at her ease with humour, and sort of succeeding. She liked his voice. There he was, a detective in the Metropolitan Police, the *London* police, and yet he was northern. When he'd turned up at Hayley's flat in Maida Vale – which was actually her mother's flat – she'd quite liked the look of him too. But when they'd sat down in the kitchen, and he'd passed over to her the sheet of paper that said if she lied in her statement she was liable to seven years' imprisonment . . . well, then his name had gone clean out of her head.

Hayley had no intention of telling any lies. Her main anxiety was that she might tell an untruth accidentally, or break down in tears at the recollection of what she'd seen in St James's Park. Another anxiety was her mother. Hayley had declined the liaison officer, and so her mother had wanted to 'sit in' – 'just in case you get upset, dear.' She'd bought two boxes of tissues and put them on the kitchen table, all ready for Hayley to get upset. When her mother was out of the room for a minute, brewing the expensive coffee she'd bought specially, Hayley had said to the detective, 'Do you mind if my mother sits in?' He hesitated, so she added, 'It's her flat, you see?'

That was a signal from Hayley to the detective. She was telling him she didn't *want* her mother to sit in, but had no choice about asking.

'That's . . . fine,' he said, in a way that told Hayley he understood. When Hayley's mother came back with the coffee, the detective said, 'Thank you, Mrs Buckingham,' and Hayley's mother said, 'Please, it's Patricia,' which was ominous, Hayley thought.

At first, the detective didn't write down what Hayley said, but she knew he was listening closely, as the bright Maida Vale morning gave way to the horrible scene in her memory . . .

'Well, it was early evening,' she said, 'and just getting dark. I was with Christophe. He's my . . . Well, we were sort of on a date.'

'Your second date with him, wasn't it, dear?' her mother put in.

'Yes,' said Hayley, and she looked at the detective. 'We both work in Mayfair, so St James's Park seemed like a good place for a walk before dinner.'

The detective said, 'Do you know what time you entered the park?' and she was glad he'd asked that, because she was able to say, 'It was exactly five-fifty.'

Christophe had taken a call on his mobile just then, and

she remembered looking at her own phone to check the time when that happened . . . because she'd been pissed off. But of course she didn't say that to the detective.

'*Eh, ça va?*' Christophe had said into the phone. He received, and made, a lot of calls. At the start of this one, he had put his hand over the phone to tell Hayley he wouldn't be long, but then he'd sat down on a bench by the ornamental pond to continue talking, so she'd had to sit down next to him, feeling spare. He was saying into the phone, 'So we double-check, yeah?' because he would sometimes slip into English. Hayley believed the conversation was to do with his work.

'Christophe's French, obviously,' Hayley's mother said. 'Is that relevant? He's a designer for video games. He does the backgrounds. He specialises in weather, doesn't he, dear?'

The detective ran his hand through his hair. He was greying. He looked at Hayley's mother, and while moving his eyes in that direction, he glanced at Hayley, who gave him the signal again.

'Mrs Buckingham,' he said, 'I must insist that you remain absolutely silent throughout this whole process, even when your daughter is not speaking.'

Hayley's mother nodded.

'I should tell you, Mrs Buckingham,' the detective continued, 'that could easily take two or three hours.'

Hayley's mother nodded again. But a moment later, she said, 'Perhaps it'd be best if I sit in the other room.'

When she'd left, the detective gave Hayley a look – a nice little twinkle – that said, 'Well, that's got rid of *her*.' It was the 'absolutely' that had done it; and he hadn't called her Patricia. Of course, there'd be a row about it later.

Hayley carried on, trying to edit her emotions. On another bench to the right there'd been a woman with a baby on her knee, and she was talking into *her* phone. She was foreign in some way. 'I think you have enough black thing darling,' she'd said. *'Thing'*, not *'things'*. Must have been speaking about clothes. Then a very tall man had walked past, with a terrier that was pulling on its lead, so the tall man kept yanking on the lead and shouting, 'Heel, Baxter, heel!' in an American accent. 'Give the poor animal a break,' Hayley had thought. Then, because she was angry at Christophe, she'd tried to think of someone *she* might call or text. In the end, she'd texted her boss, Sue, because the embargo date had been left off the press release about 67 Dover Street coming onto the market. That didn't really matter. Journalists always ignored embargo dates, but sending the text had been something to do.

She needn't have bothered because Christophe was still rabbiting on in French. Hayley tried her best not to mind. She always tried to see something good in everyone, and she had decided that the good thing in Christophe was that he did not look down on her for being a property PR, although of course it might simply be that he hadn't taken on board what she did for a living, being so obsessed with himself.

It was then that she'd realised she was being watched by a really gigantic bird sitting on the parapet of the ornamental bridge. He (. . . had to be a 'he', being so grotesque) had looked like an angel gone wrong, and she believed she had known then that something terrible was going to happen.

She gave the detective a heavily edited version of all that, but she did mention the bird, a pelican – and immediately felt a fool for doing so.

'I'm sorry,' she said. 'The bird's irrelevant.'

'No,' said the detective. 'I'm glad you mentioned it.'

'Why?'

'You'll see,' he said, smiling.

She had turned towards the bench to the right again to see a new person – a man – in place of the foreign woman. 'Now he's *definitely* English,' she had thought, and he didn't have a mobile phone either. He wore half-moon reading glasses and he was unfolding the *Financial Times*. She watched him as he started to read with much smoothing-out of the paper. Probably a bit OCD. There was a beautiful lamp near the bench. It had been illuminated – together with the other antique gas lanterns in the park – shortly be-forehand. It was possible the man had selected the bench because of the gas lantern.

The detective was writing quickly now, which pleased her.

After a few seconds, the man on the bench lowered the paper and took out a packet of cigarettes: a very unusual packet, brownish. He took out a cigarette and tapped the end of it on the packet. You saw people do that in old films. He was a handsome older man with swept-back grey hair, pinstriped suit . . . old school. Even though he might have been sixty, he wore black boots with elasticated sides. She liked his boots, and obviously so did he because he kept glancing down at them when he was supposed to be read-ing. So either the boots were new, or he was a vain article, or both. Then he'd apparently noticed a spot of dirt on one of them, and he'd taken out a handkerchief, a good one, shaken it, and rubbed at the spot of dirt on the toe of his boot. He then lit his cigarette and carried on reading, and she carried on watching him. Under the jacket he wore a sort of quilted waistcoat. Huskies she thought those things were called. Under that, she could see a light-blue shirt and a dark-blue tie. She had been thinking that her father ought to dress like that, instead of trying to look half his age with that leather jacket.

At this point, Hayley had pulled out the comb that held her hair. This had been for the benefit of Christophe. It was a test. The previous time she'd done this in his presence – the day before, on South Audley Street, Mayfair – he had stopped her with a hand on her shoulder and briefly kissed her. She had quite liked that: as if he were arresting her. But this time, he simply carried on his conversation. He had said into the phone, '*Comme ci, comme ça,*' and she recalled thinking that in a minute he'd probably be saying 'Ooh la la.'

It was exactly then that she had heard the sound of something . . . not *loud* but like something being unleashed; something almost unstoppable. But it *had* been stopped – by the man on the bench, who was now lying on the pathway. Everyone in the park was running away and screaming – and, again, it was not from the loudness so much as the *force* of the sound. Never mind a spot of dirt on the man's boots; now his suit would be completely ruined, she'd thought, ridiculously. In the half-light of the park, she had the idea that the man's shadow was creeping from his body and making a getaway, but that was simply the blood pouring out of his head, and he had twice moved his arm towards his head, like a sleeper in the middle of a bad dream. Christophe was swearing loudly over and over again, and all the birds were flying up from the lake. But the pelican remained on the bridge, still staring at her.

'The pelican,' said the detective, as if he had read her mind (because she hadn't mentioned the bird this time around). 'It was on the parapet of the bridge, and so facing the man on the bench?'

'Yes,' said Hayley, wondering where on earth this could be going.

'So the bird would have seen what was behind the man on the bench immediately before he was shot?'

'I suppose so, yes.'

'Then . . . what would it have seen?'

She tried to remember what was behind the bench. She mentioned a flower bed . . . actually more like a little island of quite high bushes.

'Anybody in that vicinity at all?' asked the detective.

She shook her head. 'I couldn't tell,' and she was close to tears now.

A little while later, when the detective was packing up, Hayley asked him, stupidly, 'Where are you going now?'

'I'm off to interview that pelican,' he said. He looked at her, and only when she laughed did he laugh himself. She liked that, and his name came back to her: Reynolds. Detective Inspector Blake Reynolds, and the man who'd been shot was a colleague, but apparently not exactly a friend, of his. His name was Quinn: Detective Superintendent George Quinn.

Reynolds' next appointment was actually with a man named Chamberlain, a solicitor who lived in the privileged eighteenth-century residential complex called Argrove. He met Reynolds by the front door. It was three o'clock on the afternoon of Monday 8 December and the sky was already darkening over Mayfair.

Chamberlain had led Reynolds down a long corridor with very solid-looking doors along one side. They appeared to be aiming towards a Christmas tree decorated with small blue lights.

'You must never say *The* Argrove,' Chamberlain had warned Reynolds, and Reynolds had promised not to. 'Four Prime Ministers have lived here,' said Chamberlain and he had proceeded to name them. 'Also many famous writers . . .'

. . . and Detective Superintendent George Quinn, in whose elegant, small bedroom they now stood.

The room was almost higher than it was wide, like a booth, an effect increased by the vertical stripes of the wallpaper, which was red and gold, like Christmas wrapping. The bed was a three-quarter bed, expensive-looking, with a head that curved away from the pillows – *scrolled* might be the word, Reynolds thought. The fireplace was a working fireplace, with wood and coal waiting to burn. A very easy room to go to sleep in, thought Reynolds, especially if you'd been at the whisky that stood on a silver tray on the pedestal table next to the slumped but stylish green couch. On this tray there were also two unopened packets of old-fashioned fags: Capstan ('Full Strength', they were marked, just to reassure the purchaser) and a silver tankard engraved 'Old Myrmidons Society'.

Reynolds held his detective's notebook. With pen poised, he asked, 'Do you know what the Old Myrmidons are, Mr Chamberlain?'

'It was his college dining society. He was at Merton, I was at Christ Church. They're colleges at Oxford University,' Chamberlain added for good measure.

There was a carriage clock on the mantelpiece that looked the genuine article – made in the actual days of carriages – with some invitations propped behind it. People called things like Mr and Mrs Henry Sykes would be 'at home' on a certain day. There was a letter informing Quinn that he was about to be invited to drinks on Thursday 11 December at the London Library in St James's Square. Keep the date free, sort of thing. It was from 'The Directors of the Society of Plyushkin's Garden'. Not Pushkin but *Plyushkin*. There was no sign of the actual invitation.

Chamberlain was telling Reynolds about how he'd met Quinn at some sherry party in Oxford back in 1973. They'd both been reading law, and everyone assumed Quinn had a great future as a barrister. Chamberlain himself had become a solicitor, but Quinn had amazed everyone by going into the police – everyone, that is, who had not heard of a certain inspirational uncle of Quinn's who'd been a great hero of the colonial police in India. Later, Chamberlain had inherited leaseholds on two flats in Argrove, and he'd sublet this one to Quinn.

'Any idea about the Society of Plyushkin's Garden?'

Reynolds asked Chamberlain, who frowned.

'Sounds like some secret society out of John Buchan,' he said, 'an old-fashioned adventure story, you know.'

Reynolds considered telling Chamberlain that he had not only seen the film of *The Thirty-Nine Steps*, he had also read the book. He looked again at the letter. Surely, Plyushkin's Gardeners couldn't be *very* secret if they were proposing a drinks party? There was also a small silver sports car on the mantelpiece, and a fancy glass ashtray.

Chamberlain said, 'You're a northerner, aren't you? Like Quinn?' by which he meant 'not at all like Quinn'. Quinn had grown up on a country estate near York; Reynolds had grown up on a housing estate *in* York.

'I can't say our paths ever crossed up there.'

'Well,' said Chamberlain, 'he's a good deal older than you. His mother was the daughter of a baronet, you know.'

Reynolds did know that, although he wasn't sure what being a baronet involved, let alone being the daughter of one.

'But the title goes down the male line,' Chamberlain added sadly. He contemplated Reynolds. 'Of course, he was a colleague of yours.'

'Yes, but we never worked together directly. I knew him more by . . . reputation.'

Everyone in the Met knew Quinn by reputation.

They entered the bathroom, which was all white tiles, old-fashioned and very clean, like a small mortuary. Reynolds opened the bathroom cabinet . . . and this was why the bathroom looked empty. Everything was inside the cabinet. It was no doubt the sight of medicines and pills – together with a lot of upmarket soaps and hair products –

that prompted Chamberlain to say, 'One dares hardly ask, but what are his chances?'

When Reynolds had first called Chamberlain, introducing himself as being from the West End Murder Team, Chamberlain had said, 'But Quinn's not actually dead, is he?' as if this was something Reynolds had overlooked. Chamberlain had then asked, 'How is he?' and Reynolds had said, 'He's in a coma.' Chamberlain, to do him credit, had sounded appalled at that, and Reynolds had regretted not having couched it in gentler terms, but then a coma was a coma: it was difficult to put a positive gloss on it. However, Reynolds now did try to be a bit gentler:

'Difficult to say. According to the consultant . . .'

'But is it an *induced* coma?' Chamberlain cut in.

The coma had been induced by the bullet that had lodged in Quinn's brain. He was now under armed guard at St Michael's Hospital in Fulham. His life had been saved by the swift arrival of the air ambulance. Helicopters had changed the face of murder investigation in the past ten years. Helicopters and CCTV . . . But there'd been no CCTV in St James's Park. The bullet had been fired from a pistol of fairly small calibre: 6.35. No cartridges had been found, but the angle of entry into Quinn's head indicated the piece had been fired from a clump of bushes behind the bench on which Quinn had been reading his paper. The guy from ballistics, who had presumably evaded all gender-equality awareness training, said, 'A woman could have handled that gun.' He'd also said that some weapons training was probably required to hit such a small target as the human head from that distance; that or very good luck.

The shootist must then have mingled in with the

panicked people – mainly tourists – who'd been charging about in the half-light as Quinn lay bleeding near the ornamental pond. The clump of bushes had been behind and a little to one side, so the bullet had entered the back of Quinn's head obliquely, hence coma rather than death. The bullet remained inside Quinn's head. It was unsafe, as yet, to remove it. The prospects of a full recovery were slight.

Seeing that he would get no joy from a medical bulletin, Chamberlain asked, 'Any leads so far?'

'Lots,' said Reynolds, which was another way of saying 'None'.

Quinn was a highly successful murder detective. There were any number of bad men who wanted him dead. That was assuming the shooting was not related to the new Operational Command Unit Quinn had created.

'I suppose you can't go into detail,' said Chamberlain.

'I'm afraid not,' said Reynolds. He was looking at something in a tube that was not toothpaste. 'Geo. F. Trumper,' Reynolds read, 'Luxury Shaving Cream . . . Sandalwood'; and there was a heavy, old-fashioned safety razor, i.e. not that safe, and razorblades jumbled in a little dish. Reynolds reached into the cabinet, picked up the shaving cream and unscrewed the top. So that was what sandalwood smelt like: lemon. The whole flat, Reynolds now realised, was permeated with that smell combined with stale cigarette smoke. The combination was not unpleasant.

They walked through to the living room. A fireplace with coal and wood recently burnt, and – resting on top of the firewood basket – back numbers of the *Financial Times* plus magazines: Reynolds saw *Bonham's Magazine*, *Mayfair Resident*, *Classic Car*, *Tatler*, among others – the kind of magazines you'd get in the foyer of an upmarket cor-poration. He picked up the bundle and riffled through a magazine called *Allure*. The cover featured a Fabergé egg on a white background. It promoted watches, handbags, cars, food. Everything seemed to be taking place against the deep blue of the Mediterranean or the lighter blue of the Caribbean.

The paintings on the wall of Quinn's place showed coun-try scenes of about the same vintage as Argrove. Two men in long coats and tricorn hats appeared to be negotiating over a horse in a field. It seemed likely they were good paint-ings, but whereas Reynolds rather prided himself on being well read, he knew he was out of his depth when it came to pictorial art.

When Quinn had got tired of solving murders, he'd moved into the Arts and Antiques Squad for a while. With his track record he'd had *carte blanche* to do what he liked. He'd managed to spend a lot of time in Florence, and it was there that he'd bought a panama hat on expenses. That was a famous incident because the hat had cost about three hun-dred pounds.

Bookshelves were set into alcoves either side of the fire-place. A lot of novels, nothing too out of the way: the works of Greene, Burgess, both Amises, Hollinghurst. Mainly British writers, but also Flaubert, Fitzgerald, Nabokov and Gogol. Among the non-fiction, Reynolds noted *The Gentleman's Suit* by Hardy Amies, *The Oligarchs* by David Hoffman, *The Death of Gentlemanly Capitalism* by Philip Augar, *The Oxford Dictionary of Finance and Banking*.

There was one room left . . . and it was all clothes: suits mainly, on basic metal racks, which somehow suggested that the suits were more important than the decor of the flat.

'He was – is – very particular about clothes,' said Chamberlain, 'and he's not shy about criticising the dress of others. He had a field day with me, as you can imagine.' This was Chamberlain fishing for compliments, since he appeared perfectly well dressed to Reynolds. 'He once told me off for wearing a jumper over my shoulders. I said, "Well, it might turn cold, you never know," and he said, "Make a decision now about whether it's going to turn cold or not." He thought it inelegant to make a contingency arrangement, you see. By the same token he always told me not to keep my glasses on a cord round my neck.'

Sure enough, Chamberlain did not keep his glasses on a cord around his neck. They were on his nose. Reynolds thought of the suit he himself was currently wearing. He'd bought it in a sale at Marks & Spencer. It was 'wool-rich' according to the label, but he doubted that would cut much ice with Quinn. He had spoken to Quinn twice, and the first time had been clothes-related. Quinn had come up to him in an incident room, and told him his coat, which was over the back of his chair, was touching the floor, and the floor was dusty. Reynolds had thanked him, and Quinn had walked off. His red socks had been particularly noticeable. Reynolds had been on the North London Murder Team at that point, and one of his colleagues had said, 'That guy cracks me up,' but nobody had actually laughed because Quinn was the doyen of the murder teams. That was why he had the pick of the special ops command units when he decided on a change of scene.

The second time Reynolds had spoken to him was a couple of months later. Quinn had come up to Reynolds and congratulated him on nicking 'the last-orders killer', Donnie Gray. Reynolds had been pleased with the thought processes that had led him to Donnie Gray, and what had been so thrilling about the exchange was that Quinn himself was known for his feats of pure deduction. He would post top-of-the-head comments on the HOLMES files of murder cases he had nothing to do with – and that would be the breakthrough, as team members would have to admit.

Quinn had to be good. Not only was he not a Freemason, he had always – even when starting out in the dark days of the late seventies – been more or less openly gay, or bisexual. And he was always a loner, whereas the Met motto at any hint of a joint investigation was 'Let's form a squad': that way alliances would be built and backs covered. Quinn was his own squad. Yet he'd always been a 'flier', on the fast track. Reynolds believed that Quinn had been 'acting down' as a Detective Super in order to keep free of admin. On paper he was a Detective Chief Super.

Reynolds knew that forensics had been in and taken the laptop, and that Reynolds' own immediate boss, Detective Chief Inspector Richard Lilley, head of West End Murder, had been with them. Reynolds mentioned this to Chamberlain, who said, 'Oh yes, and Victoria Clifford came this morning. His secretary.'

'Right,' said Reynolds, eyeing Chamberlain.

Quinn was not *quite* a one-man squad. He had a secretary. Her name was Victoria Clifford. Nobody quite knew how he'd managed it. Even assuming that Quinn *was* formally a Detective Super . . . that ought not to have entitled him to a personal assistant. Personal assistants came in at Assistant Commissioner level, but Quinn had had Clifford from his DI days in murder. He must have been on some special committee or review of the murder teams; or been asked to write some long report; he must have done *something* that required secretarial support.

Victoria Clifford was a clever misfit like her boss. Reynolds had the feeling she'd been a secretary in Special Branch before coming to Quinn. She watched Quinn's back, kept him clear of misconduct hearings, because he was known to cut corners evidentially, and he would take risks that would get him stood down from an investigation if anyone other than Clifford knew. Quinn seldom used the Met information bureau, or the administrative staff of whatever command unit he was attached to. Also, he had no line manager. He answered directly to his OCU commander, who in recent years was Deputy Assistant Commissioner Croft, who was number two in special ops.

Reynolds had been trying to get hold of Victoria Clifford all day. He asked Chamberlain, 'What did she want, do you know?'

'She wanted a notebook of Quinn's, said it might be important for the investigation.'

'Hold on,' said Reynolds, 'do you mean another computer?'

'No, no, when I say a notebook, I mean it in the traditional sense of a book for taking notes in. A rather handsome one too. Shouldn't I have given it her? She's with the police, isn't she?'

'She *works* for the police.'

'Quite so.'

'But she's a civilian.'

Therefore not covered by the warrant that had enabled

DCI Lilley and forensics, and Reynolds himself, to be crawling all over the flat of a half-dead man.

'What colour was this notebook, Mr Cavendish?'

'A rather attractive red.'

Regarding Chamberlain, the big question in Reynolds' mind was this: *How disingenuous is he?* If the book was red then it was not Quinn's official detective's notebook, because these were black, and – Reynolds realised for the first time, looking down at his own – not at all attractive. Anyhow, DCI Lilley would have taken Quinn's official book. So Victoria Clifford had got hold of something else.

Half an hour later, they were back at the front door of Argrove – in the lodge, as it was called. A Harrods van stood in the courtyard beyond. As he shook Chamberlain's hand, Reynolds asked, 'I don't suppose you have any idea what he was investigating?'

'But surely *you* know?' Chamberlain replied. 'He must have been briefing his superiors.'

'He didn't have that many superiors. And he wasn't briefing anyone, believe me.'

'He was creating this new department, wasn't he?'

'I wouldn't say it was a department. I mean, he was the only one in it – him and Victoria Clifford.' It was the smallest OCU that Reynolds had ever heard of: two people, and one of them wasn't even a copper.

'But more officers were going to be brought in?'

'I suppose so.'

'What was it if it wasn't a department?'

'A unit. An operational command unit.'

'And it was to keep tabs on the so-called "super-rich", I believe?'

'That's it.'

'I wasn't going to mention this because . . . well, you know how Quinn could get? He could become . . . rather grandiose, speaking for rhetorical effect . . . after a few drinks.'

'What did he tell you, Mr Chamberlain?'

'Well, I'll *tell* you what he told me.'

'Please do,' said Reynolds, waiting to make a note.

' . . . for what it's worth,' said Chamberlain.

Reynolds eyed Chamberlain. He wondered whether he'd ever heard of section 5 (2) of the Criminal Law Act 1967: wasting police time, punishable by six months in prison to the best of his recollection.

Chamberlain said, 'He told me he was onto just about the biggest money crime you could imagine. That's got you thinking, I can see. Oh, and murders as well, he said. That's murders, plural.'

'But no details?' said Reynolds, because what Chamberlain had said seemed at once too much and too little to note down.

'None at all, I'm afraid.'

4

'He seems to have been fixated on Mayfair,' said Reynolds.

Five hours after leaving Quinn's flat, he had finally got hold of Victoria Clifford. They'd met up at the Yard, and she now faced him across a little table with arms determinedly folded. They were in Mayfair themselves – in the relatively scruffy part of it called Shepherd's Market. If Mayfair had a 'wrong end', this was it.

In choosing this basement Indian restaurant, Victoria Clifford had been making a point – something to do with expenses. In tacit acknowledgement that Reynolds was a small-timer in this area, she'd selected the cheapest of the many restaurants she frequented with Quinn. He knew for a fact that in the past month alone, the two had dined at some of the best restaurants in Mayfair (certainly Nobu and La Gavroche, which even Reynolds had heard of).

But even though this would be a cheap dinner, it was still *dinner* and he was paying for it, with money he wouldn't get back for a month, and that only after a tussle with his finance manager, if past experience was anything to go by. It wasn't just dinner, either. When they'd stepped out of the Yard, Clifford had looked with a sort of longing at a taxi going past, so they'd come to Mayfair in that instead of by Tube. Well, it had been raining heavily, as Reynolds would be telling his finance manager. As far as he knew it was raining still. He couldn't tell from this basement which was greenish and full of plants, like an aquarium. Reynolds' black notebook was on the table. He had made a few notes on arriving at the restaurant and Clifford had asked, 'Is it good or bad when you make a note of what I've said?' Realising that she retreated further into herself with every new note, Reynolds had closed the book.

'How do you mean, fixated?' Victoria Clifford now asked.

'He socialised here, set up his new unit here. In Down Street.'

'He wanted to investigate the High Net Worths. Where do you think he *should* he have gone? Tooting?'

A very, very few people, Reynolds believed, called Victoria Clifford 'Vicky'. She was the sort of person who made him acutely conscious of his northern accent. 'He seems to have done all his socialising here. His flat is here – in The Argrove. I mean *Argrove*. It's in Mayfair, anyhow . . .'

'I think you'll find it's on Piccadilly,' said Clifford. 'And it's not called a flat. It's a set.'

'Whatever it's called, I went there this afternoon,' said Reynolds.

'Haven't forensics cleaned it out?'

You should know, thought Reynolds, *since you went there this morning.*

'His laptop and so on,' said Reynolds.

'They won't find anything on *that*,' said Clifford.

'Well, it's gone to data recovery.'

'He could barely turn it on,' said Clifford, 'let alone hide any data on it. He hated using it. All those things popping up all the time.'

'Do you think he could delete his search history?'

'Probably,' she grudgingly agreed.

'Did he have online banking?'

'What's that got to do with anything? And no he certainly did not.'

'I've asked to see his emails and anything material.'

Reynolds had asked DCI Richard Lilley. Whether, or how soon, Lilley would comply was up in the air. Lilley was tougher than his name suggested, and he was wary of Reynolds.

'I suppose you went through all his cupboards,' Clifford said.

Reynolds was waiting to see if she would mention taking the red notebook. It appeared she would not. He said, 'There were a lot of suits.'

'At least thirty.'

'All made to measure, I suppose?'

'*Bespoke*,' she said, icily.

Reynolds picked up the menus, handed one to Clifford. He asked a question that he knew would annoy her: 'How could he afford to live in that flat?'

'He was on one of the old leases.'

Reynolds put the menu down and eyed Victoria Clifford. 'You mean sort of two florins a week?'

She was deciding her response when the waiter came up. The waiter was a nice man, and he was very sorry to hear that his good friend Detective Superintendent Quinn had been shot. 'I hope he is as well as can be expected?'

'He's in a coma,' Victoria Clifford said, looking at the menu.

'I do not like the sound of that,' said the waiter. Much to Reynolds' surprise, Victoria Clifford then introduced him to the waiter and almost touched his hand in the process: 'Ravi, this is Detective Sergeant Reynolds. He is on the team investigating the shooting.'

'Good to hear it,' said Ravi, and he turned to Reynolds: 'He was the top man for you people, wasn't he? A real Sherlock of the force.'

'He was a very special copper,' Reynolds said, while Victoria Clifford stared at him, apparently with disgust.

'I think it is one of these Mayfair millionaires who have shot him,' said Ravi, who was evidently up to speed with the new unit.

'Yes,' said Reynolds. 'So do I,' and he looked towards Victoria Clifford, who was now examining the menu. Ravi took their order. Both Reynolds and Victoria Clifford declined his offer of free poppadums, Reynolds because he didn't want to eat what was basically a giant crisp in front of Victoria Clifford. He had asked if she wanted wine, and she gave a short nod. 'I dare say I can run to a bottle of house white,' he said.

'Very gentlemanly of you.'

There were two reasons why she might be blocking him. One: she thought he thought Quinn was on the take, corrupt, and was trying to protect him. She hadn't liked the question about his banking arrangements. Two: she thought the unit would be closed down, having barely begun its operations, and she – a woman of a certain age – would be out of a job. When the wine came, Reynolds decided to probe in the first area. 'Can you tell me about the panama hat?'

'What panama hat?'

'The one he claimed three hundred pounds expenses for.'

Victoria Clifford sipped wine briefly. 'He got a lot of stick about that. But you should have seen the way he beat down the seller.'

'All the way down to three hundred quid.'

'Three hundred and *fifty*. It was *un véritable panama*: a Montecristi.'

'I thought they were cigars.'

'You're thinking of Montecristos. It was made according to the true Ecuadorian principles.'

Reynolds eyed her.

'About two thousand weaves per square inch,' Clifford continued. 'It can hold water, and if you scrunch it up into a ball, it still comes back to its original shape.'

'No wonder the finance manager put it through.'

'He *did* put it through, once the whole background was explained to that not very intelligent man. It was essential for Quinn to look like somebody who would lay out fifty thousand pounds for ten forged Picasso prints.'

That was *some* sort of excuse, Reynolds supposed. The starters arrived. Clifford said, 'You were in the Clubs Squad, weren't you? Before Murder?'

Reynolds nodded warily. This was her revenge for his questions about the hat. He wondered how much she knew of his time in the Clubs Squad.

Clifford said, '*Quinn* was in the Clubs Squad, when *he* was a DS.'

Reynolds knew that. In the early eighties, Quinn had been awarded the Queen's Medal for Gallantry for disarming a man in a club off Piccadilly.

Clifford asked, 'What was the music like in your day?'

'It was called trance.'

'Did you like it?'

'Nobody liked it. You weren't meant to like it.'

'Did you see the records in Quinn's flat?'

Reynolds shook his head.

'He loved Schubert,' she said. 'And KC and the Sunshine Band. He went to *see* KC and the Sunshine Band once.'

'In his three-piece suit?'

'Yes. He had a disco suit.'

'You mean a sort of *white* suit?'

'Of course not. Just a good, lightweight suit. He was a real raver in his thirties, you know. More wine?' she said, filling her own glass.

'You knew him then?'

'Yes, mainly socially. I was with Special Branch at the time.'

'Doing what?'

'Secret,' she snorted suddenly with laughter. She was probably about fifty-five. She had sort of honey-coloured hair, possibly dyed, and a neat, squareish face with quite a pointed nose. She was pretty, and she reminded him of a vole. She had nice, rather approachable breasts, but she seemed to want to define herself by the prim cardigan she wore.

Reynolds said, 'Do you have any idea at all what he was working on? Any persons of interest?'

'He was setting up the unit,' she said, avoiding the question.

After leaving Art and Antiques, Quinn had put to his mentor, Assistant Commissioner Croft, the idea of a unit based in Mayfair to keep tabs on the super-rich, and Croft had given the green light. It was partly a PR move. Eighty per cent of new properties in central London bought by foreigners, or whatever it was; and the billionaires didn't seem to play by the rules. There were political vendettas, brothel-keeping, unlicensed gambling. Jewel and art theft had become a very live issue in Mayfair. There was money laundering through diamonds, art and antiques. There had been the murder in late September of the young hedge-fund analyst, John-Paul Holden, although the killing – he'd been stabbed in the eye – had occurred in Hampstead. Therefore it was being investigated by North London Murder. But Holden had worked in Mayfair. Increasingly often, the money trails followed by the financial investigators started or finished at a brass nameplate in Mayfair rather than the City. So the plan had been for Quinn to bring in a couple of DS's from the Economic and Specialist Crime Command, and a couple more from Central e-Crime. There'd been talk of Detective Superintendent Hugh Jenkins, Quinn's old boss at Arts and Antiques, coming out of retirement to work with him.

Quinn's new unit had been announced Met-wide on 31 October. The following week, a press release had been put out. But for a good two months beforehand, Quinn and Clifford had been acclimatising themselves with lunches and dinners and general party-going. Quinn's taxi bills were said to be particularly amazing, given that he lived within five minutes' walk of his office.

It remained to be seen what was on Quinn's laptop, but he hadn't posted on Crimintel since setting up the unit. He hardly ever responded to the daily briefings from borough command or the Yard – most likely didn't even read them. As for the missing notebook . . . Reynolds would give Victoria Clifford a little more time to come clean about that.

He asked her, 'Did he use a mobile phone?'

She nodded. 'Disposable ones. What's it called? *Pay-as-*

You-Go. He'd say, "Vicky darling, would you mind nipping out for a mobile phone and a packet of fags?"'

'So he didn't want his calls traced.'

'That must be it.'

'And you've no idea who he was calling?'

'A lot of things he didn't tell me in order to protect me.'

'Do you think he felt under threat?'

'Yes. But he was fatalistic about it, and if he complained to Croft, then Croft would have to take him off the case . . . whatever the case was.'

The main courses came. Clifford handed Reynolds his napkin, which he'd been ignoring.

'Now you've spoken to Lilley,' he said, to cover up his embarrassment.

'Twice over coffee at the Yard. He didn't offer lunch or dinner.'

Probably because this was the Metropolitan Police and not some lonely hearts club.

'And you told him . . .'

'Just what I've told you.'

Therefore nothing.

Clifford picked at her food. She said, 'Will you excuse me?'

It was a purely rhetorical question, because she left the basement in a hurry with her phone in her hand. Reynolds thought about the notebook she'd lifted. It was odds-on she'd taken something else from the flat as well. He remembered the gun. Quinn had booked a pistol out of the Charing Cross armoury a week or so before he'd been shot, and it had never been returned. Quinn was licensed to carry. He'd done the 'basic shot' course at Bisley, and it was down to Quinn that he himself had done the same course. Quinn had recommended it while congratulating him over the Gray case. Reynolds might not be so lucky another time.

Clifford returned with rain in her hair, and her nose a little reddened. This suited her, Reynolds thought. She offered half her curry to Reynolds, and her tone had changed slightly. She said she would let him see some things that might be 'evidentially material' the next morning.

When they came out of the restaurant, it had stopped raining, and Reynolds found that he liked walking next to Victoria Clifford. She was a trim figure, in a good-quality tweed coat and surprisingly modern, stacked shoes. It seemed she didn't mind walking next to him either. They certainly took a very roundabout way to Green Park Underground. She was perhaps giving him a tour of the patch she and Quinn had been about to make their own – the territory of the super-rich – and Reynolds looked at Mayfair as if for the first time.

The entrances of the hotels and restaurants were like the entrances of coaching inns. Lanterns or flares burned before the doors, which were guarded by liveried men in greatcoats and top hats. The women were often as perfect as women in magazines, whereas a lot of the men were laughably unprepossessing given the amount of money they obviously had; but there was a consistent sleekness. If they didn't have much hair, they slicked it right back, which gave them a ruthless look. They favoured loafers and quilted jackets.

On Berkeley Square, Reynolds saw men of that type going into the private clubs, leaving their Bentleys or Rollers outside with the drivers, who were similar-looking men, but who would be spending the evening playing with their smartphones. He kept seeing cigar stubs in the gutters. Cigar smoke was also very much in the air, and when two Americans walked past, one saying to the other, 'In Bangkok, I spent twelve hundred dollars on Cubans,' Victoria Clifford touched Reynolds' arm, saying, 'He means cigars, of course.' On Berkeley Street, Reynolds found he was flattered when a Ferrari stopped for the two of them at a crossing, and he was then annoyed with himself for feeling so. They then turned left into Hay Hill, where Victoria Clifford stopped, and indicated that Reynolds should stop too.

'This was where Quinn saw the abandoned car,' she said. 'About ten days before he was shot. I was walking with him. It was incredibly low – the car – barely up to knee-height. What would it have been?'

Reynolds frowned.

'It was orange,' Clifford added.

'A Ferrari?' said Reynolds. (But weren't they usually red?)

Clifford shook her head.

'A Lamborghini?'

'That's it,' said Clifford, and they were walking on again now. 'It was parked half on the pavement. A community policeman was standing over it – just a boy. He'd taken down the VIN number and radioed it through to control, but there were no plates on the car. Quinn tested the door, which the boy hadn't thought to do, and it was open. Quinn leant in and touched a switch that opened a compartment you wouldn't have known was there. He took out an envelope, gave it to the boy. "Count that," he said, and there was ten thousand pounds in it. Then the boy carried on watching the car, occasionally looking up and down the street.'

'He was giving the owner a chance to return,' said Reynolds. 'It's recommended procedure.'

'After a while,' said Clifford, 'Quinn asked the boy, "How long are you planning to wait?"'

'And how long *was* the kid planning to wait?'

'I don't know,' said Clifford, 'because Quinn said, "I suggest this car's been abandoned, and you should get it towed away." The boy asked him, "Why would anyone abandon a car that must be worth quarter of a million, and with another ten thousand in the dashboard?" Quinn said, "That's *exactly* why."'

Now a big white Jaguar was coming along Hay Hill, going too fast. A trail of orange sparks signified a cigar stub thrown from a window, like the end of a firework.

Reynolds said, 'How did he know the money was in the dash?'

'He didn't know. But that's where the cash is often kept – in special compartments. So you see the car has to be right outside the shop – preferably on a double-yellow line.'

The owner of the Lamborghini, Reynolds thought, had been winding up the police, letting them know he was beyond their reach. Because what were they going to do? Fine him a hundred and fifty quid for illegal parking? So the moral appeared to be that Quinn hated the super-rich? But Reynolds believed there was more to it than that.

They turned into Old Bond Street, where the Christmas decorations were up . . . as if it wasn't Christmas every day for the regular shoppers here. The theme appeared to be gold, so that was about right.

By the time they reached the Tube station, it was raining again. Just inside the entrance of the station – which seemed to belong in a different city from the one that harboured Bond Street – they agreed to meet the next morning at the Down Street office of the unit. As they approached the ticket barriers, Reynolds said to Clifford, 'You have a flat in Belgravia?' because that's what he'd heard.

'Victoria,' she said.

'Then it must be easy for you to remember where you live.'

She didn't exactly laugh, but she said, 'It's also a *Victorian* flat.'

Reynolds' phone rang, and so he answered while Clifford went through the barriers alone. The caller was his line manager, Detective Superintendent Ray Flanagan of the Homicide and Serious Crime Command. Flanagan was a restless, red-faced Irishman, forever shuffling the pack of the murder teams he oversaw. He did this for reasons known only to himself, sometimes with good results and sometimes not.

'Evening, sir,' said Reynolds, as he watched Clifford step onto the escalator and descend. He had thought she might glance back his way. She did not.

'What did you make of Victoria Clifford?' Flanagan asked, in his fast, flurried way. He appeared to be at some sort of noisy social event.

'How do you mean, sir?' said Reynolds.

'Did you get anything out of her? About Quinn.'

'Apparently she's going to give me some stuff that might be evidentially material.'

'When?'

'Tomorrow.'

'Well, that's very good of her I must say. She's not there with you now?'

'She's just got on the Tube. I had the idea she doesn't see why she should be very forthcoming since the unit's no sooner been set up than it's going to be closed down. And she'll be out of a job.'

'Doesn't she want to catch the bad sod who shot her boss?' Reynolds believed that she did, but that in the meantime she was on a power trip. He said something like that to Flanagan, who said, 'She's a complicated woman. And it would be as well to bear in mind that she was probably in love with the man.'

'Has he died, sir?'

'*Died?*' said Flanagan. 'As far as I know he's in intensive care under armed guard. Look, it's late and I'm knackered so let's get this sorted now.'

This was – what was the phrase? – a non sequitur. It put Reynolds on his guard. Flanagan was accelerating towards something big.

'We play it like this,' Flanagan said. 'Quinn's unit – it's going to be carrying on. You're to be the new principal, and you'll be working from the office Quinn created in that little street in Mayfair.'

'You're transferring me from West End Murder?'

'I am. Just until Quinn recovers.'

Which he probably wouldn't.

'Does Lilley want me off Murder?'

'Nothing to do with Lilley. It's all cleared with Croft.'

Deputy Assistant Commissioner Croft of Specialist Crime and Ops: Quinn's boss.

'So now Victoria Clifford's my secretary?'

'Personal assistant. Don't for Christ's sake call her a secretary. The woman's a big feminist, you know.'

Reynolds had had her down as a Tory. Perhaps you could be both.

'I have to go now,' said Flanagan, who was threatening to be overwhelmed by whatever was making the noise in the background. 'You're telling me that so far you've no notion of what Quinn was up to?'

'Hold on, sir. Is Croft going to be my supervisor?'

But Flanagan had gone.

Reynolds moved over to the barrier, which didn't seem to know that he'd just been put in charge of an OCU, since it refused his Oyster card. His reward for topping up the card was half an hour on a packed Piccadilly Line train to Wood Green, then twenty minutes on the bus that roared noisily but slowly through the rain towards his flat. Reynolds was trying to figure out why he'd been transferred to the new unit. Was he being promoted? That would have been an obvious question to ask Flanagan. It was the first thing Caroline would ask when he got to the flat. Perhaps he'd be 'acting up' as a DCI, in which case his pay would also go up. He currently earned £57,657 per annum. Had he ever heard of a mere DI running an OCU? No.

Another way of putting the same question was to ask why he'd been given Victoria Clifford as a project. Or could it be that *she* had chosen *him*? Had she called Croft when she'd left the Indian restaurant in the middle of the meal, and said, 'I'll have Reynolds. He's passed the test'? Reynolds believed Clifford was as close to Croft as Quinn had been. Croft was elusive. His nickname was 'Undercroft', because he always went under rather than over. It was not impossible that Croft had known what Quinn was on to when he'd been shot.

There was nobody on the dark and rainy streets of what

the estate agents called the Wood Green–Palmers Green borders. The double 'green' was a provocation to Reynolds, since neither suburb was exactly leafy. The houses were not very big, and yet subdivided, and Reynolds always thought of the way corpses were stacked in the Met's forensic suite attached to the Westminster Public Mortuary . . . the very likely destination of Quinn, where the bullet would be removed from his brain without need of anaesthetic. A doctor had once told him that there was less need to remove a bullet quickly these days. The risk of infection was less because bullets had got cleaner somehow. It was progress of a sort, Reynolds supposed, as he turned into his own road.

Reynolds' flat occupied one third of a house, and this was the revelation of London life to a northerner like himself: you wouldn't even have a house to yourself.

Caroline was in the flat, with *Newsnight* turned down and the central heating turned right up. It was never the other way round. She was on the sofa, surrounded by property details because they were trying to buy a property together. At first 'property' had meant a house, but now they had lowered their sights to another flat. This present flat was Reynolds'. Caroline had another, smaller still – way beyond even Palmers Green – and currently let out. Reynolds didn't see the point of buying another flat; he already *had* a flat. He had not quite said as much to Caroline.

They kissed and she asked why he was late, which was the kind of thing he wished she wouldn't ask, which was why she asked it.

'I've been transferred to a new unit that's investigating the super-rich.'

'That's ironic,' she said.

5

In her rambling and dusty mansion flat, Victoria Clifford
opened the fridge. Was there any Sainsbury's Prosecco left?
She ought not to be so bothered. Yes, a whole half-bottle,
and she poured a glass. The cat from the next-door flat was
on the window ledge, like valuable china on a mantelpiece,
glowing white against the darkness of the night. The cat
was called Debbie, preposterously enough. It got onto the
ledge via the down-pointing branch of the big oak outside.
That branch was shaped like a fork of lightning, Clifford always thought. She put the glass on the table, and opened
the sash window. With a brief miaow that said, 'What took
you?' the cat dropped onto the kitchen lino and began slinking around. That's right, Clifford thought, ignore the person
who's just done you a big favour. She took a bowl and poured
cat food into it. The cat food was dry, and reminded her of
cornflakes, so she kept it in the cupboard *with* her cornflakes, which was the kind of thing you could do if you lived
alone. The cat had come to regard this as its second home,
which was Victoria's fault for feeding it. She would quite
like a cat of her own, but she mustn't buy one, because then
she'd be a cat lady.

Glass in hand, she wandered through several rooms,
hung with the dusty and undistinguished Victorian paintings she had inherited and never really bothered about until
recently. She had started to take an interest . . . and then
something had caused her to go off the subject of pictorial

art. She finished up in the study, where she sat down and switched on her laptop, which was old and came to life very slowly and groggily. It was quite dirty as well, she noticed; she ought to get one of those expensive packs of wipes that you were supposed to use instead of a damp cloth with a bit of Fairy Liquid on it. Then again, she might soon have to rip out the hard disk and throw it in the river, since the bloody thing could not, apparently, be destroyed. The sea would be better, being bigger, and she saw herself walking the length of the pier at Brighton with the thing in her handbag.

Reynolds . . . She liked his northern accent: quite mellifluous, even if it signified lack of breeding. She had frightened him a bit. She wasn't sure how tough he was, and he was going to have to be very tough. He was well regarded at the Yard, but not a flyer. Well, he was a semi-flyer. Not noisy or political enough to be truly airborne, but he knew his worth, and she detected a streak of vanity, negatively manifest. He saw himself as being above angling for drinks with a Chief Super. He had come top Met-wide in his sergeant's exams, or maybe second. He'd probably finish up with five years as a Detective Superintendent before retiring, which might be considered a waste of his first-class degree in law. But then she was biased on that point. She would like to have been a lawyer herself, and she couldn't imagine why Reynolds had not practised. He had a live-in partner. The two of them had a flat in Palmers Green, London N13, no apostrophe. There were no children, which was on the way to being odd, since he was forty-three.

One way or another, it was now or never for DI Reynolds, and she believed that deep down, he knew that. He'd blotted his copybook only that one time, in the Clubs Squad.

Got too close to a girl. She'd been eighteen; he'd have been in his late thirties. He'd protected her, acted in a chivalrous manner, but still . . . too close.

She had four emails. The first was from Dorothy Carter, with whom she thought she had fallen out over certain aspects of Dorothy's husband's behaviour. The Spouse Mouse, she called him. It was amazing how so meek and inoffensive a man could be so offensive. He could speak French, and therefore he did. He would speak it unnecessarily, as for instance when speaking to English people who are all speaking English. He wore a bracelet – a sort of strip of rag around his wrist. He was sixty years old, for God's sake. And he *chuckled*. It was hard to define chuckling, but you knew it when you heard it. Dorothy Carter's email had been sent from her Blackberry. 'God, Vicky,' Dorothy began, 'don't you ever switch your phone on . . . ?'

Get on with it, can't you?

'I'm up from Bucks for a meeting, practically on your doorstep. A solo jaunt so I'm free and easy. Lunch in a pub? Dot xx.' An olive branch. Another one. The first had been something about a pub quiz, and Clifford had never got beyond those two words. She obviously hadn't connected the news reports of the shooting with Clifford; or hadn't read the news reports. The second was from her better and closer – or at least older – friend, Rachel Reade, saying she was so sorry to hear about Quinn, and was there anything she could do? That was more like it. Rachel Reade said she would pray for him, which reminded her, did she want to go to Mass on Sunday? They could have lunch afterwards at Wilton's if she was in funds; or perhaps Evensong in which case dinner to follow? It was a whole year since they'd been

45

to Wilton's. And by the way here was a link to a good pedestal desk going for £600. Victoria clicked on the link . . . she didn't like the desk; and there was no Evensong at St George's. St George's was C of E. Rachel Reade was C of E. Clifford was a Catholic who occasionally attended C of E services. So why did *she* know there was no Evensong at St George's, whilst Rachel Reade . . . It was not worth going into.

The third email was from *World of Interiors*. Did she want to renew her subscription? She did, oddly enough. Clifford was trying to take her Victorian mansion flat in hand, and Rachel Reade was trying to take *her* Victorian mansion flat in hand. They would get all their fireplaces working (they had about seven between them), then the plan was that they'd invite around a good-looking man that Rachel Reade knew who was sometimes on *Antiques Roadshow*, and was a great expert on Victorian furniture. Victoria would have him for drinks, then Rachel would have him for dinner, all on the same night, poor man. Rachel's aim seemed not so much to get off with this chap, as to have him around and observe him not being grossly offended by the decor of her flat.

That was her emailing done. Nothing needed replying to immediately, and she would let Dorothy Carter stew for a couple of weeks.

She googled Reynolds' street, and was none the wiser. Some appropriately dour female poet had lived in Palmers Green. She couldn't recall the name. She closed the laptop, thinking of Reynolds. He had the figure for a good suit. Maybe she would point him in the way of Hackett's. Quinn thought the Hackett profile rather spivvy, but Victoria had liked the Prince of Wales check, and she'd got Quinn into a Hackett's suit eventually. Then of course, he'd worn it more than some of his Savile Row ones. In Brighton, he'd arrested Kennett in that suit after a proper car chase. Unfortunately for the aesthetics of the operation, the armed support officers had made Quinn wear body armour on top of the suit. She thought of Kennett, that gorilla of a man, murderer and drug dealer. He was very well connected; had friends in low places. His tentacles could stretch out from Wakefield nick or wherever he was, but she knew for certain he wasn't behind the shooting of Quinn.

Reynolds had something of the look of Quinn generally. Eventually, he'd be receding in the same way. There was something of Jude Law about him, as there had been about Quinn in his nightclubbing days. Victoria liked Jude Law. When he was *Hamlet* in the West End, she went four times, admitting only two to Rachel Reade. Reynolds did not shiver his leg while sitting down, and she believed that he would not whistle, even if feeling happy. A lot of detectives whistled.

Victoria was in the kitchen again, watching the cat cleaning itself under the table. Water. She filled a bowl, and put it near the cat. The cat got up and walked away from the water. That was it. She picked the cat up, and set it back on the window ledge. The cat tried to look as if it couldn't handle this situation, but Victoria knew very well that it could.

She closed the window and went into her bedroom. She opened the locked drawer, and took out the red notebook and inspected it carefully. She thought about putting it under her pillow. But she put it back in the drawer alongside the Glock pistol. She locked the drawer again. She sat on the edge of the bed, and took the handkerchief from the sleeve of her cardigan. She blew her nose, and closed her eyes. On sitting down she had automatically crossed her legs as she tended to do. Now she uncrossed them and smoothed her skirt. She closed her eyes tighter. She was praying for Quinn.

6

On that same night of Monday 8 December, *Queen for a Day* was bounding east through the Straits of Gibraltar, fully rigged in twenty knots of south-westerly wind, which was more than enough for her to have passed two big motor cruisers since Malta. That, Captain Grant Williams hoped, would have been a salutary experience for those aboard the cruisers: to be outstripped by a craft both morally and aesthetically superior. The *Queen* flew with white wings, and was just about the most gorgeous craft Captain Williams had seen afloat, let alone worked on. She was three-masted, like a modern-day clipper, but with an Alustar aluminium hull and full automation. All evening, as he'd been standing at the wheel, Williams had been enjoying watching the automatic foredeck lights coming on in stages. First came a gentle illumination to mark the coming of dusk and keep the navigation lights company. Then the compass in its housing had begun to glow a pretty orange, after which appeared a few more fairy lights for cocktail hour, followed by a mellower, bluer ambience for any late-night smooching. But there were no cocktail drinkers, diners or dancers this evening, just Captain Williams and his skeleton crew of seven.

First mate Vaughan, who was on the next watch, was asleep in the master cabin, which he was not really supposed to be occupying, but they were two nights out of Monaco before Captain Williams *realised* he was occupying it, the *Queen* being so big . . . So Williams had let that go. Vaughan liked the master cabin, as you would do, given all that bespoke carpentry in Burmese teak and the sixty-inch plasma screen. Phillips, the bosun, was up in the crow's nest. It was the first time Phillips had been on a boat with a crow's nest as high as sixty metres, and an elevator to reach it by, and he was still not over the novelty. He'd said he wanted to look at the lights of Tunis from what was the equivalent in height of a twenty-storey building, but Captain Williams believed he was smoking weed.

On the bridge deck with Williams was Jones the cook. Jones wasn't normally a watch-stander, but he'd brought Williams a hot chocolate and a cigar, and then just hung about. Actually, he'd gone away for a minute, only to return with a can of beer, which he ought not to be drinking on the bridge any more than Phillips ought to be getting stoned in the crow's nest, but he was savouring the *Queen* from the best vantage point, centre-stage, and Williams had thought, yes, the guy should look and learn.

You couldn't handle an eighty-metre schooner like *Queen for a Day* with any fewer than eight, even with everything being automatic, but they weren't exactly over-taxed. An even less strenuous time had been in prospect: a month of sun-worshipping as sole occupants (apart from the servants) of the owner's villa at St Barth's, before all the guests turned up. But three days previously, when they were just off the Azores, Williams had received a call on the satellite phone from the owner's private office. Williams was to turn around and head back to Port Hercules, Monaco. It was not his place to ask why. 'Might I know the reason?' was the nearest you came to it with those sorts of guys, and you were only allowed a couple of *those* before you were out on your ear.

He'd seen the madness on the days when the *Queen* was fully staffed, and cruising off the Riviera in party mode. Fifty miles out in the Med, one of the guests would say he wanted all the black towels replaced with white ones even if that meant calling in at the next port . . . or all the black towels replaced with other black towels that had to be exactly the same except not the same actual towels. He'd seen that sort of perversity, and the more you saw it, the less you questioned it. Williams regarded himself as the captain of a cruise ship where all the cruisers were psychologically disturbed, unhinged by money, so that the pillows on their beds had to be propped up vertically or they'd have a fit; no bottle of toiletries must ever be less than half full; the temperature of the hot tub must be tested in advance by means of a servant sitting in it, like the person who tasted the king's food.

In most cases, it would do your head in to even *wonder* why. Maybe Williams had been asked to turn back because something was wrong, but what could be wrong when you had a couple of billion stashed in the Caymans, as Captain Williams believed was the case with the owner? Would the owner be waiting to board in Monaco? He could just as easily have 'coptered out to Gib and Williams could have called in there to collect the guy. If all he wanted was a lift to the villa at St Barth's, then why wasn't he jetting out from Northolt? If he wanted to cruise there, then why hadn't he joined the *Queen* when she set out a fortnight ago? When you had that sort of cash, the options were limitless; therefore you might very easily miss the best option. You might actually find that you had more money than sense.

51

But Captain Williams doubted that the owner wanted to cruise out to St Barth's. That would take three weeks, and the owner had never spent more than two or three nights aboard as far as Williams could recollect. Williams liked the owner. Unlike many of his spoilt guests and other associates, he was a class act, restrained, indulging in nothing more decadent, from what Williams could see, than black tea and reading books. He was never seen in the media lounge, more often in the library. Williams too would often browse there. The owner had all the right nautical titles: Conrad, Forester, O'Brien. The dude was actually the spitting image of Joseph Conrad, Williams liked to think, and Williams knew about Conrad, because he was the only truly cool person to have lived in Lowestoft, where Captain Williams had been born. Whether he could really sail himself, Williams had never talked to the owner long enough to discover, but he did have the looks of a sea dog, with that cap of grey hair, neatly trimmed grey beard, deep-set blue eyes, and he was always beautifully turned out.

But in May of last year, Williams had found him in the water, about thirty yards off the stern when they'd been half a mile off Nice, going nowhere in particular but having a cruise about the Riviera. The owner's business partner had been on board at the time: Rostov, the original Russian bear. Also Porter, slathered in sunblock and wearing his pressed khaki shorts. Williams himself had gone out for the owner in the tender. He'd said, 'Sorry to put you out, Captain. Absurd business – sat on the railing; slipped.' And that had been all that was said.

One of many mysteries about the owner was why he had no wife or long-term partner. At the age of sixty-three or so he must be one of the two or three most eligible guys on the planet. He'd had a wife once, evidently, hence that very hot daughter of his. Williams had spent a very happy half hour a couple of years back watching her playing about in the infinity pool while they drifted aimlessly in the Leewards.

The *Queen* took a mighty – but still graceful – leap forwards, and glittering spots of spray flew onto the illuminated windows of the wheel house. Any more of that and the six wiper blades would start swinging. 'Might want to power down those topsails,' observed Jones the cook.

Williams grinned back but he was shaking his head. This force five was undoubtedly strengthening, but for now he was running free with his hundred-and-fifty-million-dollar *Queen*, and he meant to enjoy the moment.

7

On Tuesday morning, Reynolds was heading along Old
Bond Street, which was to the south, he realised for the
first time, of *New* Bond Street, but he believed it was all
just 'Bond Street' to the super-rich. It had turned cold
overnight, and the slow-moving clouds threatened snow,
but there were also golden gleams in the sky, matching the
gold of the Christmas decorations overhead, and the gilded shop signs: Prada, Tiffany, Cartier, Rolex . . . whose
golden clock showed ten past ten. Most of the shops had
banners or flags, twisting in the occasional gusts, like the
flags of embassies. It made a change to be coming to work
this way, rather than along the battered, windy streets of
Charing Cross, which had taken him to the headquarters
of West End Murder.

Come seven o'clock in the morning, he thought he'd
hardly slept, the flat being so stuffy. But he must have
slept at some point because he was suddenly in Quinn's
flat, in the little bedroom, and it had become one of those
mocked-up historic rooms you see behind glass in a museum. There had been a waxwork figure in old-fashioned
clothes lying on the bed: Quinn. The figure had come to
life, sitting up and opening a locker by the bed, and taking out a book, a sort of ledger, and this had contained
all the details of the investigation Quinn had been engaged upon at the time of his shooting, and all the details
that accounted for his shooting. He held out the ledger

for Reynolds to take, and there the dream ended.

Reynolds watched a long black Bentley going north along the street, as if window-shopping. It was impossible to see inside because the windows were tinted. The registration was DUBAI 1563. The owner would presumably get round to giving it a British registration before too long. The car was a deeply polished black – 'lacquered', that was the word, like a grand piano. Reynolds was glad not to see a recklessly parked Lamborghini in the street, being attended by a young constable of the Safer Neighbourhoods team, because that would be an indication he was set on exactly the same course as Quinn. And look how that had ended up.

Reynolds walked on, thinking of that one proper conversation he'd had with Quinn at the Yard. Donnie Gray had been what you might call a problem drinker, in that he stabbed people in cheap pubs when drunk, twice with fatal results. Quinn had very charmingly asked questions about the case in a way that allowed Reynolds to shine. After Reynolds had given a description of Gray, Quinn had said, 'So he was an alcoholic?'

'And a miser,' Reynolds said. 'It was always the cheapest pubs. That's how we tracked him.'

'But there are many cheap pubs,' Quinn had said.

'But Gray would look for the pub that was *absolutely* the cheapest in any given area of North London.'

'By what benchmark?'

'The price of a pint.'

'A pint of what?' Quinn had asked, smiling.

'London Particular. A real ale, sold all over London. At first we just thought that's his favoured tipple but it began to seem that . . .'

'He never drank anything else?'

'Exactly. We knew he was committed to it, because he once assaulted a barman who told him it was off.'

'And he never revisited a pub where he'd done an attack?'

'No. So then he would have to find the next cheapest pub that sold London Particular. We had a lot of help from the brewery.'

Quinn had smiled again, nodding. A less classy individual would have said, 'Good work,' or some such thing; come over all CEO. Reynolds had liked to think that Quinn had identified in him a possible successor or protégé; and perhaps that really had been the case.

Reynolds stopped and looked at some diamond-encrusted watches in the window of Cartier. He was joined by a futuristic-looking Japanese woman, who might actually be able to afford what was in the window. Reynolds turned away . . . and saw a Person of Interest.

The Person of Interest was looking into the window of Graff, the jewellers over the road, while taking a long time about lighting a cigarette. He wore the slicked-back hair popular in New Bond Street and his coat was over his shoulders: mafioso was probably the intended effect. The man was looking at a diamond necklace that had an entire small display window to itself. The doorman stationed outside Graff did not look at the man, but he had an earpiece in his ear and a microphone on his lapel, through which he now spoke to someone inside the shop. 'Standby,' Reynolds supposed he had said, whereupon the Person of Interest lit his cigarette, and walked on, pleased. That was all he'd been trying to do: wind up the doorman, just like the Lamborghini man.

As Reynolds himself walked on, the sky was darkening over Bond Street, and something very like snow was beginning to fall.

8

In the office at the top of the tall, thin house in Down Street, Victoria Clifford waited by the window with arms folded. She looked down through slowly descending sleet at the disused Tube station. It had closed in 1932. The mystery, for Quinn, had been why they'd built it in the first place. 'Nobody in Mayfair ever needed the Tube,' he would muse. They preferred chauffeur-driven cars, then as now.

You wouldn't have thought residents of Mayfair – even at this scruffier western end of it – would need a newsagent-cum-sweetshop any more than they'd need a Tube station, but one of those now occupied part of the facade of the closed-down station. Mini-Mart, it called itself. There was an appealing dowdiness about Down Street, a forgotten quality. Up at the north end, there was a tapas bar that kept itself to itself, and opposite that was that blackened church that didn't appear to have an entrance. The church stood on the corner of Brick Street, which harboured an outpost of Justerini & Brooks, Wine Merchants, just to remind you this was Mayfair.

She had set Quinn's desk up at right angles to the window. The idea had been that he could watch the door, or look down into the street. His desk, like hers, was a tacky, veneered job brought over from the Yard by one of these white-van men who seemed to do so much back-up for the Met, and who, she wouldn't have been very surprised to learn, was actually some sort of detective.

The sleet, or whatever it was, had stopped. The sky was now straightforwardly purple. Somebody had written a song about Down Street Tube station, oddly enough. Steve Harley and Cockney Rebel. She and Quinn liked Cockney Rebel. *Come Up and See Me.* In her mind's eye, she saw Quinn dancing at Tramp in about 1979. He had a subtle, shuffling style, always with fag in hand, and sometimes with a suspicion of eyeliner. She began thinking of the half-dozen times she'd slept with Quinn. While doing paperwork at the Yard, on days very much like this, they would both be overcome with the urge to behave badly. So Quinn might buy a bottle of wine, and they'd check into one of the many dowdy little hotels near Victoria. Quinn would climb into the bed, and she might sit on a chair with no clothes on, and she'd accept one of his cigarettes, and they'd talk, both before and after the sex. Why had that stopped happening? She supposed that she and Quinn had become more respectable, like those little hotels near Victoria. And in both their cases, those afternoons had represented a divergence from the norm – that being homosexuality for Quinn and celibacy for her.

Victoria Clifford looked away from the window. She'd hung a couple of decent coats on the back of the door. They were old ones of Quinn's, but might be considered unisex. She'd placed Quinn's Lalique ashtray on what was to have been his desk. He'd want it there if he ever came back. She'd taken the ashtray from Quinn's flat, right under the nose of the man Chamberlain – also the notebook, and . . . a couple of other items besides. If Quinn died, then Chamberlain would execute the will. That was a bad look-out, since he was an idiot. Big computer terminals sat on each desk, and each was like a ball and chain, by which she and Quinn were to have been kept connected to the Yard, via email and intranet. The white-van man had installed these, and the telephones . . . and he'd obviously made the old-fashioned entryphone work because it was buzzing now. She picked up the receiver, pressed the button.

'Victoria?' she heard. 'It's Blake Reynolds.'

Blake. Ridiculous name – a little flash of romanticism from the suburban parents. They must have been thinking of Sexton Blake.

'Top floor,' she said, and she pressed the button to admit him. He'd sounded a bit nervous, which was all to the good. She waited a moment before replacing the receiver, in case he should mutter to himself, or clear his throat, or show some other sign of weakness. He did not, but a few seconds had passed before she heard the door slam behind him. Perhaps his eye had been caught by the brass plaques announcing the other tenants, and he'd read the names: *Al Hasan Risk Modelling*; *Fincham Acquisitions*; some estate-management firm and *D'Arblay Fine Art*. In spite of all the money implied by those names, the lift didn't work. So Reynolds wouldn't appear for a while.

There was a small mirror on the mantelpiece; it had mainly been put there for Quinn's benefit, but she walked over to it now and straightened her hair. She'd walked through the rain to get here, and she wanted to look her best for Reynolds, who did bear a slight resemblance to Jude Law, after all. She then walked over to the desk she had designated for herself. On it lay the notebook, on top of that the two memory sticks, and the invitation to the drinks given by Plyushkin's Gardeners. She heard footsteps on the stairs, and then in the corridor. Reynolds, in his Marks & Spencer shoes. He was a decent man, so he would knock. She heard the knock. 'Enter,' she called out, and there was Reynolds in the doorway. He hadn't slept much the night before. He wore a mac that didn't suit him and he carried an unforgivably telescoped umbrella and a fairly reprehensible laptop bag. But his hair was wavy and grey in just the way she liked. It was actually better hair than Jude Law's. He looked around the room, then at her, blushing slightly. He smiled.

'The good news is: this unit's not closing down,' he said. 'The bad news is: I'm your new boss.'

He'd rehearsed that speech.

'I know,' said Victoria Clifford.

Silence in the headquarters of the Super-Rich Unit.

'The lift's not working,' said Reynolds.

'I know,' said Victoria Clifford, and feeling somehow like a little girl, she handed him the notebook and the two memory sticks. He blushed again; was palpably grateful, which he ought not to have been, not least because she'd taken the precaution of carefully slicing two of the pages from the notebook. He set down the laptop bag, and took out his laptop, which was no better than her own. He then found the kettle on the filing cabinet, but saw that it was just that: a kettle. No 'tea and coffee making facilities' as the Victoria hotels daintily had it. He began looking about. He wanted a coffee. It was very important to her that he should ask for one.

'Since you're now my personal assistant . . .' he said.

'Yes?'

'I don't suppose you'd fancy getting us both a coffee, would you?'

'Yes,' she said, 'I would.'

She smiled at him, and he smiled too – laughed a bit, in fact. She walked over to the window. They sold takeaway teas and coffees in the Mini-Mart. Tea was seventy pence; coffee ninety. She would go over in a minute.

'They do them in the place across the road,' she said, 'I'll go over.'

'You really don't mind?' he said, blushing again. He must learn not to be so pleased about his little victories. 'No sugar, just milk please.'

'I know,' she said, and as she left the office, she saw that Reynolds was opening the notebook.

9

'This lovely embossed leather screen,' Margaret heard herself saying, 'is Spanish. It dates from the late nineteenth century, and each fold is decorated with three gardening scenes.' She hardly ever mentioned the screen on her walking tours – it was badly scratched and probably not worth more than about a thousand pounds – but her mind was elsewhere. She was on auto-pilot. Margaret and her party – the Tuesday-afternoon walking tour – continued through into the ballroom, which usually drew a gasp, with the lovely satinwood sitting-out chairs all along each wall, and the two overmantle mirrors at each end. But the ballroom had not caused much of a stir on this occasion, and Margaret realised she'd forgotten to say that if you looked at yourself in one of the gilt ballroom mirrors, you'd see your reflection reflected in the other mirror, and so on into infinity. They were in the dining room by the time she realised, and she almost thought about taking everyone back so she could do it. But she would do it next time, on the next walking tour, which was to be held, for the first time, on a day other than Tuesday. It was to be held on the coming Friday.

She would be pulling out all the stops for that, because it would be the last-ever walking tour of Gladwish Hall. The new owner had agreed to let Margaret have her swansong, but he obviously hadn't wanted to wait until next Tuesday to be rid of her. It was abrupt to say the least, and it was such a shame. Gladwish was, if not the most beautiful, then certainly one of the largest Victorian country houses in the south of England, and with an unusually large estate for the county of Surrey: four hundred acres. The house had a whole page to itself in Pevsner's guide to Surrey. The exterior was usually described (by Margaret) as 'a seigneurial brand of revived Tudor'. Inside, the theme was Jacobean, and the oak panelling in the entrance hall and lobby was really very fine, as was the carved oak staircase, although she'd once had a man on the tour – an architectural historian, he *said* – who claimed it was only 'pretty good'. This in the very week that Margaret had made a pilgrimage to the Jacobean house called Maybury Place in Sussex, to see the staircase that had inspired the one at Gladwish, according to Christopher Rye. Christopher Rye had written a little history of Gladwish Hall and the family, the Turners, who had owned the house until last year, and who had made their money in the railway boom of the eighteen-forties. Before that, the male Turners had all been doctors. People talked about the nouveaux riches today, but when you thought that in the eighteen-forties, directors of railway companies were considered the worst sort of opportunists . . .

Mr Rye, like Margaret, lived in Camberley, which was the nearest town to Gladwish Hall. He was more against the new owner than Margaret was. It was the knocking down of half the maze that had been the last straw for Rye, whereas the lovely dovecote had been the benchmark for Margaret, and the new owner hadn't touched that so far – and she didn't mind too much what he was doing with the sunken garden, about which Mr Rye had written an anonymous letter to English Heritage (because Gladwish was Grade Two listed).

She was in the morning room now, with what she called her 'guests', and she was pointing out the Turner family portraits. She hadn't been able to find out if he – the new owner – would be present next Friday. It didn't do to ask any of his staff because, after all, he was the owner of the house, and he could come and go in his helicopter or his fleet of black cars any time he wanted.

Ten minutes later they were back in the entrance hall, where the tour started and finished. The dinner gong was located here, and Margaret always left that until the end. 'It's Burmese,' she said. 'As you can see, there are six gilded warriors on the face.' She stopped herself saying, 'Now would anyone like to bang it?' because the half-dozen faces staring at her had an average age of about seventy-five, and it was the children who liked to bang the gong. She hoped there would be some children for the last tour. There were further family portraits in the hall, and a couple of questions were asked about them. And then came the inevitable: 'Who's the new owner?'

'The new owner,' said Margaret, 'is a Russian gentleman: Mr Rostov.'

'Is there a picture of him?'

'Yes . . . well, not a painting, which is a shame because he has a lovely wife and three absolutely lovely children. But there is a photograph.'

She walked over to the mahogany side cabinet and picked up a silver picture frame that held a photograph of a thick-set, cheerful-looking man in his early seventies. He had flyaway hair, and quite a red face. He wore jeans and a green T-shirt. 'This is how he dresses,' said Margaret, 'always very informal.' She hoped no one would ask for a close look at the photograph because there was a slogan written on the T-shirt, and it wasn't in Russian. It said, 'All this, and brains too!'

'What's he like?'

As far as Margaret knew, Mr Rostov had once been in the KGB, which did not bode well for anyone who, like Margaret, read a lot of spy stories, but Mr Rostov had been perfectly polite, if a little distracted, on the two occasions they'd spoken, on both of which he'd asked her how she was. 'And the kids?' he'd asked in addition, even though Margaret's 'kids' were in their thirties and long since moved away. When she'd asked him how *he* was, he'd replied, 'Doing great. Hundred per cent!' But her own reply might seem strange if she'd had to tell someone how *she* was in Russian. Also, she wasn't absolutely sure that it was Rostov himself who had brought the Tuesday walking tours to an end. According to Mr Rye, he had been put up to it by Mr Rostov's head of security, who was an Englishman called Porter, who'd been a major in the army.

Margaret opened the big front door to let her guests out.

'Oh dear,' she said, 'rain.'

It wasn't just the rain, but also the mess made of the lovely terrace by the cement mixers and diggers . . . and all those big, black cars. On the whole, she would have liked Mr Rostov a lot more if she hadn't seen the bin-liner full of discarded mobile phones in the stable yard, and if, perhaps, he had been more like his business partner.

This other man was the senior partner. She believed that he had even more money, and certainly better taste, than Mr Rostov. She had seen him once, when he had come to Gladwish for the dinner Mr Rostov had held to celebrate his purchase of the house. That had been on a Tuesday, and Margaret had heard a helicopter landing while she was leading the walking tour. Then two lorries – not vans but *lorries* – with 'Fortnum & Mason' written on the side had turned up, and they had brought the dinner. There were to be a hundred guests, and they had been gathering in the drawing room and the ballroom, but she had seen Mr Rostov's business partner sitting alone in the library. She had left her handbag in the library, and the moment she entered the room, he had stood up and very nearly bowed at her. He had been so charming, and his English was almost perfect. He had been so beautifully dressed; he was handsome too, with distinguished grey hair and deep blue eyes. She also believed he was modest – in the way he'd been sitting alone in the library, and with just the one reading light switched on. Margaret had to admit it: she had rather a crush on Mr Andrei Samarin.

The notebook was smaller than the one Quinn had given him in the dream, and whereas that might have been a sort of faded blue, this was red – expensive red leather with pale blue pages. There were little gold capitals on the front. Reynolds read out, 'TOP SECRET'.

'That *is* rather camp,' said Clifford, looking up from whatever she had started typing on her return from the Mini-Mart. 'He usually bought the one marked "Engagements". Or sometimes "Wine Notes".'

'What did he do with the old ones?'

'Don't know. He'd have one on the go at any time. It's from Smythson of course. One of their soft notebooks. They're known as floppies.'

'I've heard of Smythson's.'

'*Smythson*. No 's'. Have you never had a Smythson diary? Your partner – what's her name?'

'Caroline.'

'Caroline. She should be buying you one every Christmas. They tell you things like when Glorious Goodwood starts.'

'But this is not a diary.'

'I've just told you what it is. Guess how much it cost.'

'Seven hundred pounds.'

'Now you're just being silly. Sixty. It's not A5, you know.'

'I never said it was.'

'It's a format unique to Smythson. Every page is watermarked with the design of a feather.'

'That's useful,' said Reynolds. The notebook was not *very* floppy, it seemed to Reynolds, and Clifford seemed to read his mind.

'The true Smythson floppy is actually a bigger format,' she said, 'but he used to say they'd ruin his pockets. The official notebooks ruined his pockets as well. That's partly why he never really wrote anything in them.'

Reynolds tried to think of the rule that said a detective had to write in his detective's notebook. He couldn't.

'He regarded them as a snare,' Clifford continued. 'He used to say that if any case rested on what you'd written in your notebook, then you weren't going to win that case. But it didn't work the other way. The opposing barrister could always trip you up on what was in the book. So Quinn stuck to the floppies. He would doodle in them, usually while smoking. He said it got his mind working, like dancing at Annabel's.'

'Why did you take it from the flat, just out of interest?'

'To secure it.'

And so saying, Clifford stopped typing, folded her arms and looked down, as if she'd gone on strike in protest at the question.

'Are you all right?' said Reynolds.

'Fine.'

Unlike the book in his dream there appeared to be no useful information in this real-life version. It was blank except for the first five pages, which were crowded with a dense scribble: a jumble of words, mostly illegible, and some doodles. The largest of the doodles looked like a primitive drawing of a round-faced king wearing a crown. There was what looked like an elaborate '88'. There were letters that might have spelt, 'SERG E I', with gaps before and after the second 'E'. There was what seemed like the word 'Carlton' followed by 'HT'. There was also 'Jenkins' plainly enough, the surname of Quinn's old boss in Art and Antiques. And there was the word 'Sfinsk', if that *was* a word.

'What do you make of all this?' Reynolds asked Clifford, who had started typing again, albeit slower, so that he wondered if she was one of these bipolar people. He took the book over to her desk, and began turning the early pages.

She said, 'It's going to be very hard to say. He'd write almost unconsciously.'

'You mean subconsciously?'

'Possibly.'

'This looks like a fat king wearing a crown.'

'Which it is obviously not,' said Clifford.

'Jenkins must be Hugh Jenkins.'

' . . . who's been in a monastery near Venice for the past month, writing a thesis on some Renaissance painter. I managed to get him on the phone last night. He last spoke to Quinn in late October. They had a drink at the Athenaeum. Jenkins said they discussed private matters, not to do with any case.'

'This looks like an eighty-eight,' Reynolds said, pointing to the doodle.

'It says B. B.'

'Could be Barney Barnes?'

'Yes, it could.'

Barney Barnes was also ex-Met, also retired like Jenkins. Barnes had finished as a DI. Serious and Organised Crime –

Flying Squad for most of his time. He was a big man, bursting out of shiny suits; an overt hardcase, who talked a lot about football. He was the opposite of Quinn, in other words.

'Quinn spoke to Barnes early in October. It was about *that*,' she said, pointing to one of the memory sticks.

'How do we know they spoke?'

'Barnes heard about the sweep. He got in touch.'

'When?'

'This morning.'

A Met-wide sweep had been put out, asking any officer who'd had dealings with Quinn in the weeks before the shooting to contact Lilley. But it seemed Barnes had come straight to Clifford. She indicated her screen. 'He emailed that he's happy to see you as soon as you like, so I've set up a meeting for Thursday.'

'At La Gavroche, presumably?' said Reynolds.

'It's going to be in The Audley. That's a pub near the Connaught.'

Clifford turned the pages of the notebook. 'What you call the fat king is pretty obviously a diamond ring.'

Reynolds indicated the word 'Carlton', followed by the 'HT'. 'What about that? The Carlton Club? Was Quinn a member?'

'He was not.'

Reynolds eyed her sceptically. From what he'd heard of the Carlton, it was the sort of place Quinn might very well be a member of.

'Go and ask if you don't believe me, but they won't tell a DI. You'll need a letter from Croft. If not a warrant.'

Reynolds had to admit this was probably true. Then it came to him: 'Carlton HT – must be Carlton House Terrace.

It overlooks St James's Park . . . which is where he was shot.'

'I hope to God you think faster than you talk,' Clifford said.

'And why have you given me this?' Reynolds asked, holding up the invitation.

'You're going to it,' she said.

'But the invitation is to Quinn.'

Clifford held out her hand and Reynolds passed her the invitation which she had obviously lifted from Quinn's flat, leaving behind on the mantlepiece the letter announcing that an invitation was imminent. She crossed out Quinn's name and wrote in Reynolds'. 'I've called them,' she said. 'I told them you'd be coming in Quinn's place.'

'What *is* The Society of Plyushkin's Garden?'

'A sort of literary salon. Are you going to look at the memory sticks now?'

She eyed him until he went back to his own desk.

'Start with the one on the left. It was sent round by forensics just before you arrived. It's Quinn's email inbox and outbox, taken from his laptop.'

'Have you looked at it?'

'I told you, it was sent just before you arrived. Lilley got first sight of it of course, and the fact that he's letting us have a look means there can't be anything material on it. By the way, have you noticed that he's blocked the HOLMES file on the case?'

Reynolds had done. He'd tried twice to log in and find out where Lilley had got to with his investigation. He'd probably be given the password if he asked nicely. It was a game quite often played by the fliers, forcing people to ask: 'Can I have a look at your crime, please?' The blocking might mean Lilley had something. More likely, it meant he'd got nothing and was trying to look like he'd stumbled on some matter of national security. A terrorist plot to take out senior Met men.

'What about Quinn's search history?' Reynolds asked Clifford.

'Evidently he did delete it.'

'Can it be recovered?'

'Apparently yes, if they spend about a million pounds. The other stick – the one on the right – was requested by Quinn from Flying Squad on 24 September. It's the one he talked to Barnes about.'

If it was from the Flying Squad, the memory stick must relate to a robbery of more than about ten grand in cash or goods. But why had Quinn wanted to speak to a retired rather than a serving officer about it?

Reynolds uploaded the first memory stick.

It seemed Clifford was right about the emails and she didn't bother to look over Reynolds' shoulder as he viewed them, possibly because she had already viewed them and then lied about it. She said from her desk: 'Quinn never sent me an email in his life.'

It was a Gmail account – a new one for what had apparently been a new laptop – and hardly used. There were several emails from a man called Napper who lived on a farm in Devon, and wrote in response to Quinn's enquiry about a classic car: an Austin Healey 3000 MK which, according to Napper, had a 'Fast road spec, restored to concours standards' – whatever *they* were – and a giveaway at £65,000.

When Reynolds read this out, Clifford folded her arms

again. 'He couldn't afford it. A pipe dream.'

'Did he have a car?'

'He said why have a car in London when you can just get taxis everywhere and claim them on expenses? He has a car at his dad's place in Yorkshire.'

'A classic car?'

'Define classic. It's practically a vintage car. A Sunbeam Alpha. I mean, *Alpine*. Cost practically nothing.'

Quinn had received more emails than he'd sent. The inbox was like a more upmarket version of Reynolds', which featured many messages such as 'Your Tesco Clubcard points are about to expire'. Quinn's contained promotions from tailors, who had names like firms of solicitors: 'Dawson, Howe and Fletcher' was one. Quinn had been invited to browse the e-store of John Lobb, bootmaker. He had been invited by 'Events at Berry Brothers' to 'An exceptional evening of fine Burgundy.' The only Met-related matter was an email from a Trevor Kennedy of the Yard that appeared to be about expenses. It was dated 2 November:

In the absence of any reply to my phone messages, I am obliged to email your personal account. I do not see how the dinner at Le Caprice for yourself and a mysterious 'contact' is claimable, let alone the purchase of a new shirt at a cost of fifty pounds for attending said dinner. Let us assume you were in desperate need of a certain shirt in order to 'look the part'. My wife, who buys my own shirts, informs

me it is possible to buy something perfectly respectable from Marks & Spencer for half the
price you paid.

Reynolds read this out to Clifford, who said: 'Trevor
Kennedy is Quinn's finance officer. Unfortunately he's one
of the old-fashioned Trevors. He's also going to be *your* finance officer, I'm afraid. You'll notice he marks all his emails
with a star. Any problems go to Cresswell. He's our SPC in
the Business Group. He's obsessed with flow charts but he's
on our side.'

Reynolds eyed her.

'Oh, I should have said. The terms of your transfer have
just come through.' She indicated her computer screen.
'You're going to be acting up as DCI, but you remain on the
same pay grade. Also, the local paper wants to speak to you.
The *Mayfair Gazette*.'

'I don't know that I want to speak to *them*.'

'The *Mayfair Gazette* was founded in 1779 so I think you
should.'

'Eh?'

'It's not some website; it's a very august publication.
I've cleared it with Croft and the Press Bureau. They think
it's a good message to send out. You know, business as
usual. Press Bureau thinks the *Standard* will probably
pick it up.'

'I think I'd better speak to the Press Bureau myself.'

'Be my guest, but don't call them Press Bureau. They're
Media Desk now. Speak to the American woman: Jodi. Say

we're informing public debate about policing issues. Tell her we're being proactive.'

'What's this paper going to be writing about me? Here's the next mark to take a pot shot at?'

She eyed him. He knew she was wondering whether he was scared.

'They've sent me a draft and I said fine. They just want you to fill in a quote.' She began reading from her screen. '"The work of the Mayfair-based police unit dedicated to investigating the 'super-rich' – that's in inverted commas – "is to continue in spite of the shooting of the officer heading it up." Well, I didn't say it was *elegant* . . . And they want a photograph, but they can come here for that after we've got you a new suit. Now look at the other stick.'

He removed the first one and put in the second one, eyeing Clifford as he did so. 'Will you kindly forward that email about my promotion?'

'You'll be getting it on paper to your home address in the usual manner.' The memory stick was taking a long time to load. '. . . In triplicate!' added Clifford. As the loading continued (the screen was at least now admitting that it was loading), Reynolds took out his own detective's notebook. Victoria Clifford came over from her own desk and crouched down very nimbly by his chair. It seemed that she too would be watching the screen, and watching Reynolds as *he* watched.

11

The memory stick was a CCTV grab.

The screen showed a small, cluttered shop with two counters facing each other and a fancy chandelier hanging down in the middle. The bulbs of the chandelier appeared blurred. It became apparent to Reynolds that this was a jewellery shop. The counters were glass-topped with jewellery beneath. Underneath the chandelier stood a good-looking, bored-looking woman with arms folded. Some numbers appeared in the bottom right-hand corner: a steady 1417, and other, incessantly changing figures alongside to show the passing seconds. Unmoving figures showed the date: 22 September – about ten weeks ago. Like all CCTV, this was a silent film. Data protection. Suddenly Reynolds saw the woman from a different angle, and now she was fiddling with a necklace she wore. She still looked bored. She was probably in her late thirties. This new angle gave sight of the shop door, and the window display of jewels, viewed from the shop interior. It was now 1418 and counting.

'Where is this?' Reynolds asked Clifford, who seemed to be maintaining great poise in her crouching position.

'Shop in that arcade going north of the Ritz.'

Reynolds made a note in his book. The screen seemed to give a jump, and it was now 1420 and counting. The shop door opened and a man came in. He wore a sort of fur coat. He had thick glasses, and a lot of dark hair.

'I think the coat's alpaca,' said Reynolds, 'and I think

the hair's a wig. It's a good one, though.'

The man went up to the shop assistant, and the two of them went over to the window display. The man began indicating some items, and the pair were seen from a new angle: the side.

'Who put this together?' Reynolds asked.

'Ward,' she said. 'Do you know him?'

Reynolds had vaguely heard the name.

'Flying squad DS,' said Clifford. 'Always wears a mustard jacket which, with his colouring, he shouldn't.'

Ward, in other words, had edited the CCTV footage given him by the shop.

The perspective jumped back to the angle that had shown the man entering. Now a woman also entered. She was younger than the shop assistant. She looked like a beautiful woman trying to look un-beautiful, and not quite succeeding. Or maybe it was some high-fashion statement. She wore a shapeless woollen hat ('beanie hat' was the term, Reynolds believed), and a pair of those thick fifties glasses that were in fashion. She wore a coat that was obviously a *good* coat, precisely calculated to be neither short nor long. She wore narrow trousers and low shoes like ballet shoes, only with something fancy about them. The shop assistant turned towards her and said something that was probably, 'I'll be with you in a second, after I've helped this gentleman,' and the new woman said something like, 'Don't worry, I'm only browsing.'

The assistant had taken some things out of the window, at the request of the man in the coat. The two walked over to the counter on the left, and the new woman appeared to head off in the direction of the counter on the right. Now the view was side-on again, allowing Reynolds to see the man in the coat and the assistant at the left-hand counter, but not the new woman.

The assistant had put three little boxes down on the counter. They were like little oyster shells with their lids up. All held rings, diamond rings presumably. They would have to be valuable, otherwise Flying Squad would never have been involved. The woman took the rings out of the boxes, and laid them on the counter. They all had little tags on them.

'Watch carefully,' said Clifford.

The man picked up the first ring with his left hand; moved it to his right hand, lifted it towards his face and examined it. He moved it back to his left hand, put it down on the counter. He did the same with the second ring, and with the third, shaking his head this time. He was not attempting to try on the rings. They were obviously women's rings, and he hadn't liked any of them, as he was presumably now explaining to the sales assistant, who had been in view, watching the man, all this time. There was a jump to the higher angle, and the man was seen leaving the shop. This angle also showed the new woman walking over to the sales assistant, who was putting the rings back in the boxes. The two spoke briefly. The new woman then left the shop as well and the screen went black at 1426. Reynolds was developing a slightly sick feeling.

'What was lifted?'

'A two-and-a-half-carat yellow diamond ring. Worth about thirty thousand. Watch it again.'

This time she pointed things out. When the coated man approached the window display with the shop assistant,

Clifford said, 'See how he puts his left hand in his coat pocket, and takes it out again. I think that's important.' When the man was inspecting the rings at the counter, Clifford asked, 'Why do you think he moves them from one hand to the other?'

'At some point he palms the ring, I suppose. Substitutes a fake.'

'The third time,' said Clifford. 'And watch the assistant. Wait . . . as he holds the third ring, she glances over to the right, and I think the other woman does or says something at that point, as a distraction. Stop it there.'

Reynolds clicked pause.

Clifford said, 'Ward told us there was footage of her at the other counter, but just a couple of seconds because that camera kept going on the blink. We can see it in a minute. It comes after the black. Press play again.'

Reynolds clicked the arrow for 'play'. He watched the man make his excuses and leave. The younger woman came over to the assistant. Reynolds watched her leave, and Victoria Clifford was watching him watch.

'Now skip forward,' she said.

After a short period of blackness they were back in the shop. A different camera showed the woman in the beanie hat over at the right-hand counter. They had gone backwards in time to 1424. The camera observed her from side-on as she looked down at the counter. As she leant over, she was kicking the back of her right shoe with the toe of her left shoe. She looked extremely relaxed, but with a kind of formality, like a ballet dancer at rest. A couple of times, she may have half turned towards the opposite counter; the second of those times, she might have spoken, saying something like, 'Excuse me,' and then, 'Oh, sorry,' when she saw that the assistant was still attending to the man in the coat.

Reynolds was thinking himself back to his Club Squad days, and to one long-gone nightclub off Hanover Square. It must have been seven years ago. What was it called? A provocative name: Noise Pollution or something. There were too many under-aged women in it, so the owners were suspected of pimping. A young woman was being followed about by a big guy three times her age. Reynolds had asked, 'Is that man bothering you?'

'Yes,' she had said, 'but there is nothing to be done about it.'

'Why not?'

'Because he's my bodyguard.'

She had had a Russian accent, but not strong (and he would later discover there was a bit of French in it). Reynolds had asked for her ID, and she had shown him an obvious forgery. On Reynolds' recommendation, she had left the club, taking the bodyguard with her.

Reynolds had met her again, in other clubs; and she had found out he was a policeman. She would come over to him, and take the mickey out of her friends. Pointing to a bottle of champagne being brought to a table, she would say, 'That will be eleven hundred pounds please.' She had pointed to one girl, who was in tears, and being consoled by another. 'That one has issues. Affluent issues.' Then, moving closer to Reynolds on the banquette seat, 'You see, no one ever said to her "*no*". Well tonight . . . someone said *no*.' She would offer tips, which he didn't know whether to believe, and never followed up. 'He's mafia . . . That one's just tried to sell me a pill.' He had taken these remarks to be a form of flirtation, which was perhaps arrogant of him. He'd also assumed that saying such things gave her a thrill. The final time, he had danced with her. Afterwards his colleague – because Club Squad officers always operated in twos – had said he'd gone too far, as Reynolds admitted was the case. The colleague was Lilley, so therefore the entire Club Squad, including management, got to know; and certainly Victoria Clifford knew. There had been no reprimand for Reynolds, but Lilley had moved ahead in their mutual race.

The young woman was called Anna, and she was the daughter of a Russian billionaire called Andrei Samarin. Being a Russian woman her name was spelt 'Samarina'. The purpose of this variation was unclear to Reynolds, but it seemed to beautify the name.

Reynolds was almost certain that she was the young woman in the CCTV grab. Whereas she had been seventeen when he met her, she would now be twenty-four or -five. It was the leaning on the counter and the kicking of the heels – the restless but graceful way of doing it – that had given her away.

Reynolds turned to Clifford. She was eyeing him.

12

'What's the shop called?' Reynolds asked Clifford.

'Wilmington's,' she said, half smiling.

'Did Quinn go there?'

She shook her head.

'I'll go there now.'

It was something to say; something to do. He wanted to get away from Clifford, who obviously suspected he was acquainted with the woman in the film, and generally knew far too much about him. He stood up and reached for his mac, but Clifford was at the door, holding out a different coat. It was long, and white.

'Quinn's old Aquascutum,' she was saying, while holding it out for him like a valet. 'You're a thirty-eight so it should be fine.'

Going red, Reynolds stepped into the coat.

'Quinn never liked the Burberry lining,' said Clifford.

Reynolds glanced at the lining.

'The Burberry lining of a Burberry *coat*, you twit. When it comes to raincoats in town you can only have an Aquascutum or a Burberry. Or a Barbour in certain circumstances. It looks fine,' Clifford continued, 'but don't do it up. They look wrong done up.'

Three minutes later, Reynolds was walking fast along Piccadilly. He had not done up the coat. He was carrying his notebook, but he didn't know why. Grey clouds swirled over Green Park, making up their mind about what to do next. The sleet might be renewed as snow; or the default option of rain might be preferred. The golden gleam had gone, but that had just been the folly of the morning. There was a cold grey slime on the pavements, and Reynolds was thinking of Russia, a place he'd never been. The Society of Plyushkin's Garden. He brought it up on his phone. It was a charity founded in 2012 to promote a wider understanding of Russian literature, and foster East–West cultural links. He clicked on 'our friends and partners', and saw many worthy names of British culture. If corporate, there was a logo; in the case of individuals, a headshot. Eventually Reynolds read: 'Founding Partner: the Samarin Foundation. President, Andrei Samarin.' No picture and no logo.

Reynolds clicked back to 'About'. The society was named after a wild Russian garden described – and evidently very well described – in Gogol's novel, *Dead Souls*. Reynolds might once have read *Dead Souls*, but it had the sort of baleful title generic to Russian novels. Happening to glance left into the dark window of the Mercedes showroom, Reynolds saw the reflection of a man in a good, white coat; a man who looked as though he half belonged in Mayfair. It was an advance on what he'd seen in the window of Cartier.

Whether the Arcade counted as indoors or outdoors – that was ambiguous. It was open at the ends, had a glass roof, and a silent red carpet, like a corridor in an old-fashioned hotel. Overdressed Christmas trees had been placed at intervals along the carpet; and there was a shoe-shine boy, cleaning the already-clean shoes of a man talking Italian into a mobile phone.

Wilmington's was one of several jewellers in the Arcade.

Reynolds was buzzed in to find himself on the film set, so to speak, of the CCTV grab, and there was the bored-looking woman, looking just as bored as before. Reynolds produced his warrant card, and she said something like, 'I get my boss for you.' Reynolds could not guess at her nationality, but the man who escorted him up a narrow, thickly carpeted staircase, past a tiny office and into a lounge above the shop, could easily have been Mr Wilmington. He was not, however. His name was Savoury. He was small, neat and tanned, and very good-humoured for a man who had recently had a valuable ring stolen from his premises.

'Would you like a coffee?' Savoury asked. Reynolds declined with thanks. 'This is the third time I have entertained the police here – in my VIP room.'

The first would have been from the borough; then Ward of the Flying Squad. Reynolds explained that he'd seen the film, and wanted to ask a few questions about it. He took out his notebook and his pen, and laid them on the table. But as Savoury began speaking, Reynolds knew that by taking a note he might be tying his own hands. He was already in Quinn territory.

'I was watching the man come in myself,' said Savoury, who gave no more than the briefest quizzical glance at the unemployed pen and book. 'On the screen in my office. Aisha – the lady downstairs – saw no reason not to let him in and he certainly did not raise my hackles.'

'What would you have done if he had?'

'I would have gone downstairs and asked him if he'd had an appointment. If he'd said no – which he would have to have done, since we never *give* appointments – I would have said, "I'm sorry sir, but we are appointment *only*," and I

85

doubt he would have tried to make one. In retrospect, he was clearly a professional. I'm told he left no prints. The substitute was tagged in just the same way as the original.'

'Explain about that, would you, Mr Savoury?'

'All our rings are tagged with the GIA number. I am speaking about the number given to the stone by the Gemological Institute of America. The certificate travels with the stone, as proof of title. Also on the tag would be the cut, in this case round brilliant, and the weight and the colour, in this case 2.3 carats fancy intense yellow.'

'Who writes out your tags?'

'I do, or Aisha. Or my partner, Mr Moore.'

Reynolds said, 'To make the copy tag, would he have to imitate the handwriting on the original?'

'Well you see, not exactly.' Mr Savoury fished in a pocket and produced a tagged ring. 'You can buy these tags by the gross in Hatton Garden.' The tag was half the size of a postage stamp, and jumbled with letters and figures. 'It's so cramped, you see – it's not like forging a letter. That said, he produced something very like the original, I can assure you. The figures might have been a little unclear, but it would have been unfair to expect Aisha to spot the discrepancy.'

'I'm sorry to ask this, but I assume you have complete trust in Aisha?'

'I should think so! She's my wife, you see!'

Reynolds smiled, went crimson. 'And the perpetrator had an accomplice?'

'An accomplice?'

'The young woman who came in at the same time.'

'Ah. Maybe, yes.'

86

It was difficult to say whether Savoury had entertained this thought before, perhaps not, since he was beginning to look at Reynolds with a sort of amused admiration.

'What was the substitute ring made of, Mr Savoury?'

'Zircona. Cubic Zircona. With a coating of gold oxide. I only wish I could show you it, but your forensic people took it away!'

He seemed positively delighted about that.

'What's it worth?'

'Well, I won't be asking for it back, let's put it like that. Fifty pounds perhaps – as costume jewellery.'

'And the ring that was taken?'

'A nice piece. Cut and mounted in the Deco style. Very *Great Gatsby*, which is fashionable right now.'

'Worth?'

'It was on sale at £35,000.'

What had been perplexing Reynolds was the thought that Anna Samarina did not need to be involved in the theft of such a ring. She could easily have bought it. And he did not doubt that the man in the alpaca coat had been stealing it *for* her. He was not stealing it for himself with her assistance . . . Because surely most things that happened around Anna Samarina happened for her benefit.

'Where does that put the ring, in the scale of prices?'

'Well, it's not mega-mega.'

'It is *mega* though, isn't it?'

Savoury considered: 'It's entry level for Mayfair.'

'You're covered by insurance of course?'

'Naturally.'

'You sell new and second-hand diamonds here?'

'Well of course all diamonds are very old, so that's not

87

the terminology. But yes. We sell what you might call pre-owned diamonds.'

'And was this diamond pre-owned?'

'It was. The stone was – how to put this? – a pre-owned, non-vintage diamond presented in a vintage style.'

'How could you tell it wasn't really vintage?'

'Excellent question! The round brilliant cut was too perfectly angled to be what you might call an "old" cut. A new cut brings in more light, whereas an old cut gives a more limpid appearance. And the mounting – a platinum loop – showed no signs of wear.'

'Where did you get the stone from?'

'It came in off the street.'

Reynolds had an image of Quinn's fat king walking.

'What do you mean?'

'I mean that we bought it off a member of the public who . . . sold it to us!'

'Who was that?'

Savoury sat still and smiled. 'Ah,' he said. 'Now you're the first person to ask that.'

Reynolds was pleased; tried to hide the fact. 'Do you know?'

'Not offhand, but I can find out.'

Savoury went into the little office again. He came back holding a flimsy piece of paper and a more important-looking document, laminated. It was headed 'GIA Coloured Diamond Grading Report', and there was a drawing of the stone looking a bit like the rough doodle in Quinn's floppy book. The date on the certificate was 16 December of the previous year. Savoury then held up the flimsy paper. 'Now this sort of reinforces the certificate. Anyone who sells to us has to sign one.' Reynolds saw the bad thing coming as Savoury began to read from the paper: 'I hereby declare that the undermentioned goods are my own personal property and are not subject to any charge. Signed John-Paul Holden.'

Savoury handed the paper to Reynolds who saw that Holden's name had been printed in capitals beneath the signature. The paper did not give the price the shop had paid for the ring but there was a date: 12 September, just over eleven weeks ago.

Reynolds wondered whether Savoury had noticed that he was not taking a note of these disclosures. Reynolds did not want an official record of the fact that he had unearthed a connection between Anna Samarina and John-Paul Holden.

'Mr Savoury,' said Reynolds, handing back the two documents, 'towards the end of September a man called John-Paul Holden was murdered.' Savoury's smile did not disappear, but it became frozen. 'The Mayfair Hedge Fund Murder. You might have heard of it?'

'I have now that you mention it. I wonder if it's the same man?'

'I should think it is, Mr Savoury. Did you buy the stone yourself? I mean do you have any recollection of the seller? Holden was in his late twenties. He was apparently very good-looking.'

'But I didn't buy this stone. My partner bought it – Mr Moore – and he's on holiday at the moment.'

Good, Reynolds was appalled to find himself thinking, *I can use that to buy some time.* He said, 'I'm surprised I'm the first person to ask who sold it to you, because surely the person who sold it would be best placed to have the copy made?'

'But you *saw* who stole it, and there was no young man involved. The stone had been in the window for ten days before it was taken,' said Mr Savoury. 'Anyone could have photographed it and made a copy from that. Although I admit they got all the detail right on the tag. So yes . . . most likely someone who knew the stone.'

'And where did *Holden* get it from, do you think?'

'Well, I'll ask Mr Moore when he comes back, but it's very unlikely he'll know. Sometimes a seller volunteers the information. We might be offering twenty on a stone, and they'll say, "Oh, I paid forty for it at Tiffany's." But to put the question . . . It would be tantamount to an accusation you see, and remember we do ask for the certificate, and they do have to sign the declaration of legal title.'

'Could the ring we're talking about be an engagement ring?'

'Spot on,' said Savoury. 'It's a classic engagement ring.'

There seemed nothing more to ask. Under the quizzical eye of Savoury, Reynolds re-pocketed his notebook. It was almost as ridiculous an act to put it away as it had been to take it out. As he walked down Mr Savoury's plush little staircase, Reynolds was thinking of Detective Chief Inspector Xavier Hussein of North London Murder. Hussein always wore white shoes. You'd think a man in white shoes would be flamboyant, but everything about Hussein contradicted those shoes. You might also say that everything about him contradicted everything *else* about him. He was small, neat and monosyllabic. His accent was partly Midlands and partly something else. Well, he was obviously Middle

Eastern in some way but if he was a Muslim, he kept very quiet about it. Reynolds thought it not impossible that he was an Iraqi Kurd, but he had a feeling that no Kurds could be called Hussein. Possibly as a result of the white shoes, with their suggestion of informality, Xavier Hussein was known as Zav. He didn't seem to mind being called Zav, but he called *himself* Xavier. He was reserved, but then again not standoffish, and he had not blocked the HOLMES file on the Holden case, unlike Lilley with the Quinn case. Therefore Reynolds knew that Zav Hussein had nothing: no witness, no motive, no DNA, not so much as a footprint, about which he was entitled to be very pissed off, given that Holden had been found on a muddy track on Hampstead Heath – optimum territory for footprints. But the point was *Hussein had nothing*. If Reynolds told him what he'd just discovered, then he'd have *something*. In particular, he'd have the name Anna Samarina. But Reynolds would not be mentioning her name to Hussein. Not yet anyway, because she'd very likely be on a murder charge the moment he did.

13

When Reynolds stepped out of Wilmington's, he saw two people staring at him: the shoeshine boy, and Victoria Clifford. He actually flinched, took a step back. Were they somehow in league, like Sherlock Holmes and the Baker Street Irregulars? But no. The shoeshine boy was just bored, whereas it was the opposite case with Clifford. She walked fast up to Reynolds, took hold of his elbow, and began marching him along the red carpet.

'Did you ask where the stone came from?'

'Yes,' said Reynolds, with a fatalistic sort of sigh.

'I knew you would. If you hadn't I'd have sent you back in. It was Holden, wasn't it? The murdered boy?'

He nodded. They were on Piccadilly. Rain remained highly likely.

'We knew that,' said Clifford. 'Quinn and I.'

'For Christ's sake,' said Reynolds, but Clifford wasn't listening. She was watching the street. What the hell was she going to do? Hail a taxi? She was always likely to do that, and there were plenty going past, their lights already seeming a bright orange at barely noon. But she was pointing at a café over the road. Patisserie Valerie. Reynolds had often passed by, never been in.

'Let's get a coffee,' said Clifford, and she was dragging him across Piccadilly.

In Patisserie Valerie, Christmas was encapsulated in warmth, redness, tinsel, cakes. Clifford had recommended that Reynolds order himself a gluten-free brownie, and she was now eating it.

'It's noisy here, so we can talk,' she said. 'Holden was engaged to the girl in the CCTV. You know her, don't you? From the clubs?'

Reynolds eyed her. Now they were coming to it. 'Yes,' he said. 'I know who she is.'

'Samarina,' said Clifford, 'daughter of Samarin. Quinn sort of knew Samarin.'

'How?'

'Various cultural events in Mayfair. He was interested in him.'

'You mean he was a *person of interest*?'

'Not exactly,' said Clifford, 'but there were rumours.'

'What rumours?'

'I don't know. That something was amiss. Quinn had met the girl a couple of times as well; he liked her.'

'I thought Samarin was a recluse.'

'Yes. But he does good works, so he's got to leave the house occasionally. But please just answer this: did you know that Anna Samarina was engaged to John-Paul Holden?'

'No.'

'Obviously you didn't, because if you did know you'd would have spoken up. You'd have gone to . . . who runs North London Murder these days?'

'Hussein.'

'You'd have gone to Hussein.'

'How did *Quinn* know she was engaged to Holden?'

'*Tatler*,' said Clifford. 'Gossip item. "It is believed the gorgeous Anna Samarina has become secretly engaged to the delectable John-Paul Holden." Or vice-versa.'

'And how come Hussein's team don't know it? Because from the HOLMES they don't.'

'Because *they* don't read *Tatler*. Quinn believed in magazines, you know – more than the internet. He thought more love went into them.'

'Yes, but why didn't Quinn *tell* North London Murder about the engagement?'

'I've just told you: he liked her. What I mean is: he didn't think she could have killed Holden.'

'Well, that's right. Because . . .'

'*Exactly*. The dates don't make sense. Here's a man who meets her very demanding requirements. He's apparently successful, charming, very English, which she probably wants after all that Russian chaos. So they get engaged; he gives her a ring. A ring she likes, the value's not so important, and it symbolises an achievement. He then *breaks off the engagement*. Quinn said you were a reader. I'm thinking of a novel by Trollope . . .'

Reynolds thought: What is this? A game of charades? For a minute he wondered whether she was going to stand up and act it out amid the cakestands. But then he realised he knew the answer: '*The Eustace Diamonds*.'

She looked sidelong, smiling. 'It's different of course because there's a marriage and the problem comes up after the husband dies, but Lizzie Greystock – is it? – won't give the stones back to the family of the husband. She believes they're hers. So you can imagine Anna Samarina . . . she tricks her brain into thinking the stones are hers. She's not stealing them, she's taking back what's hers. Of course, we can't *know* about her motivation. All that's . . .'

'Guesswork.'

'No. It's a dart. *You* can make darts.'

Reynolds drained his cup. 'I've *played* darts,' he said, 'in pubs and so on. I can't say I've ever made them.'

'This is drollery, I assume? A northern thing? I'm talking about a lunge after truth. You make the lunge and go where it leads. Fill in the gaps, get the evidence, answer for the consequences . . . *later*. Do you want another cake?'

'You said the dates don't work.'

'She steals back the diamond on 18 September. She then supposedly kills him on 26 September. Surely that can't be right? She's executed her revenge. She's got the stone back. That draws a line under it, wouldn't you say? The one crime is of a completely different order from the other.'

'What if she killed Holden because he discovered she'd stolen the diamond back?'

'But *how* would he know? And he didn't lose anything by that, did he? So why would he broadcast the fact? He'd sold the stone to the shop and been paid a good price for it. He got what he wanted. I mean, I can't say for certain and nor could Quinn. The question really is this: how mad is Anna Samarina?'

'You brought me into this because you thought I'd protect her, didn't you?'

'No. Well, yes. Partly. But you see this all leads somewhere else. It's a bigger picture than one wayward girl, and if we get to that, we'll find out why Quinn was shot.'

Reynolds recalled the words of Chamberlain of Argrove: the biggest money crime you could imagine, and murders plural. He said, 'What if Holden was killed on the girl's behalf? On the orders of the father, because he'd stumbled on . . . whatever was amiss?'

'It's a possibility. But I think this secret is buried pretty deep. The boy would need to have had some sort of proof; and by killing the boy they put the girl in the frame for his murder – to anyone who knows about the engagement.'

'Do you think she shot Quinn?'

'That's in a way more likely, but still *un*likely, I think.'

They both sat back, momentarily becoming normal customers at Patisserie Valerie. Then Clifford leant forward again. 'I thought you might be able to find out the big picture, and it *is* big. You must understand . . . At first, Quinn was very happy to talk to me about the girl, about Holden, but then, in early November, he went very quiet. He took to spending a lot of time at Annabel's. You could always tell Quinn was preoccupied when he was taxi-ing off to Annabel's every weeknight.'

'What would he do there?'

'What do you *think* you do at Annabel's? Quinn would dance, preen about in his latest suit, pick up . . . people. It was like his equivalent of Sherlock Holmes's pipe, or his violin. He would go there to think, and believe me, if he thought the way to get at what lay beyond the diamond was to hand over to Flying Squad about the robbery or North London Murder about Holden, don't you think he would have done that? He wasn't a complete egomaniac. So we try to follow where he led. We've got a few days before we have to go to Hussein and Lilley with what we know.'

'Do we have Croft's blessing on this?'

She looked at him sharply. 'We'll be fine with Croft.'

Reynolds was beginning to see the usefulness of Clifford: as a sort of unofficial conduit to the top. She was now typing into her phone, which she kept in the most expensive sort of case – calfskin or something.

As she typed, she was saying, 'The sweep has yielded . . . Eaves . . . financial investigator, and narcissist. He's just back from leave. He spoke to Quinn by phone in late September.'

'Has Eaves contacted Lilley?'

'Forget Lilley. He's on the wrong trail. I called Eaves back. He's extremely busy; he told me that personally. But I've pinned him down on Thursday. He's happy to tell you about what Quinn asked him.' Clifford was still typing. 'You can see him before you see Barnes in the pub. Mount Street Deli. Good coffee. Eaves knows about coffee – flat whites and all that.' Putting aside her phone, she rolled her eyes at Reynolds. 'Let's get the bill. And make sure the tip's on the receipt.'

When the bill came, Reynolds said, 'Do we know who Anna Samarina's accomplice was?'

'The guy in the probable wig? No we don't, but Quinn was interested in him. I think that's why he was in touch with Barney Barnes.'

14

Destined for Bond Street on a westbound Central Line train, Ronald Cooper was manipulating a ten-pence coin. The manipulation was called a finger-roll, and it was purely instinctive. Not wanting to appear in any way magicianly – in light of what he'd recently been up to – Cooper stopped as soon as he realised he was doing it. But then he noticed that a little girl, sitting opposite with her mother, had been watching him. She had been smiling, so he started the finger-roll again.

Only the girl was watching, not the mother. Pretty little thing in pink earmuffs – Indian or Pakistani. So it was their secret. She smiled at him, and he looked away, as if rather put out, but he kept rolling the coin, and this combination of being serious but still doing the silly thing amused her even more, as he knew it would from having performed at a thousand children's parties. A thousand? Who was he kidding? You could double that without risk of exaggeration. Cooper liked performing for children. With adults, they were impressed if you fooled them because they thought they were clever . . . So they admitted you must be quite clever yourself. But children – they were just impressed full stop.

The little girl was now laughing, so her mother clicked to what was going on. He saw it from their point of view: a coin climbing over the backs of his fingers like a little living thing, from index finger to pinkie and back. The two were seeing more skill than they knew. Cooper had devoted a good six months of his boyhood to practising the coin roll, and that had been in the pre-decimal days with the half-crown. A big coin was the half-crown, so you had the leverage. It was not so easy with a two-pence piece, the biggest coin available to the modern-day roller, and it was harder still with the ten-pence.

Why, in actual fact, was he rolling the coin? In the restaurant in Mayfair the night before – the Wolseley – he had found himself shuffling cards one-handed while waiting for the bottle of Rioja to arrive. He always carried a pack of cards. They were his calling cards in a manner of speaking, a means of showing his skills to interested parties, who might become paying customers. But he seldom brought them out in a public place without prompting. Cooper had not been showing off. He could honestly say that he had grown out of showing off. No, it must have been down to the nervous energy left over from his adventure with the Russian girl. That had still not worn off, even though it had been nearly three months ago.

They were approaching Oxford Circus, and the mother and daughter were preparing to alight. The girl still watched him though, so he wrapped up the show by disappearing the coin. 'Isn't he a clever man?' said the mother, and it did seem that the little girl agreed, because she was still staring at Cooper from the platform when the train rolled away.

Bond Street next stop, and Cooper would be back in Mayfair. He ought to keep away: stick to his home turf in East London. Better still, take the foreign holiday he could now afford. He fancied the Algarve – for the golf. In Mayfair, he was only putting himself on more and more CCTV, but he was beginning to feel he belonged in Mayfair, in his new outfits, with the restaurant guide always in his pocket, together with that certain other item. Mayfair had been the scene of his greatest triumph; it was just a pity he couldn't walk around in the alpaca coat, but Almond had warned him off wearing it ever again; and he wasn't to sell it or give it to Oxfam either. He ought to have been insulted because the idea of the coat was to cover up Cooper's suit, which was his cabaret suit (he'd been told to wear his best one). But that had not passed muster with Almond or the girl. He had to admit that the alpaca had really done something for him. With all that hair – on the coat and on his head – he *had* felt a bit like the yeti walking into the Arcade, but he had looked the part, he knew.

He thought of Almond's rooms, above that posh antique shop. All the cameras at the entrance, the little lift like a fancy birdcage; and then the room at the top full of all the diamond-dealing gear. Very high-tech it was: computers, scales, lights . . . Difficult to draw the man out about it though. Cagey – that was Almond. It was incredible that he'd owned such an item as the alpaca coat, even if he'd never worn it. It had been a gift, he'd said, and a sort of semi-joke. When Almond had presented it to Cooper . . . that was the nearest Cooper had come to seeing him smile. It had been the day before the job, and the girl had been present. She'd briefly taken off her dark glasses to look at Cooper in the coat: 'The power of cool,' she'd said. It was one of only about five remarks she'd made to Cooper, which included her suddenly saying she would be coming into the shop with him.

Well, she was not a girl you could say 'no' to, and it turned out she'd had an instinctive understanding of the art of distraction. When they'd come out and he'd given her the lifted ring, she'd kissed him on the cheek. 'Thank you my friend,' she'd said. He didn't know her name, and as far as he knew, she didn't know his either. She was always in half disguise, and her hair kept changing, but of course he'd know her again, and she hadn't seemed to mind about that. Presumably she knew what Almond had told him: that if he ever spoke about what had happened, or attempted to contact her, the consequences would be serious.

In Cooper's fantasy, she was the daughter he'd never had. He didn't see her very often – in this fantasy – so when he did see her, he made a big fuss of her. They were kept apart much of the time by the demands of his career. You see, he had a top-rating show on US cable and he had to keep it going for the sake of his support act, Penn and Teller. The rest of the time he was in . . . He was in the Algarve, where his golf handicap was . . .

It was silly.

He was standing in Hanover Square, on the west side, and he hardly knew how he'd got there. He stopped and checked his top pocket. Yes, still there – the forty grand's worth. A motorcyclist was sitting on his bike nearby, watching him – Cooper thought – through the dark visor of his helmet. So Cooper walked fast to St George Street, the exit from the Square to the south side. The motorcyclist pulled away, so it was just Cooper in St George Street, with the grey church of the same name, the grey sky . . . and a very attractive-looking restaurant. He walked over. Like an old Pullman carriage, it was: soft lighting, cosy, with individual booths. It was empty just now, between lunchtime and evening service. There was a menu outside, and Cooper read it as the church bell began to chime four. 'Roast Norfolk pheasant, cabbage, quince compote, sausage roll.' Sausage roll! He didn't know about that. He assumed they didn't mean the sort of thing you got in Greggs.

It was lonely in St George Street when the bells had stopped ringing. He headed south, towards Piccadilly. It was always a tonic to be on Piccadilly with money in your pocket, or in his case his credit card and the forty grand's worth. In the event, he *crossed* Piccadilly and found himself on St James's Street. He was looking in a hat shop. Perhaps he should buy a fedora for a hundred and twenty pounds, bring that 'Man of Mystery' touch to the cabaret act.

He was now outside a tobacconist's. They actually had the wooden Indian standing outside – the universal sign of the tobacconist. 'Smoking lounge upstairs,' he read. Should he go in? Trouble was, he didn't smoke. He had to remember he was not one of the idle rich. There was no point nudging towards his credit limit just for the sake of it, and think of the interest. He'd better cash in his forty grand's worth sooner rather than later, he thought, as he moved towards the window of the wine merchants called Berry Brothers. It was here that he made his plan. He would buy a decent bottle of wine, and take it to Almond's place off Bond Street, and he would try to realise his forty grand that very evening. He'd need a bit of Dutch courage for that, so he'd have a couple of G & T's on the way.

15

There had been no Prince of Wales check in a thirty-eight left in Hackett, so Victoria Clifford had taken Reynolds over the road to Ede & Ravenscroft. He had wanted the chalk stripe on grey, single-breasted. But that was parody City gent, which the Russians would think absurd. He had the figure for the hourglass, so they'd come down to two double-breasteds: the charcoal or the mid-blue. She'd had some fun with the trying on. 'Put your hands in your pockets!' 'Take your hands out of your pockets!' He knew absolutely nothing of how side vents should work, but he knew he looked good. Reynolds and that full-length mirror had rapidly been developing a relationship. She'd let him make the final choice, and he'd gone for the blue, which seemed fortuitous, because Quinn had one just the same. He'd put it on his credit card. She'd tried to steel him for the fight with finance officer Trevor Kennedy. Did Kennedy really think you could deal with billionaires in a Marks & Spencer suit? He probably did because he lived in Orpington. She was quite looking forward to the fight over the suit. There was a clear policing reason for the purchase. Being well presented was an important part of being professional. The standard of dress shall be smart, fit for purpose and convey a favourable impression of the service. She was very familiar with the dress-code toolkit.

Unfortunately, the trousers had to be taken up, so the M&S suit had had to do for the *Mayfair Gazette* photo. It would be in the paper the day after tomorrow: the Thursday. The thought that she was trying to launch a new Quinn made her feel guilty about the old one. And so, at four, she'd gone to the Church of the Immaculate Conception in Farm Street, to light a candle for him. When she'd told Reynolds she would be doing this, he'd remarked, inanely, 'I didn't know you were a Catholic.' What else did he think had screwed her up?

She had been thinking about Reynolds and clothes as a way of not thinking about what she was about to see, in the private room of St Michael's Hospital . . .

The nurse introduced her to the doctor and they walked fast down a bright, pale-blue corridor. Something about the pale blueness told you it was raining outside. The doctor was talking to her over his shoulder. She knew his surname only: Henderson. He must be one of those rugby-playing types of medical men; muscular Christian: a big man, yet not big enough for the suit he wore. As a consultant anaesthetist, he was presumably excused the white coat. What was the posh sort of rugby? He would play that version of course. Half of them were called Toby. She looked down, and, yes, brown shoes. He obviously wasn't going to stand still for a minute, so Victoria talked to his back.

'Is there any prospect of a full recovery?'

'I wouldn't rule it out.'

'Have you taken the bullet out?'

'Not as yet.'

He had a lot of other things to be getting on with, no doubt.

The nurse, walking behind, said to Clifford's back: 'There's no infection, so that's good. Here we are, on the left.'

Where was the armed guard?

The doctor wheeled left abruptly, in a way that made Clifford think the nurse had been speaking for his benefit. Clifford lowered her head as she walked through the door. She thought of the big night out that she had coming up. She would wear her Jigsaw party frock; no, the faux-Chanel. She looked up. Quinn was sitting half upright. Because of the oxygen mask on his face he looked almost like the pilot of a supersonic plane, and handsome with it, although they'd brushed his hair the wrong way (which meant, she slowly realised, that his head was not bandaged). It was as if during the course of the flight he'd been hit by a strong wind coming in from the left – and of course they'd got him in some kind of green smock instead of the pale-blue silk Hilditch & Key pyjamas favoured by the conscious Quinn. In her shocked state, she must have made some remark on his posture, because the doctor was lecturing her about how it was normally thirty degrees, but in Quinn's case more for some strange reason.

Quinn, Victoria Clifford was thinking, seemed to have no shortage of visitors, but they were all robots. There were half a dozen clustered about the bed and the nurse was introducing them to Clifford: ventilator, monitor, probe . . . That last one was going into his brain, where the pressure was normal, the nurse was saying. As far as Clifford could see, all he needed to do was wake up. They needed a big brass alarm clock.

'You can hold his hand,' said the nurse. Victoria looked at the doctor, who gave an encouraging nod. Encouraging and patronising, Clifford thought. She looked at Quinn and she thought of the time she'd gone up with him to his father's house, and he'd driven off to that gay club. It was in Scarborough, for heaven's sake. And he'd picked up a man who had a little dog, as he'd told her with great relish when he'd returned. She'd chosen to believe it was an act against his father, and not against her; and you couldn't blame a man for his true nature. The anomaly was that he'd some-times slept with her, not that he sometimes slept with men. Mostly, like her, he didn't sleep with anyone. What they did was talk: in restaurants; in the Yard; in the little hotels of Victoria; at her flat; in the Buddha Room at Annabel's.

Crouching by the bed, she took his hand. Quinn, with his eyes closed, and no movement from the rest of him, squeezed her hand, immediately bringing a tear to her eye. The nurse had spotted it – hand-squeeze and tear. Clifford could tell this from a rustle behind her, and she also knew the nurse was smiling. Clifford liked the nurse, but Hender-son was on his wretched mobile phone and walking out of the room.

'I'm afraid it's only a reflex,' said the nurse. 'I'm told he's a brilliant man.'

Come on Quinn, Clifford thought, *don't let me down*. But the tense wasn't quite right there. What she really meant was: *you'd better not turn out to have let me down*. Clifford found herself thinking of McKenna, a respectable business-man, or at any rate the owner of a minicab firm.

He'd had a veritable murder factory in a lock-up garage in east London. Middle-aged working-class women: he stabbed them, and burnt them in barrels of petrol, when they weren't necessarily dead, but perhaps only full of stab holes. McKenna had been Quinn's serial killer, the only one he ever came up against, and he'd stopped him after

106

three deaths. Without Quinn there might have been a dozen. Clifford herself had nudged him in the right direction, she had to admit. She'd pointed out that all the women worked late – two of them in bars – in jobs that allowed them to claim the costs of a cab. Well, it had been Clifford's special subject: expenses! This was before the extension of the Tube to that part of London: public transport was almost non-existent, and everything came back to minicabs.

But the true dart had come when Quinn realised that none of the victims used McKenna's firm, even though it was the dominant one in the locality, and the nearest to their homes. This was unconscious. They weren't deliberately avoiding McKenna. Perhaps they hadn't even known about his firm. If they had done, and they'd used him, they'd have been on his phone records and so on, and he wouldn't have touched them.

The way Quinn had squeezed her hand. It was like the way he told a joke, with no fanfare. You sometimes didn't know it was a joke until later. Looking at Quinn's closed eyes, she thought of the word 'comatose'. It had been flowing in a sinuous way through her head, and she knew why: it was used in the song by . . . She couldn't recollect, but she and Quinn would dance to it at Annabel's. It was one of his regular requests. Another – more of a smoocher, for later in the evening – was called 'If You Leave Me Now'. She turned away quickly from Quinn. She must act. It appeared that his protection had devolved to hospital security personnel, who were neither armed nor in evidence at the present time. She'd get on to SO1, Specialist Protection. And she'd see about getting this Henderson replaced.

16

'So I have the fake finger-palmed in the right hand. Held in the fingers but with the fingers *straight*.'

Peter Almond lit a Silk Cut. 'So you're not clutching it?' he said, because he thought he'd better seem interested.

'It's not a clutch,' Cooper said, 'so it's more natural than the true palm, where it's actually *in* the palm. Pick up with the left hand, transfer to the right to examine – then back to the left hand for the set-down. It might seem an unnatural movement the first time, but by the second it's normal, and the third you don't notice. It's the rule of three – it's a flow thing. The third time, I release the fake, transferring *that* back to the left hand for the set-down, while keeping the target stone in my right hand.'

Almond nodded.

'*Game over*,' said Cooper, pouring himself more wine. 'Now I didn't go straight for the pocket with the target stone,' he continued. 'The hand goes down to the side. The hand relaxes. I go for the pocket a couple of minutes later.'

'And the girl was there with you?' said Almond. 'That seems rather crazy.'

Cooper shrugged in his chair. 'Insisted on coming with.'

'But why?'

'You tell me. Maybe she didn't trust me; thought I'd walk off with the stone.'

'That would not have been very wise.'

'Maybe it was for the thrill. But it wasn't such a big risk

when you look at it. We're both disguised, and there's nothing to connect us except . . .' He waved towards Almond. 'I said to her, not wanting to sound big-headed or anything, but even if the shop bod is looking straight at my hand when I do the switch, he won't *see* the switch.'

Almond was thinking about his connection with Cooper. He'd booked him to do a show for his kids – the oldest boy's thirteenth birthday. He'd known even then that he was dodgy. Not a kiddy-fiddler of course, which you might suspect from his line of work. No, Cooper had done time for pickpocketing, and it had become apparent to Almond that this must be the sleight-of-hand expert who'd palmed a biggish stone in an Hatton Garden shop in about 1995. He'd nicked it to order for some thug, and it had been beautifully done, which might also be said of his work in Wilmington's. But the guy's success had evidently gone to his head. Three months on and he still hadn't got over it. He was shaping up as a loose cannon, which was dangerous in light of what had happened.

'I said to her, "If you're coming with, we might as well use you."'

Almond nodded again.

'So she did the distraction. I told her to—'

'It was a good day's work for the two of us,' said Almond, trying to make it sound final. He stood up, and walked over to his workbench without any idea of what he was going to do when he got there.

'I wonder if they've tumbled yet,' said Cooper. 'I know I shouldn't go back to look.'

'You shouldn't, no – and you don't need to. They *have* tumbled. The fake's gone from the window. They'll have spoken to the police.'

Almond began fiddling with a lantern. It occurred to him that Cooper was within range of a stray business card of Almond's that featured his phone number. He'd walked over and pocketed it. He returned to the workbench.

Cooper watched him. He said, 'How do you think they could tell?'

'The excess fire of the CZ. It would become apparent when it's put next to the genuine article.'

'Really?'

A silence fell. Almond put out his cigarette in a way intended to signify: this meeting's over.

'I'll be off in a tick,' said Cooper. 'But we might as well finish this wine.'

Interesting that he said 'we', given that he'd downed two-thirds of the bottle on his own.

Cooper said, 'Would you mind just telling me, old man, how the whole thing came about? Because I couldn't really ask the girl, and I do want to get it all straight.'

Cooper reached for the bottle. Almond lit another cigarette. 'I can tell you some of it,' he said, 'then I'm going to have to head off, I'm afraid.'

Cooper nodded, grateful.

'She came to me with her fiancé,' said Almond.

'And what was he like?'

'I'll show you a picture of him in a minute. They looked at some stones for a ring, mainly whites, but she was always after a yellow. Her mother had liked yellow diamonds, or something. She'd seen a picture of her mother wearing them. The mother meant a lot to the girl because she died giving birth to her.'

Cooper frowned.

Almond said, 'She fell in love with the yellow I showed her. Everything about the stone: the brilliant cut. All facets warming up the yellow. We agreed it would look perfect in a vintage setting.'

'Where did you get it from?'

'Never you mind.'

The original stone was from South Africa, illegally traded.

'I acquired it as rough,' Almond continued, 'got it cleaved and polished up in Antwerp.'

'Sounds big.'

'It yielded two principals and . . . a parcel of smaller material. She chose it, he paid.'

'*How* did he pay?'

'That's confidential,' said Almond, and Cooper looked at him sadly. Almond relented somewhat. 'Half in cash,' he said, whereas in fact the guy had paid the total sum in cash: two instalments of ten grand, for which he'd earned himself a ten per cent discount. It occurred to Almond that he would have to erase the CCTV footage of Cooper's arrival. 'Two weeks later, the boyfriend came back. He said the engagement's fallen through, and would I like to buy back the stone? I said no. I sent him to the Arcade, and he sold it there. *She* then saw it there, so then I had *her* knocking on my door. She said the stone was hers. I said, "He gifted it to you?" She said, "What is 'gifted'? He *gave* me it." She asked if I could get a paste copy made, and did I know anybody who could do the switch.'

'You said no to him and yes to her,' said Cooper.

'A woman's wiles,' said Almond.

'Why didn't she just buy it back?'

'As she saw it, the stone was hers already. And she's a bit of a nut.'

It was Almond's turn to ask a question. 'What were your wages?'

Cooper produced a stone from the inside pocket of his jacket. He'd actually been *carrying* it there, for God's sake. He passed it to Almond. A two-carat e-colour flawless. Might fetch forty, but a man like Cooper would probably not be offered more than early thirties. Even so, he'd done well. Rather better than Almond himself.

'Can you give it the once-over for me?' Cooper asked.

Almond laid his cigarette in the ashtray; he angled his lantern, put a loupe in his eye and held up the stone against a sheet of white paper.

'A little sleepy,' he said, handing it back, 'but it ought to fetch thirty grand with no trouble.'

'I was wondering whether you might want to make an offer.'

Almond shook his head. 'Not my kind of goods.'

It was exactly his kind of goods, but he couldn't have any more dealings with Cooper or anybody in the nexus of the yellow stone. He said, 'She gave you the cert as well, I assume?' Cooper nodded, looking sadly at the stone. 'Then try Hatton Garden. But give it a few months if you can hang on.'

'When the dust has settled, you mean?'

'It could be a while,' said Almond.

He stood up, and eyed Cooper. All the merchandise was in the safe except for a one-carat white on the side. He wouldn't insult the guy by moving it. He walked through to his storeroom, returned with a carrying sling and a back number of the *Evening Standard*.

'If you must carry the stone about, put it in that, and wear it under your shirt.'

'Right you are,' said Cooper. 'I suppose you think I'm crackers to have it on me.'

Trying to be kind, Almond said, 'You'd be amazed what walks up and down Bond Street.'

Cooper was removing his shirt, exposing a not very pretty sight. Almond handed him the newspaper. It was open at the right page: the report of the murder.

'That's the boyfriend,' said Almond, 'the fiancé.'

'Bloody hell,' said Cooper. 'Are you saying she killed him?'

'I'm not saying that, no. On balance I'd say probably not. But it's become very messy, and you ought not to come here again.'

Almond put out his cigarette, this time with finality.

17

At midday on Thursday 11 December, Reynolds watched the rain from the high window of the Down Street office. He was about to go to Mount Street, for his meetings with financial investigator Eaves, and ex-copper Barney Barnes. He had no idea where Victoria Clifford might be.

Open on his desk was the *Mayfair Gazette*. A picture of himself occupied half a page. There might have been some consolation in the fact that the *Mayfair Gazette* had a small readership, whether in print or online, but that had been removed by the appearance on the streets about an hour ago of the *Evening Standard*, which had run a variation of the story, albeit over just a quarter of a page. Reynolds thought of all those hundreds of thousands of copies being thrown out of vans on rainy street corners for distribution free to the populace, and then all the clicks on all the laptops, tablets and smartphones. Clifford had telephoned from somewhere. 'The picture looks much better smaller,' she'd said.

It had been raining for more than twenty-four hours, and there seemed no reason for it to stop. It was 'set in', as people said in York, but probably not in Mayfair. Yesterday had been a quiet day, but with one big jolt. He had taken the Tube from Green Park to St James's Park, in order to visit the Yard, where he intended to browse various databases and paper files at the Information Bureau. In St James's Park Tube station, he'd been queuing at the ticket office, in order to get a printout of the journeys made on his Oyster card. It was his habit to tick off the ones made on Met business, and claim for those. He was about to be served when he saw a pair of ghostly feet: a small, neat man in white shoes stepping into the station from the south side. Xavier Hussein had obviously come from the Yard. He looked, Reynolds suddenly thought, like a golfer. His facial expression – a moderate frown – suggested he'd found no new leads on the killing of John-Paul Holden, but with Zav Hussein you never knew. If he ever decided to maximise that enigmatic quality, he would be more than just a semi-flier. In a minute he'd see Reynolds. The ticket clerk's hand was outstretched to receive Reynolds' Oyster card, but Reynolds withdrew the card, turned about and left the station by the north entrance. He stood on Broadway, breathing heavily in the swirling grey rain. He wouldn't bother going back to itemise his journeys. He'd just claim for the cost of the whole bloody card, like every other detective on the force.

In the Yard, he bought a coffee for a contact in Serious and Organised Crime Intelligence Support, and so learnt a little more about the career of Barney Barnes.

Barnes had joined the Met in the early seventies. He had failed his sergeant's exams first time around, then joined the Flying Squad as DS at a time of corruption scandals. Barnes had never been prosecuted, but he'd been close to some of the blokes who *were* done, which was probably why he'd remained stuck at DS for fifteen years.

Whilst at the yard, Reynolds had also wandered into Foreign Office Liaison to ask whether they had any Russian speakers on the premises. They did not, but he was referred to a guy who did Technical Support for covert policing who'd just been in the Liaison office and was now probably in the canteen – and so it proved.

He turned out not to be Met. He was a service provider, some sort of electronics expert. He was called Gregory and he was half Russian and half English. Since he was not actually MPS staff, Reynolds ought not to have shown him an item that should have been securely bagged and tagged in an evidence room, but he seemed a perfectly nice bloke, so Reynolds showed him the written-on pages of the floppy book, asking, 'Is anything there in Russian?'

'None of it is Russian,' Gregory said, after a quick inspection.

'No, but I mean transliterated Russian, if that's the word.'

Gregory looked again. He pointed to 'SERG E I'. 'Sergei,' he said. 'A Russian first name.'

'But why the gaps?'

Gregory shrugged. 'Could be an abbreviation of Sergeant, and then the initials E. I.?'

Reynolds said, 'Good idea,' but he'd already thought of that, and there was no one at all on the MPS Directory with the initials 'E. I.'

Gregory looked again; this time he pointed to the word 'Sfinsk'. 'Means "Sphinx" in Russian,' he said.

Again Reynolds thanked him, but the mystery of the word was only increased if the word itself *meant* mystery. (Or as good as.)

There was nothing on any Met database about Andrei Samarin or Anna Samarina, so Reynolds had repeatedly googled them both, finding more about her than him. She would come up alongside photos of parties, fashion shows, art fairs, auctions, but the text was often in Russian. Her father's name came up in bland lists of oligarchs. He was low-key, and he gave a lot of money to the arts in London, Russia and France. He had once written a very obscure book about the planning of modern industrial towns in Russia, and almost everything to do with that was in Russian. Samarin might have qualified as the 'shadow oligarch' or the 'intellectual oligarch' but those roles were already taken.

Most of the coverage for Samarin was about his boat, *Queen for A Day*, which appeared to be his biggest extravagance if you discounted the Mayfair mansion, the chateau near Nice and the bolthole in St Barth's. The *Queen* was raved about on superyacht websites. She was one of the dozen biggest sailing superyachts in the world.

There was marginally more about his business partner, a man called Viktor Rostov. He had just bought a big house in Surrey. His name also brought up a story from a local newspaper in Northumberland about the shooting of a 'much-loved' dog on a country estate. The dog had been shot by a gamekeeper called Michael Fleet. It had evidently been harassing sheep and 'out-of-pen pheasants'. Mr Fleet had been found not guilty of criminal damage in respect of the dog, which he had shot three times with a double-barrelled shotgun. That had been in 2013. The article concluded by mentioning that 'the owner of the estate, Major Graham Porter, is a security consultant to some of Britain's wealthiest businessmen, including the Russian oligarch, Mr Viktor Rostov. Major Porter was out of the country at the time of the drama.'

Reynolds googled Porter. Only scraps, and no doubt

Porter liked it that way. He'd evidently done a bit of motor racing. Nothing on his army record. Putting in 'Samarin' and 'Rostov' together brought up a silent YouTube clip of a giant earth-mover attacking a mountain of snow-covered coal under what appeared to be a night sky. There were no comments.

18

The gothic brickwork of Mount Street was a scrubbed, pale pink that appeared livid against the darkening sky. The shop fronts had sprouted dark-green foliage – a Dickensian-Christmas look.

Reynolds had walked there in the Aquascutum, carrying the disapproved-of umbrella, and wearing the M&S suit, Clifford having insisted he keep the new suit in reserve for the drinks with Plyushkin's Gardeners. At the north end of Down Street, a man had fallen in step behind him, talking Russian loudly into a mobile phone. He wore a bad suit, and was angry: he was probably only talking business, but it seemed to Reynolds that all the turmoil of the Revolution, Stalingrad, and the Gulags was in his voice. Reynolds stopped outside the Curzon Cinema to let him go by, but the man stopped there too, shouting under the same canopy. It was there that Reynolds saw the first man in a black four-by-four looking directly at him. If the man was English there was nothing English *about* him. The shouting man now moved away, his work of agitating Reynolds having been taken up by this new person.

Reynolds walked on, heading into the heart of Mayfair. Cars moved slowly behind him in the pretty, rainswept, Hansel-and-Gretel streets. Reynolds was regretting his appearance in the *Evening Standard*.

The cars parked outside the Mount Street Deli were all, without exception, black Range Rovers. Some had people –

men – in them, behind the smoked windows and swishing wipers. There was also one expensive-looking red bike, locked to a lamp post. That would be Eaves's. Reynolds saw Eaves, sitting on a high stool at the shelf-like table against the window. His fluorescent cycling jacket was folded neatly on the stool next to him, and he was talking into his phone. The Deli was chalet-like inside, mock-rustic with wooden walls, cosy on this day of rain. Bespoke Christmas Hampers were advertised. A blackboard announced hot sandwiches involving things like Brie and rocket for six pounds. Smoothies were four pounds. Eaves had ordered a smoothie. Eaves *was* a smoothie. He had a lot of curly black hair with a few raindrops sparkling in it; his black roll-neck jumper was possibly cashmere. Reynolds wondered whether Quinn would have approved of that jumper, and of Eaves in general. All he knew was that Quinn had called Eaves, and asked him for information. Eaves was saying, 'It's good on the hilly stuff, yeah, but there's an issue with the front mech.' He was talking about his bike.

Detective Sergeant Stephen Eaves was about thirty, and he was a flier. Reynolds was old enough to think of him as Fraud Squad, but Eaves would never use that term himself. He was number two in a Financial Investigation team under the Economic and Specialist Crime Command. As Reynolds sat on a high stool alongside him, Eaves put his hand over his phone, and said, 'All right fella?' The person at the other end was looking something up. Reynolds said he'd order, and Eaves asked for a double espresso. He wouldn't eat; hadn't got time . . . So none of this was very promising. Eaves, like most of the fliers, was hard to pin down. He'd always be in a meeting when you called, and when you met him he'd *still* be in a meeting, albeit by phone. There was a newspaper on the high table near him: the *Wall Street Journal*. Reynolds wondered whether it belonged to Eaves or the Deli: could easily have been either.

A man stood in the rain over the road. He was conspicuous by virtue of not being in a black four-by-four. He wore jeans and a black blouson jacket. He was big, athletic; his hair was a blond brush-cut. He could have been a basketball player.

Eaves was holding up his phone as Reynolds brought the coffee over. It showed the footage of the giant mechanical digger that Reynolds had already seen; but Eaves knew more about it. 'Here's one of Samarin's mines from a few years ago,' he said. 'Open-cast. Somewhere near the Ob River, just this side of the Urals. Not exactly a holiday resort.'

'It was Samarin that Quinn wanted to talk to you about?'

'That's what he told me. Can't remember the date, but I was tied up over the next few days. Then he got shot.'

Reynolds asked, 'Any idea *why* he wanted to know about Samarin?'

'Not a clue.'

Eaves did not seem to have been very curious on the point. Reynolds also hoped he would not be curious about why he in turn wanted to know about Samarin. He was betting heavily on Eaves's lack of curiosity, which he believed stemmed from his egotism. Eaves would not believe that anything anybody else was doing could possibly be important.

'Tell me what you know about Samarin,' said Reynolds, sitting down, and he was gratified by the way that Eaves did not look askance at the absence of a notebook. Reynolds had gone right off his notebook.

'It's Samarin *and Rostov*,' Eaves began. 'They're business partners. Sort of like . . . Jagger–Richards.'

'Best mates?'

Eaves shook his head. 'Don't really get on. Very different characters but they're stuck with each other. Samarin's reticent, tasteful; got the reputation of an intellectual. Rostov's a heavy – ex-KGB and looks the part.'

Reynolds looked over the road. Brush Cut was now sitting under the canopy outside Scott's restaurant. He was the only man under the canopy. He sat amid the decorative torches that burned there, and he didn't look as if he belonged. His eyes met Reynolds' and so they were into a staring match as Eaves continued: 'It's the classic double act. Samarin was the ideas man, Rostov brought protection, which you needed in Russia in the early nineties because it was, you know, the Klondyke.'

Eaves's phone rang. He was good enough to suppress it.

'It's called *krysha*,' he said.

'What is?' said Reynolds, who'd lost the staring match, looking away first from Brush Cut.

'The protection. It means ceiling. There's no formal contract, just an understanding. Others had legal battles over this sort of arrangement. Samarin and Rostov seem to have avoided coming to blows about it, and they've spent the past twenty years cashing in their chips and putting all the grubby stuff a long way behind them, including the coal. What you've got now is two respectable citizens. Samarin's based mainly here, in Mayfair, just around the corner, in what is considered the finest private house in SW1.'

'Who considers it that?'

'A lot of people who've never been inside it. Rostov's just bought a big place in Surrey. They've both got places in the south of France and the West Indies or wherever. Samarin's got a big boat. They probably did well in hedge funds in about 2000. They're in property now – lot of developments along the river here, and some projects in Russia to keep Putin happy. Samarin's a philanthropist . . .'

'In the arts?'

'Yes, but also research into clean technologies. Carbon capture. He'd probably say he was putting something back, if he ever talked to the press.'

'What are they worth?'

Eaves shrugged. 'A billion apiece?'

'Can you tell me how they earned it?'

Eaves picked up his phone, checking the time. 'Quick overview,' he said, 'but keep in mind most of this is speculation because they're not people of interest as far as we're concerned. Back in the early nineties, when things were taking off in Russia, Samarin got into frozen foods. You'd think that was a big thing in a country with terrible cuisine that's half frozen anyway, but apparently not. Distribution systems were poor, and a lot of – I don't know – cabbages and potatoes were just rotting away in Moscow warehouses. So Samarin got that going, big factories in Moscow and St Petersburg, but with his personal base and the holding company always out east. Not quite Siberia but nearly. He's from an island in the Kara Sea, which is an obscure sea up there that's frozen most of the year. Then I think he lived in Tomsk, which is in Western Siberia. He moved around a lot because of his father's job.'

'What was that?'

'On the railways, I think. Then the father died and he was brought up by some female relative. But nobody really knows about this stuff. Rostov's from Moscow. KGB, as I said, but I think he saw he was onto a loser there, and he was out of it by the end of the eighties. I don't know how he met Samarin, but he probably thought, this guy's my meal ticket for life. When the frozen-food thing took off, Samarin got into coal, and he started buying up state coal mines. He got them for next to nothing, but the price of coal was falling at the time, so it looked like a mad strategy. But he must have banked on China and the developing world going for growth and not being too particular about burning coal.'

'Why should they be particular?'

'Global warming.'

Reynolds had forgotten about that. Brush Cut was still looking at Reynolds from the terrace of Scott's. The staring match was on again, and this time war was being declared between the two of them. A waiter was approaching Brush Cut.

Eaves was saying, 'Samarin starts up a bank, the Moscow stock exchange being so crap at the time, and he grows the business. He hooks up with Rostov, and Rostov becomes the sort of public face. But they run the business at arm's length.'

'How's that done?'

'They avoid sitting on the boards of their own companies for one thing.'

'Why?'

'Probably because in the early years the whole thing's volatile and likely to go phut. Then they'll end up in jail or dead. It's safer to be out of Russia, so the two of them move to France for a couple of years, then they come over here. Meanwhile coal's sparking upwards and they start cashing in their chips like I say. Some of the companies begin to be registered here; others are kept in Russia. I mean they don't want to look unpatriotic. They bring some of the sub-sidiaries to market in London, testing the water, then the holding company. The first IPO's about 1998, can't remember the exact date offhand. And of course they're shuttling the equity offshore, probably to the Caymans.'

'How do you know?'

'Educated guess. The nominee companies that owned the listed companies were registered in the Caymans.'

'That had to be disclosed?'

'Yeah.'

'So it's likely that's where the proceeds of sale went?'

'Yeah. But I mean so what? We're talking about vast un-touchable personal wealth. It's going to be held offshore, does it matter where? Most of their time now is probably spent managing their personal wealth, and building luxury flats, mainly in London.'

'And they've invested shrewdly in London property?'

'How shrewd do you have to *be* to invest in London property?'

'What about Samarin's daughter?'

'She's terrifically good-looking.'

'How rich would she be?'

'She's going to be minted one day. I mean she's the sole heir. Meanwhile she's probably getting ten grand a week from a trust, or maybe not so much. It's said that she's not spoilt. But these terms are all relative.'

'Why did Quinn want to talk to you about Samarin and Rostov?'

'No idea, fella. No idea whatsoever. I half thought it might be a sort of test. Because he was looking for a financial investigator, wasn't he? All academic now anyway.'

Eaves clearly did not consider that Reynolds himself might be looking for a financial investigator, no doubt because Eaves saw very little future for Quinn, Reynolds or the new unit. Reynolds paid the bill and the pair of them moved towards the door. Reynolds saw that Brush Cut had been ejected from under the canopy of Scott's. He still stared at Reynolds, and he was now making a mobile-phone call.

19

Reynolds thanked Eaves, and watched him cycle off. A sort of shift-change was going on beneath umbrellas near one of the black four-by-fours. Some men in suits were leaving the car, others were going into it. It was about as big a Range Rover as it was possible to buy, which was saying something. There seemed no prospect of anyone driving it anywhere. Reynolds couldn't tell if there was any connection between Brush Cut and the four-by-four lot.

Barney Barnes was approaching the pub from South Audley Street, fag in mouth. He hadn't seen Reynolds, probably wouldn't have recognised him if he had done. They'd spoken only a couple of times at the Yard. Reynolds looked at Barnes through Quinn's eyes. He wore trainers, which no man over thirty ever should; his trousers were probably called slacks, and they were too short. His socks were fawn; his upper half was bursting out of a shortie mac. He'd miscalculated on the cigarette front, arriving at the door of the pub with most of it left to smoke, so he had the choice of finishing it off in the rain or going into the warm. He threw down the fag in apparent fury before entering the pub. Reynolds followed him, and Brush Cut's head turned, like a slow machine, as he observed.

Barnes was at the bar. Reynolds touched his arm. Barnes turned and recognised Reynolds without enthusiasm.

'This weather,' he said. 'Gets you down, doesn't it?'

They carried their drinks over to a little table that looked particularly little when Barnes sat down at it. 'Been busy?' said Barnes. 'What's Flanagan doing with the murder teams? Tell you what, forget I asked, I don't want to know.'

So Reynolds didn't tell him.

'So you're with this new OCU?' Barnes said. Reynolds didn't like to say he was running the show. 'Quinn's outfit. Poor bastard. What's the point of it again?'

'Keeping tabs on the super-rich.'

'The super-rich?' Barnes drank a lot of his beer. 'What a lot of cunts they are.'

Barnes was now coughing.

'Are you all right, Barney?' asked Reynolds, although he wasn't sure whether first-name terms were appropriate.

'Not really,' said Barnes. 'Heart. It's not imminent, but I've had one attack, and another's on the cards, according to the doc. I've been on antibiotics. Does you up. Makes you very weak.'

He didn't look weak; just ill.

'You follow football?' asked Barnes. 'My team's QPR. We've got this centre-half. Didn't fucking *exist* the other night. Didn't touch the ball more than twice the entire game.' He eyed Reynolds for a while. 'Fucking super-rich. Arabs, Nigerians, Russians, Yanks, bloody *French*. My brother gets them in the cab, putting their feet up, lighting cigarettes. Treat him like dirt. The most obnoxious, greedy, arrogant . . . And do you think they tip? You've got to be fucking joking. They always want to go places like Bournemouth – you can get on a private jet at Bournemouth. They'll stop him at midnight in the King's Road. Put the bags in the back, and take me to Bournemouth fucking airport, and if he says he's sorry but he's off to bed, they start fucking screaming at him. But there's nothing you can do about it.'

Reynolds realised he wasn't going to be bonding with Barnes, so he said, 'Quinn wanted to talk to you.'

'Quinn, yeah. How is he? Still got the bullet in, from what I've heard. That ain't good. We were in a squad once, me and him. Manhunt. Lee Chubb. Now he was a bad man. What kind of cunt takes a sawn-off shotgun to steal fifty quid from a corner shop? Eventually, the thing goes off. Twice. We're in the incident room with some forensics boys, and Quinn's looking at my legs. I said, "Excuse me, but what's your fucking problem?" He told me I ought to get longer socks. Said he could see my leg.' Barnes drank most of the rest of his beer, '. . . and he didn't *want* to see it. Well, fair enough. You'd take that from Quinn because who do you think it was nicked Lee Chubb in the end? Two thousand exhibits in that case when it came to court. I don't believe Quinn saw one. Everything we considered evidence, he didn't. The other day he called me. Wanted to talk about jewels. Wanted to know who could get a fake ring made for a switch done by, you know, manipulation.'

'Do you know the case he had in mind?'

Barnes shook his head. 'Retired, ain't I? And he wasn't saying. But I gave him a name.'

'What name?'

'Almond. As in the nut. Slightly dodgy jeweller, and clever with it. He'll get hold of a biggish rock. Twelve, fifteen carats of rough. Not too particular about where it comes from. Anything bigger than that's out of his league. And he'll cut the fucking thing. There's very little cutting goes on here now. It's all done in Amsterdam.'

Barnes completely finished his pint. 'Not Amsterdam,'

he said. 'Antwerp. But he can do anything with a diamond, and he can produce the fakes. You got a pen?'

Reynolds gave Barnes a pen and the back of a receipt to write on. Barnes wrote down an address, saying, 'It's off Bond Street.' The piece of paper happened to be the receipt for the new suit: £550, and Barnes happened to turn it over; he eyed Reynolds. 'Excuse me for asking because it's none of my business, but where are you getting this sort of money?'

'I bought a suit,' said Barnes. 'I'm claiming it back on expenses.'

'You'll be lucky.'

'It's necessary to look the part.'

Barnes eyed him. 'Quinn,' he said, '. . . we all knew the score.'

'How do you mean?'

'Secret squirrel. Law unto him-fucking-self. Gay – you'd have to say. But I mean where did the secretary fit in? She's a funny girl.'

Barnes leant forward. He was speaking to someone standing behind Reynolds. 'Excuse me mate, would you like to come and join us?'

Reynolds craned, and saw Brush Cut. He did not appear to have a drink. He carried his head very high, which made him look haughty, trying to rise above the pub fray.

Barnes spoke again. 'I said, excuse me mate, would you like to come and join us? It would be easier for you to listen to our private conversation if you sat down here.'

He patted the stool next to him.

'I stand here,' said Brush Cut. Yes, he was probably Russian.

'Come and sit next to us,' said Barnes, 'or fuck off out of it.'

Brush Cut said, 'I go outside right now.'

'Excellent,' said Barnes.

'You also,' said Brush Cut.

Barnes got to his feet. 'You're fucking *on*, pal. What are you doing? Calling for back-up?' Because Brush Cut was dialling a number while walking to the door.

So there had been a short-circuit. Instead of squaring up to Reynolds, Brush Cut was going after Barnes. But who did Brush Cut represent? Perhaps just himself. Reynolds rose to his feet, holding up his warrant card: 'Now hold on, I'm a police officer.'

'For Christ's sake give it a rest,' said Barnes, and he was following Brush Cut out of the pub. Through the stained-glass windows, Reynolds saw the blurred, multicoloured shapes of the two men . . . and the gap between them was widening. One of them was walking off. Reynolds knew it wasn't going to be Barnes, and when he himself stepped out into the dark afternoon, he saw that he was right. Barnes stood alone, lighting a cigarette.

'Where'd he go?' asked Reynolds, and Barnes pointed towards South Audley Street. 'Legged it. Twenty years ago, I would have given chase. I tell you what, *six months* ago I would have. Shame really,' he said, blowing smoke through the rain, 'but there's nothing you can do about it. Best of luck pal,' said Barnes, and he too began drifting off towards South Audley Street.

At length, Reynolds followed, thinking how Brush Cut must have been called off by the telephone conversation. Or was it all just coincidence, owing nothing at all to the new

131

unit or Reynolds' appearance in those newspapers?

In South Audley Street, Reynolds walked past what looked like a modern art exhibition but was in fact a shoe shop. There were about four shoes in the window; then came a jeweller with about four watches. They're so expensive, four is all you need, Reynolds thought, confusedly. Next was a shop selling vast sprays of lilies and pale flowers, such as could not be picked up by a single person. It was like a supplier for extravagant funerals, and the black four-by-fours trailing ceaselessly past were starting to appear hearse-like to Reynolds. He turned left, and one of the four-by-fours broke away from the main parade, and was moving slowly alongside him. It went without saying that he couldn't see the occupants in detail. There were two of them – that's all he knew. The street was wide and silent – sleeping mansions, bigger than any house in London ought to be. Each one ought to have stood in a hundred acres of countryside, but here they were all pressed up against each other. Well, there was safety in numbers. Antiquated street lanterns illuminated small areas of diagonal rain. They did not presume to throw any light on the mansions.

In the heart of Mayfair there were hardly any people but only money. Reynolds turned a corner. The car alongside him did the same. He turned again, and the car went a different way, greatly to his relief. He was now in the street behind the mansions: the mews, an empty street of back doors and strange, small – but still multi-million-pound – houses. It seemed the done thing to have bay trees in pots outside. The roadway was cobbled. As Reynolds looked along it, the black four-by-four turned in from the other end, and it accelerated towards Reynolds, who turned and ran.

As he ran, he thought of the diplomatic protection guys. They were outside the Saudi Embassy only about two streets over, and they had automatic rifles. But two streets was too far. The words of Barnes came: 'Shame really, but there's nothing you can do about it.' The street along which he was running was all set up for a death. All the doors were black; wreaths hung on them. The car was three feet behind him as he tripped on the cobbled road; and then the car was beside him, accelerating, cornering, gone.

20

'Perhaps they followed you from here,' said Clifford. 'Of course, they were only trying to scare you, although I don't know if it's related to Samarin at all. You must be in shock, you're not speaking. I don't suppose you're going to mention this to Croft.'

'Say something that requires an answer and you might get one,' said Reynolds.

She knew he wouldn't be speaking to Croft about any danger he might be in, because then he would be taken off the case. Clifford said, 'You realise I'm going to have to take your trousers off?' Reynolds unzipped his fly, rather resignedly, Clifford thought. She did not so much remove what remained of the right trouser leg as unpick it from the skin of his knee. He couldn't have been in shock, because he was dialling a number as she did it. 'Thank *God* it was the M&S suit,' she said.

Clearly the phone at the other end had not been answered.

'Who were you calling?' asked Clifford.

'A jeweller called Almond. Barnes gave me his name. He'd also given it to Quinn.'

'Why?'

'He can make fake diamonds.'

Clifford didn't believe she'd ever heard of Almond. She said, 'An Indian chap called. He wants to talk to you.'

'Why?'

'He has information.'

'What kind of Indian?'

'A rich one. He suggested a meeting in Claridge's.'

'When?'

'Now. Well, in half an hour.'

'Give me his number, I'll get back to him.'

'No need. I agreed to the meeting. You'll have time before the Plyushkin drinks. Six forty-five. He said any of the staff will point him out.'

Reynolds was trying to look indignant, but finding it difficult without his trousers on. He said, 'I suppose it would help if I knew his name.'

'Rakesh Dutta. He works for a hedge fund.'

Reynolds' knee was basically a good knee on a good leg, but still bleeding. Clifford said, 'This is a job for the Down Street Mini-Mart.'

She went down the stairs, the lift being still broken, and over the road. She wore the Aquascutum but the rain had stopped. The moon was hanging low over Green Park, which gave urgency to her stride, but the good old Mini-Mart was still open. She bought bandage Elastoplast, Sudocrem – then plucked a bottle of Dettol, the sole known quantity from among the incomprehensible detergents. She had a lot of faith in Dettol. That was because of the smell, which reminded you of the aftermath of illness. You'd been sick; it had all been cleared up by your mother, or in her own case her nanny; you were calming back down, getting into your stride with the sickbed melodrama, and yes, you rather thought you might be able to manage a cup of hot sweet tea; and yes, you thought you could just about bear it if nanny came back with the coal scuttle in two minutes and lit the bedroom fire. If there were two words that meant happiness in the cold houses of her girlhood they were 'bedroom fire'. Why had she not followed up with the fireplaces in her own flat? But she always lit the fire when she went to Quinn's place.

She ran back from the Mini-Mart. She loved the brightness and functionality of the Mini-Mart. If they couldn't have a Tube station in Down Street, then it was a worthy heir. It anchored Mayfair, reminded her of the days when it was still part of London: a kind of faded grandeur about the place, fewer residential houses and more offices, which of course all closed at five. So it was a different kind of emptiness. If you walked to Annabel's from Green Park station, it was just you and – ideally – your plus-one. In those days you were very aware of the big trees in the Mayfair squares. Regent Street was all travel agents, usually with model planes in the windows, and strange-coloured lumpy maps on the wall. Dinner at the Ritz was within the range, as an occasional treat, of any Detective Sergeant; it was before the grotesquery of the hundred-and-fifty-pound glass of champagne.

Reynolds was now some way along the road that Quinn had travelled. She had watched him when he came into the office with the injury. He had been a little pale, but not shaking, and she was satisfied that she couldn't call him off now even if she wanted. Surely they had been trying to scare him, not kill him. She believed they would be trying another tack soon. Curious thing though . . . The whole business that had just occurred might not be connected to the conspiracy that Quinn was pursuing. From Reynolds' account, it might be explained by his having antagonised the man with the brushed-up hair.

She patched Reynolds up. She enjoyed splashing on the Dettol. Well, she'd given him the classic warning, 'This may sting a little,' and he'd have been disappointed if it hadn't. She had kept him in his boxer shorts for only a little longer than strictly necessary; then she'd got him into the blue suit with the new white shirt she'd bought him as a gift. (Shouldn't say gift: 'present' was the word.) He'd then spent a long time looking at his reflection in the window. She had created a monster.

She sent him off to see the Indian chap, and she believed the doorman at Claridge's would not look twice at Reynolds. He would say, 'Good evening sir,' but not the fatal follow-up, 'Can I help you?' which the badly dressed were always likely to hear.

She'd never heard of Rakesh Dutta, and a Google search had thrown up nothing except the fact that he'd played in the Oxford–Cambridge cricket match at Lord's. But if he was a regular at Claridge's she'd be able to find out more.

She looked down at the Mini-Mart. Its lights were going off. It modestly beat a retreat when the Mayfair nightlife began. It was half past five. She would be seeing Reynolds at the London Library for Plyushkin's Garden. Not that Reynolds knew that yet. Samarin and Samarina ought to be present. Afterwards . . . she would be going 'on'. She had a date, having been very charmingly invited to dinner by a three o'clock phone call that was almost completely un-expected. It was such a pleasant change not to be going to Fortnum's Food Hall for a discounted chicken pie for one. (Fortnum's discounted their chicken pies – and all pies – after five o'clock.) She would just have time to cab it back to the flat and shower and dress. She would have a glass of

Prosecco and she would put on some music. Simple Minds. For a bunch of funny-looking Glaswegians they could be very elegant. Her favourite of theirs was 'Don't You Forget About Me'. She and Quinn often played that while having pre-drinks at Argrove. Perhaps she would be allowed to take it to St Michael's Hospital and play it for Quinn there, whereon he would rise from his bed in Pavlovian manner, run a bath, put on his suit and go off to Annabel's with her. Once in the club, she would be asking him about a certain painting.

21

Outside Claridge's, Reynolds counted the Christmas trees mounted on the canopy over the door. Five. But they were all quite small. The principal tree was in the lobby. It had been placed alongside – and was as high as – the curving white staircase. It seemed to have been steeped in blurred gold. There were also giant bouquets of lilies wrapped in silk bands. A very clean fire burned behind a transparent screen. Orange sparks would occasionally fly upwards like a sort of special effect. Almost all the guests coming through the revolving doors carried branded shopping bags. A woman in what looked like a zebra-skin coat carried a Harrods bag no more than six inches square, like a normal Harrods bag drastically shrunk. But no doubt there was a diamond in there. Most of those who came through the front door went upstairs. Reynolds decided that those coming down the stairs looked like guests on an old-fashioned chat show.

At six-twenty, afternoon tea was still going strong in a mainly green-and-white area behind glass. It had the feeling of a conservatory and the two most perfect blooms were immediately apparent in the form of two young Asians. The young man was drinking tea, the woman a pink concoction – it was perfectly possible that it was pink lemonade. The young man was imperious, crow-like, with a high black quiff. Reynolds could have looked at the woman for hours. In practice, he gave repeated, furtive glances. She was perhaps slightly too thin. She smiled at him and looked down. Demure, that was the word, but women only ever *looked* demure. It was more of a word than a genuine quality. The young man was advancing towards Reynolds.

'Hello sir, I recognise you from the newspaper. I wanted a very quick word. Shall we go this way?' He indicated one of the hotel bars, which was behind glass doors to one side. It seemed they would be leaving the woman behind, which was a shame. Perhaps she not only did not drink alcohol, but also couldn't bear to be near it. Rakesh Dutta bent low and whispered something in her ear, and she nodded, smiling.

The bar had that expensive, controlled darkness that only the top hotels can manage. Reynolds heard an English voice: 'For a serious lunch it simply *has* to be Gavroche'; then an Arab-sounding voice: 'You would fit right in and the money is very likeable.'

'How are you?' asked Rakesh Dutta.

'Very well,' said Reynolds, wondering whether the question had been prompted by the reek of Dettol coming off him. 'You?'

'I have had a mediocre trading day, otherwise good. No complaints. This is my treat,' he added, as they looked at the drinks list.

'Thanks,' said Reynolds, 'I'll have a glass of white wine.'

He would need to enter it in the Hospitality Register. Tea or coffee could be accepted at any time from anyone. It was all right to accept an alcoholic drink or similar if to refuse would 'cause offence or damage working relationships'. But the drink must be entered. This could be done by filling in a form, either on paper or via the appropriate intranet portal. Quinn had made no entries by either method since setting up the new unit. Reynolds had checked.

'Which wine exactly?' asked Ravi.

'Just the house.'

'Can I take the liberty of mentioning the Muscadet? It is particularly good.'

Reynolds had thought Muscadet was a sweet wine, but it turned out not to be. Dutta had a glass of champagne. Reynolds had noted the price of a glass of champagne: thirty pounds. It seemed reasonable to assume that his own wine would also be unreasonably expensive. He would put it down at twelve pounds. When Dutta ordered there seemed to be a note of familiarity in the waiter's, 'How are you, sir?'

'I will come down to it straight away,' Dutta said. 'A very good friend of mine, John-Paul Holden was killed, murdered, nearly two months back. That was in Hampstead, yes, but he worked in Mayfair – in the world, you could say, of the super-rich, and hence my call to you. We met as Cambridge undergrads, and we went into the financial world at the same time. John-Paul did very well.

'He had a first-class degree from Cambridge. *I* had a first-class degree from Cambridge. These laurels come your way. They are ten a penny in this world. But you need talent for finance just as you need it for football or music or anything else. It is not only a matter of brains. In his first job, in management consultancy, John-Paul was *on* it, and he was an outperformer. He could see what a business needed, and he could put the people in place to bring that about. I mean he is twenty-two, and he is turning around the turnaround guys, so he gets all the laurels again, and he decides on a new move. He goes to work for a hedge fund. It's called Rolling River, and it's run by a very heavy character from the South of America – I mean the American South – name of Eugene Crawford. He is formidable, you could say, but he has a very impolite manner, and if you falter with him there will always be repercussions. I have met this guy, and believe me, he does not have a funny bone; a very bad guy to be on the wrong side of.'

He leant closer, speaking more quietly.

'Eugene Crawford did not rate John-Paul in his new job, and it is true, John-Paul was probably too conservative in his trades. I would say he was a natural long-position guy. It was not the job for him, and he had made the wrong jump.

'Eugene Crawford begins to marginalise my friend, and believe me, that takes its toll. Under pressure, he makes a mistake, and does a trade that is basically illegal because of inside information. He goes to the compliance officer and puts his hands up but he is told "Forget it, because we can't afford the scandal." But before, or after, that I'm not sure, he turns himself in to the regulator. You must know this . . .'

Reynolds explained that he was not investigating this particular case.

'Then the investigating people must know it by now, and Eugene Crawford must know it. And, he must have known it before John-Paul was killed.'

'And you're saying that's why he was killed.'

'Insider trading . . . If that is found to have occurred that fund is going down; those people are going to be on the streets. I do not say that Eugene himself is a killer, but a man like that has people to do his bidding, and maybe one of them went over the top; like way over.'

142

Reynolds asked further questions for clarification, and told Dutta he would pass on his name and contact details to the team investigating the killing of John-Paul Holden. This had been a gratifying conversation. Reynolds was glad to be able to do *something* for Xavier Hussein. This Crawford seemed a legitimate suspect, and Reynolds very much hoped he *had* killed John-Paul Holden on Hampstead Heath, because then Anna Samarina wouldn't have.

'I am fine with that,' said Rakesh Dutta, and he shook hands with Reynolds before retreating to the glamorous woman in the tea-drinking area. As Reynolds approached the front door, he was nearly knocked over by a man who barked at the doorman, 'Do you have an umbrella for me?' But in fact it was not raining. It was a beautiful, blue night with a full moon tracking over the West End. With Christmas only a fortnight away, it was also one of the big party nights of the year, Reynolds thought, watching the Claridge's doorman despatching and receiving the fast succession of taxis. He himself did not take a taxi, but walked in the direction of the London Library.

When he reached St James's, he took a detour, towards the stately clubs of Pall Mall, most with golden flares burning outside. He headed east, and turned into the street called Carlton House Terrace. The building of that name – to which almost the entire street was given over – was silent and largely dark. It offered no clue as to why Quinn had written down its name, albeit in abbreviated form. Once, famous aristocrats had lived there. Now it was mainly the offices of money companies. Through basement windows, Reynolds could see dark, bland committee rooms. The street turned a right angle into a square, overlooked by the end of the terrace. There was work going on at this end of it, some sort of refurbishment. Notices read 'Site Safety Starts Here' and 'Construction Sites Are Dangerous'.

St James's Park lay across the Mall, which was illuminated, Reynolds noticed for the first time, by lights that were oddly white and luminous: gas lights. For the tourist. It was a Royal Park, and so must be kept beautiful, hence no CCTV either in the park or along the Mall; hence the shooting of Quinn. In spite of those tourists the park would be a spot worth thinking of for any bold shootist who knew Quinn's habits. (Clifford had said he liked to go there alone to read a newspaper and smoke a cigarette.) At the Yard, Reynolds had picked up gossip about Lilley's investigation. After many hours watching CCTV of cars on Constitution Hill and Trafalgar Square – which was where the CCTV kicked in at either end of the Mall – he still apparently had nothing.

Reynolds turned again to the terrace. If you were going to shoot a man sitting on a bench more or less centrally located in that park with a well-sighted rifle, you might choose the south-facing top-floor rooms of this end. Perhaps the assassin was an engineer with access to the offices of the Royal Academy of Engineering, or a pathologist from the Royal College of Pathologists, because there must be pathological pathologists, and both organisations were accommodated in Carlton House Terrace. But Reynolds had been shot from relatively close range with a pistol. In any case, why would anybody write down the name of a place from which they might be shot?

22

The London Library: from the name, it sounded open to all-comers. All *Londoners* anyway. But Reynolds knew that it, like most Mayfair institutions, was for members only.

From across the dark square, he watched taxis pull up: five in two minutes, almost a Claridge's-like rate. Parked near the railings of the square were some black four-by-fours, encamped like a wagon train. He supposed they were something *more* than high-end four-by-fours. They would be bulletproof, maybe bombproof, with harder suspension to cope with the weight. They were crude really, like a cross between a taxi and a tank. As he closed on the Library, he saw that most of these vehicles were occupied by bored-looking, probably foreign, men. In the security business, this was called 'overt presence', and Reynolds couldn't believe it was all for Samarin. He was known to be low-key, a 'discreet presence' guy.

Reynolds entered the library while holding up his invitation, just in case anyone wanted to see it. Someone did. The invitation was checked at the library counter by a bespectacled woman in a spangly dress, and his name was ticked off a list. So Victoria Clifford had fixed that all right. She had wanted him to come to let the Samarins know they were not off the hook.

The main flow was towards the wide red-carpeted staircase. A couple of men in suits were not part of the flow, and might have been Samarin's security. One of them glanced at

Reynolds, but possibly only because Reynolds had glanced at him. On the stairs were waiters holding drinks. Reynolds took a glass of champagne. Then he saw a particularly attractive middle-aged woman on the staircase crowd. Victoria Clifford. She carried a small black-and-gold hand-bag, not her usual big, jangly one; her black dress was quite minimal. She wore black stockings and green suede, quite high, shoes. Her hair was different in some way he couldn't understand, but it certainly worked. He tapped her on her bare shoulder, and rather enjoyed doing so.

'Smart outfit,' he said.

She turned around. 'How much have you had to drink? We go in here – the Reading Room.'

'You never told me you were coming.'

She ignored that.

The Reading Room was like a room in a gentleman's club: oil paintings, dark wood, more red carpet. The books were mainly works of reference, but candles in glass cups had been placed among the dictionaries and encyclopae-dias in a way that relegated those books to the shadows. Everyone was either Russian or English. The members of the inner circle stood over by the fireplace. There was a Christmas tree, and a lectern with a microphone. Reynolds saw Andrei Samarin, recognised him from the internet. He was speaking to one of the most English of the English women, who – judging from a distance by gestures – was trying to draw him out, while he was politely not being drawn out. His left hand was in his pocket. He was paler and greyer than the internet photograph had suggested, but still more elegant. Reynolds was pleased with his own suit, but Samarin's was better.

Clifford was also watching Samarin. Then a man who was evidently something to do with the library came up to her. When he'd moved on, she said, 'They have a lot of parties here now. The members are annoyed about it.'

'Is that what he told you?'

'No.'

'Are you a member here?'

'Yes.'

'And was – is – Quinn a member?'

She nodded, and Reynolds pictured them sitting side by side and reading, like two kids in infant school.

'Is that why you were both invited?'

'If that had been the reason they'd have asked all eight thousand members. Quinn was invited because he knows Samarin, and Samarin wanted to keep tabs on Quinn just as Quinn did on Samarin.'

A tray of champagne glasses was before them. They took one apiece.

'By the way,' asked Reynolds, 'do we have to enter these drinks on the hospitality register?'

Clifford said, 'Attendance at schools, lunches, dinners, receptions, or comparable functions organised by Embassies, cultural organisations, professional bodies and their equivalents, where attendance was in the capacity of MPS representative, *need not be entered*.'

'That's exactly what I thought,' said Reynolds.

Reynolds saw a very famous playwright. Whose name he could not remember. 'You say they're annoyed? The members.'

'Because they're usually not invited to these events. And the next day there are wine stains on the carpet. It's class war. Old Mayfair against new. Tell me about Claridge's.'

'Hold on. You can borrow books from this library, right?'

'You can take them out for months on end, if no one else wants them.'

'We could ask what books he had out. We'd have authority from the warrant for the flat.'

'Quinn never took books out of the Library.'

'Why not?'

'He thought it was bad form. Like having a takeaway coffee.'

Reynolds eyed Clifford for a while. 'You know, sometimes I think he deserved to be shot.'

'He read the books *here*. *In situ*. He usually worked in a room through there,' said Clifford, indicating a different entrance to the Reading Room. 'It's called the Sackler Study. Now tell me about Claridge's.'

When he'd finished, she quickly took a black fancy notebook out of her black fancy handbag; she wrote something down, put the notebook back in the bag. She had enjoyed doing that, Reynolds could tell. She said, 'Where did you talk to Dutta?'

'In Claridge's. You know that.'

'Yes but where exactly?'

'A sort of little, dark bar.'

'The Fumoir,' she said, looking over his shoulder at the people coming through the door of the Reading Room.

'It's all done out in purple.'

'Aubergine.' She leant over and adjusted one of his pocket flaps. 'Keep that *out*,' she said. 'You could smoke in the Fumoir until about 2006. I used to go there with Quinn, but that was back in the eighties. The drinks were affordable and they had these tremendously good crisps. Well, cheese and onion. You didn't even have to *buy* a drink. If it was pouring you'd go into Claridge's and stand in front of the fire to get dry.'

Samarin was now closer to them. All Reynolds could gather from his quiet remarks to the Englishwoman who'd collared him was that Gogol was evidently pronounced 'Goggle'. About five people stood in a queue behind the Englishwoman, wanting to talk to Samarin. A waiter came up, and Reynolds exchanged his empty glass for a full one. A pamphlet was also put in his hand. It was half in Russian and half in English. The first page spoke of 'our grateful thanks to Mr Andrei Samarin . . . the literary connection has always been the strongest bond between our two nations . . .' And yet Plyushkin's Gardeners were independent of either the Russian or British governments, so this was Samarin being a non-partisan goody-goody. He did not look very relaxed about it.

'Look at the way he keeps his hand in his jacket pocket,' Reynolds whispered to Clifford.

'*Suit-coat* pocket,' said Clifford.

A gloomy-looking Russian with shaggy grey hair and beard had now taken possession of the lectern. He would be holding forth about Gogol. Just as everyone was supposed to be shutting up, Reynolds heard a tall young Russian woman saying very clearly, 'Yes dear, we are going on. This is the pre-drinks in effect.' The lecturer had heard this as well, and didn't much like it. After very sombre thanks to Andrei Samarin, whereupon everyone looked at Samarin (much to his apparent distress) the lecturer began talking, in a depressed tone, not so much about the book Gogol had written

149

as about the books he had not written – all the intended sequels to his masterpiece, *Dead Souls*, that had never appeared. It was heroic of Gogol to persist in trying to live in the world of his imagination, even when he had no imagination left. The speaker complained about the way *Dead Souls* was generally taken to be a comedy, but Reynolds hadn't found it very funny when he'd read it. Because he remembered now that he *had* read it, years ago. It had seemed to him sub-Dickensian: a portrait of rackety and corrupt Tsarist Russia. But if you read it in Russian, it was no doubt as good as Dickens. There was something exceptionally Russian about Gogol, the speaker was suggesting. He had written in Russian, not French, which was the language of Russian literature at the time. Yes, he had considered Russian society horrific, but this seemed to be the hallmark of the Russian character: you didn't much like Russia. Andrei Samarin was listening with his eyes closed, in a manner that suggested great satisfaction or great exhaustion. His left hand was out of his pocket, and Reynolds saw that the little finger stopped at the first knuckle. It made a poignant sight: the runt of the litter. It made the next finger look extremely long, which it was not.

Reynolds could not believe the details of Gogol's career could have any bearing on the shooting of Quinn, and when the speaker said, 'I am going to read this passage in Russian . . .' Reynolds drifted over to the second entrance, pushed open the door, and he was in a kind of vestibule. Another refugee from the speech was making a mobile-phone call. Reynolds saw further double doors, with a notice above: The Sackler Study. He entered a high-ceilinged room with one long table down the centre, reading lamps at intervals.

He had half hoped to find some of Quinn's fabled stationery lying next to a pile of the books he'd been engaged in reading. Then he saw a shelf next to the fireplace marked 'Books Aside'. It denoted a dozen stacks of books, each with slips of paper protruding, upon which members had written their surnames. These were books they wanted kept back, not reshelved, so they could continue working from them. In the distorted handwriting familiar from the floppy book – and the same expensive black ink – Reynolds saw 'Quinn'.

Five books. *The Overcoat and Other Stories* by Nikolai Gogol; *Dead Souls* by Gogol; *Russian Emigration: A Historical Survey*; *The Russian Diaspora* and *A Natural History of Siberia*. He opened each, and scanned the indexes of those that had indexes. The *Natural History of Siberia* (a skimpy book for such a big place) did not have an index, and nor of course did the Gogol, being fiction. Towards the end of the final index he checked – that of *The Russian Diaspora* by a certain Michael Berg – something leapt out. It was under 'S':

Sfinsk (**Max Aktin writing as**).

Sfinsk/Aktin was represented by a single quote. This occurred in the midst of a dense passage giving the figures of emigration from Soviet Russia by Jews and others in the mid-seventies:

> It seems likely that the harshness of the quotas did not truly reflect Soviet priorities. It is possible they were by way of a bargaining chip, and yet an increase in the quotas was a prize never played

151

for by the governments of Western Europe in their diplomatic games with the Kremlin.

And there was a footnote. Michael Berg had written:

This was the last word from Aktin on Soviet emigration. He was killed in a fire in his London flat later in the same year.

Reynolds had to turn to the back of the book again to find the date of the quote: 2001, and it came from a magazine called *Refusnik*. He made a note of all the books Quinn had been reading, and stepped back into the Reading Room. Victoria Clifford was watching him as he re-entered. She looked annoyed that he'd been away. The speaker seemed to be winding up; Clifford was indicating the other double doors of the Reading Room.

Anna Samarina stood there.

The very tall young Russian woman, who'd said about 'going on', was making her way towards her. When she got there, the two kissed and whispered.

Anna Samarina – and everyone else – was now applauding the speaker. Questions were being invited. Reynolds looked at Anna Samarina until she noticed him, which took about half a minute. She smiled, apparently delighted. He nodded at her, going red in the process – partly because he in turn was being watched by Victoria Clifford. There had been only one question for the speaker, and now the event was a drinks party. The tall young woman, and a new young woman, were speaking to Anna Samarina, who kept eyeing Reynolds.

Under the eye of Clifford, he walked towards her.

The new young woman – an American – was saying to Anna, 'I totally love your father.'

Anna Samarina smiled; she was holding a glass of champagne. Her tall friend was speaking Russian loudly into her phone.

'Mr Blake Reynolds,' said Anna, and they somehow both kissed on both cheeks. Her Russian accent had faded, he believed, since he had last spoken to her: it was now more a matter of Russian inflections. Her looks had not faded. As far as Reynolds was concerned, she might as well have stepped down off the top of the Christmas tree. She wore slipper-like shoes, a pair of black leggings beneath . . . well, it was a sort of white ballet skirt or tutu. On top she wore a white blouse and a black leather jacket. She wore no jewellery at all. She effortlessly transcended the strangeness of her outfit.

She said, 'How are you? You're not in the clubs these days?'

'I was transferred to a murder team.'

'Lovely!'

'And now I'm with a new unit.'

It was impossible to tell whether she knew about the new unit, but he was sure that she did. The former head of it might have been investigating her crime, or crimes; and it had been in the papers.

'When was the last time I saw you?' she enquired.

'I think . . .'

'It was a white Christmas.'

He frowned. It had certainly been winter.

'For London, I mean – a sort of off-white.'

153

Her tall friend was now speaking *English* into her phone. 'It is what it is, darling!' she was saying.

Anna nodded towards the lectern. 'In ten minutes there will be another speaker. He will be talking about Dostoevsky. I am told he is very interesting.' She actually said 'interestink', but as a kind of joke.

'But we are going, however,' said the tall friend, who had finished her phone call.

Anna did the introductions. 'This is my good friend Detective Blake Reynolds. But what is it by now? What is your rank?'

Detective Chief Inspector,' he said, blushing. 'Well, *Acting* Detective Chief Inspector.'

'Oh well,' said Anna as he shook hands with the tall girl, 'we are all acting.'

The tall girl was called Eva.

Reynolds asked Anna, 'Will your father be speaking?'

'Now what do you think? Does he *ever* speak?' and she was smiling because her father had come up alongside Reynolds.

He had been followed by a line of people who wanted to speak to him, but he was shaking Reynolds' hand.

'I was extremely distressed to hear about George Quinn,' said Andrei Samarin. 'I knew him a little, and I admired him a good deal. Recovery is not out of the question, I understand?'

Reynolds said something like, 'So I believe.'

'And now you have stepped into his shoes?' Anna Samarina put in, so she did know. 'Papochka can lend you a bodyguard or two,' she added.

Samarin was frowning at his daughter.

154

'They come with or without Ray-Bans,' she said, accepting more champagne.

Reynolds asked her father, 'Where did you meet Quinn, Mr Samarin?'

'Is that an official question?' the tall girl put in, and Samarin eyed her for a moment.

'I don't quite recall. Some place like this,' Samarin said eventually.

'Gatherings of the intelligentsia,' said Anna, but in the Russian way, with a strong 'g'.

Just then they all overheard a woman saying, 'Wow, your Van Kleef is amazing.'

Samarin shook his head and smiled.

'Frieze Art Fair?' said Anna. 'Serpentine Party? No. A Russian art . . . *evenink* at Christie's. One of – what? – three occasions last year when you attended a social event, Papochka.'

'We are ready to go,' repeated the tall Russian girl. She was very insistent on this.

'Where to?' Samarin asked his daughter.

It was the tall girl who answered. 'That is up in the air, Andriusha. It is a movable feast.'

Anna explained to Reynolds, 'She collects English expressions. It is very annoying.'

She then kissed her father, saying, 'Don't worry, Papochka, I will not be driving.'

Samarin was then taken away by all the people who wanted to speak to him.

'It is all right for him,' said Eva. 'He is driven everywhere.'

'So am I and so are you,' Anna pointed out. But she

155

added, for Reynolds' benefit, 'I sometimes go on the Tube these days. It's very cool.'

Eva finished her champagne. She said something to Anna half in Russian and half in English. Anna said, 'In fact, Papochka *can* drive.'

'Really?' said Eva. 'That is contrary to popular belief.'

'He bought his licence fair and square in Petersburg. And he has an electrical car, amongst others.'

'He has gone green?' suggested Eva.

'Literally. He'll be riding a bike next.'

Reynolds asked Anna. 'Does your father drive around in the electrical car?'

'No, because there is only room in it for his driver.'

Eva's phone rang. In the act of answering, she sort of swirled herself into an exaggerated listening position. Anna Samarina walked over to say something to her father. He was still being besieged but, as his daughter, she had the right to an immediate audience. They both looked back at Reynolds; then the other people closed around Samarin again. Eva was standing next to Reynolds, eyeing him with dislike. You'd almost think she was the one who'd stolen the yellow diamond. Her phone rang yet again, and she answered, 'Da!' She was made for that phone, and vice versa. This time she spoke entirely in Russian, stepping away from Reynolds . . . to be replaced by Victoria Clifford.

'They're going,' said Reynolds. 'They've been going for some time.'

'*Where* are they going?'

'On.'

'Try to go with them. But remember the Special Demonstration Squad.'

That was an undercover Met unit, some of whose members had slept with women they were investigating. Reynolds eyed Clifford, wondering: is she jealous? But she was the one urging him on.

'What about you?' Reynolds asked Clifford.

'I'm going off straight away to read *Dead Souls*.' She finished her champagne and gave him the real answer. 'It might surprise you to know that I have a date.'

'It doesn't surprise me at all.'

'Yes it does.'

In fact, it did. He had thought they would go off together after the event, drink a glass of wine on expenses while discussing the Samarins and their possible involvement in the shooting of Quinn.

'Can I ask who you're having dinner with?'

'I believe you just have done.'

Anna Samarina came back, and put a rather steely grip on Reynolds' elbow.

'Come with,' she said. This meant he was to follow her and Eva down the stairs. They began speaking in Russian, with glances back to Reynolds. Sometimes they broke into English. Reynolds heard the tall girl say, 'I give you fair warning.' He followed on, feeling spare; behind him, the Dostoevsky lecture had started. He was forty-three whereas Anna and her friend Eva were about twenty-five. He was English and they were Russian. He was a detective and one of them, at least, was a criminal. He was also beginning to think they were both coked up. It was not a very promising situation.

23

The party to which the Russians went on was like a determined attempt to recreate heaven . . . Or a long Georgian winter banquet on white tables in a hall lined with white fluted columns . . . Or Scrooge's house when he's visited by the Ghost of Christmas Past. It was a white-and-gold scene, much of the gold being champagne, much of the white the tuxedoes of the men, who tended to wear them with distressed Levis.

The name of the place was The Orangery. It was in Kensington Gardens, and Reynolds had vaguely heard of it as an expensive party venue. They had been driven from St James's Square in a black four-by-four. The driver was called – or referred to as – Nicky, and he struck Reynolds as being too big a man to have that name. They had all sat in the back. The front passenger seat was for Nicky's mobile phones. Was this the car that had raced towards Reynolds in the multi-millionaire back streets of Mayfair? It was impossible to say with black four-by-fours. They all looked the same.

Reynolds asked Anna, 'Your father is particularly keen on Gogol?'

She nodded.

'What are his favourite works?'

'Of Gogol: *The Overcoat*, and especially *Dead Souls*.'

Quinn had taken out both.

'Why does he like that so much?'

'The main character, Chichikov. He finds a kind of . . .' and she said something in Russian.

'I don't speak Russian.'

'No, thank God.'

'So what does that mean?'

'Look it up, Acting Chief Inspector Blake Reynolds.'

She wandered a little way off. Reynolds had somehow thought she would be swept into some private meeting, or placed on a white throne with suitors all around. But she was simply talking to some new Russian woman, albeit very fast, while knocking back champagne. He heard a Russian accent enquire, 'Have you been to the Cotswolds?' An American accent replied, 'No, but I've been to the Lake District,' and it seemed that would do instead. Then an English accent: 'But the Russians were denied an aristocracy . . .'

Anna returned to Reynolds. 'She organised this event,' she said, nodding towards the departing woman. 'She is in fact an Events Organiser. How is your relationship going? I assume you are in a relationship.'

The question was both exactly what he wanted, and exactly what he didn't want. She was very radiant, even though only about five foot three. Being only five foot three she would be very easy to enclose or encompass.

'Could be better,' he said.

'Clearly, it is your fault. You are married to the job.'

They both watched the party for a while.

She looked down at her glass, which was empty.

'Excuse me, I want another. You can't, I think, if you are on duty.'

He could drink, but he would have to log his drinks,

since this was very definitely a party, and very definitely not a cultural event.

'You should eat something,' he said. He indicated all the food, and she shook her head.

'It is all icing and no cake. But thank you, doctor.'

She drifted away again, looked back, smiled, drifted further.

Reynolds himself wandered a little way through the room, hearing, 'We get overcharged three times just for the accent,' and, 'I think it is the major cocktail city.' After five minutes, Anna came back, having hooked up with tall Eva again. 'We are keep on going,' Anna said to Reynolds, in her put-on Russian.

'Heading for undisclosed location,' Eva added, in case Reynolds should think of accompanying them. 'It is on need-to-know basis.'

'Even I not know,' said Anna, still in her comedy voice.

As she was leaving, she said, 'Come and see us. Papochka and me. You know where we live. Get into touch and we can talk over everything.'

'I don't know your number.'

She told him. 'Write it down in your policeman's notebook.'

She then stood in a line with Eva, who was at least a foot taller – probably a model, Reynolds belatedly realised – and two others. They prepared to have a group photo taken by the phone of another woman whose nationality was not clear from the accent with which she spoke English. She called out, 'All the beautiful Russian ladies!' at which the subjects tipped up their heads and closed their eyes. The photographer didn't mind this. She seemed to have expected it, and was very happy with the result. Then they all made for the exit, with Anna Samarina giving a special smile to Reynolds that told him she knew far more than had been said.

He walked over to a white table and picked up a glass of champagne. He was very sad that Anna Samarina had left, and that was not good.

24

Reynolds wandered through Mayfair. He had quit the party half an hour before. Since then he had been walking through streets in which many other parties were continuing. No doubt somebody had paid for the moon to be full – and tinted a spectacular orange – over the number one cocktail city.

He had found himself in South Audley Street, off Mount Street, and then – two corner turns later – in the mews where he had nearly been run down. It did not look a particularly innocent street, even in the absence of the car, and two of the decorative bay trees still lay on their sides, as if a great wind had blown through. Their owners were not around to set them upright, being in the Caribbean, or wherever was the best place to be at this particular time. He was pretty sure that was London, but some of the rich had jumped early to the next square on the board. On behalf of all Londoners, he had thought: *Let's wait until they all go, then reclaim their houses.* But he wasn't really a Londoner himself. He wasn't sure that any such person existed any more. There were just ten million people spinning in the whirlpool of money, of which he was currently in the centre.

He turned a further two corners, and there was the house he knew to be Samarin's. It was off Berkeley Square, a perfect Georgian house, neat and well proportioned, but big. The bricks were painted black, and so it looked like a present wrapped in black crepe paper. The doorbell looked highly sophisticated: biometric, perhaps. The house suggested both Jane Austen and James Bond – the latter because an Aston Martin was parked outside: a metallic grey classic in perfect condition; James Bond's car. Reynolds believed that this was about the most expensive 'classic' car it was possible to buy. It was worth possibly half a million quid. It might have been Samarin's because he was notoriously tasteful. There was no sign of an *electrical* car, but that could be in the mews at the back.

The interior of the Aston was flawless, like the exterior. But there was one stray item: a folded tabloid newspaper poised on the edge of the cream leather back seat. Reynolds did not recognise the typeface. So it was a local paper, or a trade paper. He looked up and down the street, which was empty. Samarin's front door remained shut. The house seemed asleep, since the shutters were closed. The fanlight over the door was illuminated; that didn't mean that Samarin was in, but looking up to the roof, Reynolds saw a thread of smoke coming up from the chimney. Samarin was perhaps making an offering to the carbon gods that had made him rich.

The Aston dated from the sixties. It might well not have an alarm. Reynolds shoved the edge of the roof with the palm of his hand. The beautiful car immediately began shrieking with indignation, and Reynolds walked away fast towards Berkeley Square. Even if he didn't quite run, it was undignified to move so rapidly. But the newspaper had fallen off the seat, and its name had been revealed: the *Northumberland Guardian*. How many men associated with Samarin and Rostov would also have a connection with

Northumberland? He believed this car belonged to Porter, whose gamekeeper had shot the dog.

He walked to Piccadilly, watching the slow black river of taxis. He crossed the road, picturing a little pub tucked away in the back streets of St James's, and thinking of it as a haven, where everything would be all right for half an hour, and he would be able to decide what to do about Anna Samarina.

He was in front of the big restaurant on the south side of Piccadilly: the Wolseley. The girl who'd been witness to the shooting of Quinn had been planning to go there with her French boyfriend. The Wolseley was a good-time venue. Yet it was all black marble, like a funeral parlour; the doormen wore black. Come to that, so did most of the diners. Looking through the smoked window his eye snagged on a silvery, distinguished-looking gent. He recognised the man, but couldn't put a name to him. He could put a name to his dining companion though: Victoria Clifford, and she provided the context for him to name the older man: Deputy Assistant Commissioner Croft, the boss of Quinn, and now the boss of Reynolds himself. Clifford was sipping wine rather than eating – she never really did eat – and doing all the talking. Croft would nod occasionally. Every so often he'd lay down his knife and fork especially in order to nod. Reynolds knew that if he stared at Clifford for long enough, she would look up and see him, because she noticed everything eventually. Therefore he remained in place by the window. Judging by the look the doorman was giving him, he might have to flash his warrant card in a minute. His eyes met Clifford's; then she leant towards Croft with pretend animation. Reynolds walked on, looking for the pub.

When he found it, he ordered white wine. He asked the barmaid, 'Are you Russian?'

'Ukrainian,' she said. 'Some people think it's the same.'

'Do you mind if I ask you to translate a word?' and he pronounced the Russian word that Anna Samarina had told him to look up: '*Ny-ev-in-ov-nost.*'

The barmaid said, 'It means . . . "innocent".' He thanked her.

When Reynolds had sat down with his drink, she came over collecting glasses and said, 'No, different. It means "innoc*ence*",' and he thanked her again. He sipped his wine, and googled Anna Samarina once again. He put in her name alongside the name Eva. A picture of the two together came up. They were at a fashion show called Rus Looks. He searched under that for a while and found somebody's blog, some intercontinental airhead. 'So, Rus Looks, my friends. Thursday 4 December, 5 p.m. to 8 p.m., Plaza Inn, Heathrow. All proceeds to children's charities. And I am just SO excited!!!' Reynolds set aside his phone. Quinn had been shot at soon after six on that day. He imagined that Heathrow Airport was about as far outside central London as Anna Samarina ever went, except for those times when she actually boarded a plane there. She could not have been in St James's Park shooting George Quinn, and partying at the Plaza Inn – not that he ever thought she *had* shot Quinn. It was nice to have it confirmed though, and he repented of his animus against the intercontinental airhead.

25

Reynolds let himself into the hallway of the flat, where, after Mayfair, everything looked cracked and faded; and the place was far too hot, in a cheap sort of way. 'Hello!' he called out, but no answer. These domestic Hellos came out as 'Hullo' in a silly way he didn't like. He caught a glimpse through the opened kitchen door of the scrubbed pine table. There was an unconvincing Victorian-farmhouse theme to the decor, and it was his fault since he'd furnished the flat himself. Everything needed replacing, and he realised this accounted for the fusty smell: it was the smell of unreplaced items; the smell of lack of money. He walked through to the living room where in the half-light the armchairs and sofa looked overstuffed, like so many fat, faded dead men. Caroline was sitting on the sofa, under the orange standard lamp. She wore her pyjamas, which normally she did not. Reynolds walked over to kiss her.

'Are you ill?' he said.

'I called you.'

'Sorry,' he said, and he took out his phone to look.

'It's too late now,' she said, 'I mean you're *here* now. Where were you?'

'At a party. Two parties. It was noisy. Actually, at the first one I had to turn it off, because it was in a library.'

That didn't go down very well.

'Where did you get that suit?'

'Place in Jermyn Street.'

'This new job of yours . . .'

'As I said, I've been transferred to—'

'Are you sure you haven't been transferred right out of the police and into a PR agency? Or a film-production company or something?'

He always liked Caroline in her pyjamas; she looked like somebody ready for a nocturnal adventure in a storybook. But he knew something bad was coming. She had assembled all her bedtime things around her in a very poignant way: alarm clock, cup of herbal tea and book: a biography of the cellist Jacqueline du Pré. Caroline was a talented cellist herself. She was a good writer as well, if her emails and texts were anything to go by. All of a sudden – and it was a Quinn-like, romantic thought – she struck Reynolds as someone who had accommodated herself too quickly to the banalities of life, as represented by eBay auctions, two-for-one vouchers . . . and mortgage applications.

He said, 'Have we heard about the mortgage application?'

They had heard.

'We've had an email from the agent. The vendor has had a higher offer.'

'We can match it.'

'No we can't.'

He felt ashamed of his fifty-eight thousand a year for causing her such misery. He moved towards her, but this was evidently not going to be welcomed. It was without much hope – since she had adopted a sort of combat posture – that he asked, 'Why are you on the sofa? Come to bed.'

'I'm staying here.'

'It's not my fault we can't get the mortgage, is it?'

He wondered how he could make up for two years of poor communication, frequent absence and self-absorption, and whether there was any point trying. 'Look . . .' he said, and he always knew he was doomed when he began a sentence with that word, '*I'll* sleep on the sofa.'

She just turned away, so he got up and went into the bedroom, making a point of not quite shutting the door, open to negotiation. He sat down on the bed and took out his phone. He had a voice message. He listened. 'Blake, it's Xavier. Could we speak about the Holden case please?'

Reynolds sat on the edge of the bed, holding the phone. It was half past eleven. Too late to call back? But he couldn't keep avoiding the man, and Anna Samarina could not have shot Quinn, being otherwise occupied at the time . . . which made it still less likely that she had stabbed her boyfriend. Therefore Reynolds, in protecting her, was surely not protecting a killer. He pressed call return. Hussein picked up.

'Sorry it's so late, Zav,' said Reynolds, but that didn't seem to matter. Hussein was his usual focused self.

'Thanks for putting me onto Rakesh Dutta,' he said.

'Any use?'

'He confirmed our suspicions that there might be a work tie-in.'

Silence down the line. Reynolds had to fill it. 'You already knew that Holden had been onto the Financial Conduct Authority of course?'

'Yes.'

'Have you been onto the employer? Crawford?'

'Just had him in, yes.'

'What was he like?'

'Arrogant. Came in with a big cigar.'

'Any joy?'

'Stonewall.'

'And I gather you've got no forensics?'

'No.'

'No footprints either.'

'Too many footprints. A man came out of the flats to have a look. Then he brought his friends.'

'How many friends?'

'Thirty. He was having a drinks party. Some of them were carrying glasses of champagne.'

'What were they doing at the crime scene?'

'The man was a doctor. Thought he could help.'

'But Holden was beyond help at that point.'

'He was.'

'I gather it might have been a robbery? Because the wallet was taken.'

'There was no wallet.'

'That's what I mean.'

Another silence down the line. Reynolds was starting to hate Hussein. He thought of the white shoes. The man was supposed to be a *plain clothes* detective, for God's sake. 'I'm just off to bed, Zav,' Reynolds said guiltily. 'Anything in particular I can help with?'

'The super-rich,' said Hussein. 'The Mayfair world. Holden had a lot of friends; lot of *girl*friends.'

'Well now,' Reynolds blustered, '*Quinn* would have been your man for society women. I'm on a pretty steep learning curve here.'

Another silence. Reynolds' eyes roved around the hot, battered bedroom. Reynolds could hear, from beyond the

169

door, the chink of bottle or glass. Caroline was pouring herself a drink. That meant she was steeling herself for something. Reynolds was steeling himself for something else.

'One name that has come up', Hussein continued relentlessly, 'is Samarina. Anna Samarina. Daughter of an oligarch. That name mean anything to you, Blake?'

'I'll do some digging,' Reynolds said, and he found he was talking just for the sake of getting beyond the name of Anna Samarina. 'Zav, do you want me to have a go at Crawford? I've a few contacts – a few brains I could pick. He might be intimidated to think we're coming at him from two directions.'

'He's not going to be intimidated.'

'Annoyed, then.'

'That's possible,' Hussein conceded, after a while. Maybe he actually liked the idea. Anyhow, they agreed on it.

Reynolds sat forward in his bed, turning the phone over and over in his hand. The only possible justification for not 'sharing' with Hussein was to crack a bigger case; a bigger one even than Holden's murder. And it had to be done fast. Reynolds immediately googled 'Carlton' yet again. He was pursuing the fact that there were at least three villages of that name in Yorkshire. It was Quinn's old man living in Yorkshire that had started him thinking along these lines, but he didn't see where the 'HT' came in. Surely that could only be accounted for by Carlton House Terrace? Having hit this familiar dead end, Reynolds looked at his emails. He saw that Caroline had not forwarded the one from the agent. She had wanted the drama of telling him. He stood; began taking off his suit. When he was down to his boxer shorts, she walked in. He knew she'd been emboldened by some wine. She was staring at the bandage on his knee.

This was going to be momentous, he knew.

'What's wrong with your leg?' she demanded.

Caroline was a kind person, always very solicitous if he was under the weather, or otherwise endangered. He recalled the time, soon after they'd met, when he'd come under fire while on duty. The next day, the two of them had been with another couple at Pizza Express in Muswell Hill. Everyone was talking about their week at work, so Reynolds had told the story of what had, after all, occurred within the last few days of his own working life. He'd been with Lilley, and they'd been moving in on a Turkish gangster and professional killer called (quite amusingly when you thought about it) Ender. The London Turks were interesting. Very entrepreneurial and dynamic, even the bent ones; and they kept their violence – usually heroin-related – in-house. He and Lilley had tracked Ender's younger brother – fanatically committed to Ender – to a basement social club in North London. Unlike Café Rouge, that had been a fascinating, genuinely foreign-seeming place: sort of seventies wood-veneer with photographs and paintings around the walls apparently showing handsome, middle-aged men in a diversity of hats. But when you looked closer, as Reynolds had done when he'd returned with forensics, they were all pictures of Kemal Atatürk.

Ender's brother had been waiting for them in that room with Ender's machine pistol, the Mac 11, the 'spray-and-pray'.

'What did you do?' the man belonging to the other couple had asked.

'We ran away as fast as we possibly could.'

They had been running under a railway arch when Ender's brother had emptied the entire thirty-two-round clip in their direction. That had taken two seconds. When the other man in Café Rouge asked Reynolds how he'd not been hit, Reynolds said he had no idea.

Caroline had made no comment on the story; but she'd started a campaign to get him out of the force. When that failed she'd stopped asking about his work. It was what came between them; it was also what stopped her living in a desirable property.

She was eyeing him from the bedroom door.

'It's over between us,' she said. 'I'm seeing someone else and I'm moving in with him. It's Bob.'

A longer name, thought Reynolds, would have made a more dramatic culmination. She meant Bob Ballantyne, deputy head at her school. It had always been obvious that she liked him. As deputy head, he would earn more than fifty-eight thousand; he might earn as much as seventy. Reynolds said, 'You can make a joint mortgage application with him. It'll be very romantic for you.'

'We will try to buy something, yes.'

He considered observing that she appeared to have sold herself to the highest bidder, but he didn't honestly believe that was the case. He glanced over to the wardrobe. He hadn't put the suit away straight. The suit, rather than Caroline, was his true ally in the room. He went over to the cupboard to adjust it.

'I'm going to let you sleep on the sofa,' he said.

26

'Welcome, this Friday morning, to the last of our Tuesday walking tours,' Margaret had said, making a bit of a joke of it.

There was a good turnout for the tour, because word had got round that it was the last. There were three of Margaret's Camberley regulars, and one of the women was accompanied by a child – a little boy – of about ten. Margaret couldn't help wondering why he wasn't at school, because there didn't seem to be anything wrong with him, but she was delighted anyway, because it meant the tour could literally go out with a bang, when they came to the gong. They were in the ballroom now, and everybody was looking at the reflections receding into infinity in the opposing overmantle mirrors. The little boy had to be held up by his mother to see, because he was very small. Perhaps he was too small and that was somehow the trouble. 'There's hundreds of me!' he said, in a very sweet and shy way. Some children, Margaret thought, would take it as nothing less than their due that there should be hundreds of them. Sometimes, when there were children, she would miss out the next room but one – the Blue Drawing Room – because the explanation of the panelling and the porcelain could be a little dry, but he was a bright little boy, and she was looking forward to asking him if he could spot the differences between the two elephant heads on the candelabrum vase.

Mr Rye had not come on the tour. He had discovered that Mr Rostov would be in residence – as indeed he was, having arrived by helicopter that morning – and he had declared in a very pompous way, 'I'm sorry – the house is simply not big enough for the two of us.' It was so silly because Mr Rostov was not even aware of Mr Rye's existence, and Margaret feared that would continue to be the case even now that she had given Mr Rostov a copy of Mr Rye's book, *The Turners of Gladwish: A Study in Stability*. It would have been nice if Mr Rye had signed the book, but of course he had refused point blank.

They were in the Morning Room now, and Margaret was pointing out the portraits of the Turners, and there was no stumble this time about their being 'the owners', they were very definitely the *former* owners. She added, 'We will be seeing a picture of the new owner later,' which she thought a nice touch: a little tease, and the boy had smiled at her as she said it, as though this was a most intriguing mystery.

It wasn't as if the Turners had been particularly solicitous towards Mr Rye. They had been quite a snobbish family in many ways, and had not helped him with his book.

She had not handed the book personally to Mr Rostov. She had handed it over to Mr Rostov's personal secretary, the woman called Valentina, in the office in the stable yard that morning at ten o'clock (because Margaret always arrived early to walk in the grounds before the walking tours began). Valentina had been speaking Russian on the phone in what sounded like an agitated voice, but a man in the office had indicated in broken English that the book would be given to Mr Rostov as soon as possible. At the time there had been a lot of shouting in Russian from the stable yard – not least from Major Porter, who was English of course but spoke Russian fluently. When he shouted, it was like somebody commanding a hunt. This might have been to do with the parking of the big black cars that had been turning up all morning, and were being manoeuvred around the yard just then, or it might have been to do with all the work going on in the grounds. Margaret believed that an electronic fence was to be installed around the entire perimeter – an *intelligent* electronic fence.

The cars had darkened windows, so it was impossible to see inside, but Margaret thought their arrival might have concerned the delivery of Mr Rostov's art collection from a secure storage centre in London. She had heard about this from her husband, who in turn had it from a man called Patterson he would see occasionally in the pub, and whose daughter worked on the local paper, which was trying to find out all it could about Mr Rostov, and not getting very far. An hour later, when Margaret had returned from her walk, she happened to see the man who'd taken delivery of the book. He was talking to Major Porter by the West Conservatory. Normally Margaret would have given them a very wide berth, but she was emboldened by this being the last day. She had thought she had better address Porter first, since he was English, and probably in charge.

'Excuse me,' she said, 'is this a good moment?'

Porter tilted his head half towards her. He had a rather red face, and didn't like to be looked at. 'Well, what is it?'

From his voice, she would have said he was well educated, but not well mannered. She turned to the Russian, who was smoking a cigarette, a far more relaxed character. 'Excuse me, but did you manage to give the book to Mr Rostov?'

'Of course, he have her yes.'

Margaret thanked him and, as she hurried away, she heard

Porter say, 'She is an appendage of the house, I suppose.'

It was mortifying of course, but not as bad as it might have been, because Porter was really talking to himself. The Russian wouldn't have understood an English word like 'appendage'. Porter must be very clever, but he had no 'social skills' at all. With his tweed suits and flat cap – he always looked as though he was going to the races – he was the sort of man you'd expect to own a place like Gladwish. Perhaps he was filled with bitterness that he did not. Then again, Margaret believed he had his own country estate somewhere up north.

They were approaching the entrance hall, and the end of the tour; and Margaret found that she had tears in her eyes. Thirty years of the walking tours were finally ending. What would she do with her Tuesdays? She thought of all the things she had hoped for at Gladwish that had never come to pass: wine tasting in the wine cellars, chamber music in the ballroom, a proper restaurant in the West Gallery as opposed to the rather irregular summer teas. She stopped. She would tell them about the funny little embossed leather screen, just to prolong the tour slightly.

But that was the work of a moment, and now she was in the entrance hall, and indicating the photo of Mr Rostov. 'The new owner!' she said, and it was all coming out broken because she was being so silly and emotional. As she spoke, she glanced at the little boy, and he was looking at the photograph and nodding gravely, thoughtfully taking it all in, the dear little thing. Margaret hurried over to the Burmese gong and handed the beater to the boy, because by now she was simply too choked to speak. The boy smiled as he took the beater, and he turned to the gong. He knew just what to do.

27

Four o'clock on the dark and cold Friday afternoon. The weather might have been made for offsetting the Christmas decorations of Mayfair, a district that had seemed full, that afternoon, of young men with swept-back hair carrying oil paintings about.

Reynolds was standing in a Mayfair courtyard, somewhere off St James's Street. On one side was the façade of the Duke's Hotel. He was supposed to be meeting Eugene Crawford, the important Texan hedge-funder, and employer of the late John-Paul Holden, in the cocktail party of Duke's. Reynolds now knew what Crawford looked like and he was waiting for him to turn up before going in himself. Reynolds had on the good suit, and what Clifford had called, as she draped it over his shoulders, 'Quinn's second-best covert coat'.

The coat had been a sort of peace offering.

They had both been late into Down Street that morning, Reynolds especially. He had not been delayed by another row with Caroline, who always left for work before he did. He had been delayed by the revelation that she had already started packing. And so he had eaten a stunned, solitary breakfast.

'Well?' Clifford had said, when he'd entered the office.

'I might ask you the same question.'

He went first. Clifford adopted a pious, and patronising, listening pose (arms folded, head down, eyes possibly closed) as he told her about the time he'd spent with Anna Samarina, holding back his personal feelings about her, which Clifford had presumably guessed in any case.

He told her that Anna Samarina knew they were on to her about something. She must know about the death of Holden, having been engaged to him and the news having been all over the papers, but Reynolds had not broached the subject, and she had certainly not brought it up, no doubt for fear of being entangled in a murder investigation. She certainly also knew about the shooting of Quinn – that equally newsworthy event – but she'd been at a party at Heathrow when that had occurred. All Reynolds knew for certain was that she'd been involved in the theft of a two-and-a-half-carat yellow diamond.

He also told Clifford about Quinn's library books and how a Russian journalist called Max Aktin, who had died in a fire in 2001, seemed to be the 'Sfinsk' of the floppy book. He told her that he believed a certain Porter was Andrei Samarin's head of security, and that he was evidently very well rewarded, since he owned an estate in Northumberland, and a half-million-pound car. He told her Zav Hussein had called him, mentioning the name Anna Samarina as being possibly connected to John-Paul Holden. He told her he'd *blanked* Hussein, and Clifford approved of that, which did not make him feel reassured. He added that he'd offered to interview the hedge-fund man, Crawford, employer of Holden, and Clifford said, 'I think that's an excellent idea.'

He wondered aloud how they could find out about Porter. Clifford said it was not easy to find details of an army service record. It was even harder – this regarding the death of Aktin – to get a coroner's report off a coroner. 'But maybe it was written up in a newspaper.' Or she might try a contact of hers in the London Fire Brigade, which she called the LFB, in a familiar way.

In return for all this, she'd given him next to nothing about her dinner with Croft: 'It was primarily social. He knows we're onto some funny Russian business. He doesn't want the detail yet, because then he might have to do something.'

'Does he know about Anna Samarina and the yellow diamond?'

She had shaken her head. Reynolds rapidly looked up the HOLMES file on the Holden case. 'Nothing's changed on that,' said Clifford, by which she meant that Anna Samarina's name had not appeared. Not yet, anyway.

After half an hour's futile pursuit of Max Aktin leads, Reynolds had said, 'I'm getting a coffee and a sandwich from the Mini-Mart. Do you want one?'

'I'll have a coffee and a Toffee Crisp please.'

As he left, she'd said, 'Thank you, dear,' and given him one of her more straightforward smiles.

*

In spite of the Crombie, he was getting cold pacing the courtyard, which was made up on three sides by the backs of other hotels. So far nobody had gone into or come out of the Duke's Hotel. But perhaps he had somehow missed Crawford. He went in again. The old-fashioned cocktail bar contained two grand American women and one white-jacketed waiter. On the wall, along with various works of art, was a framed picture of Sean Connery as James Bond. In Mayfair, all roads lead to James Bond. According to the notice under the photograph, this was the place you could get an authentic James Bond Martini. Reynolds stepped back into the courtyard.

To kill time, he dialled the number of the jeweller, Almond. No reply. That was the third time he'd called. Then his own phone rang. It was Clifford, calling from Down Street, which she was just about to leave.

She said, 'Crawford can't meet you at Duke's Hotel.'

'Why not?'

'He doesn't want to. He'll see you in Fox's on St James's.'

'What's that?'

'A tobacconist's. He'll be there in five minutes. You can be there in two.'

'What are we supposed to do there?'

'Smoke a cigar. In the smoking room. It's on the first floor.'

'I don't smoke cigars.'

'You'll get more out of him if you do. He'll probably buy you a very good one. He's not generous or anything, but he is rich.'

Reynolds had to do little more than cross the road. A beige Bentley was parked illegally outside the shop marked 'Fox's'. A wooden Indian stood guard outside. There was another one inside, together with a lot of plaques and shields commemorating feats in the making of cigars and pipes. Sort of smoking heraldry. Then he saw Crawford. He was in the humidor at the back: a 'walk-in' humidor – that was the term. So Reynolds walked in and introduced himself.

Eugene Crawford was not dressed for winter; he was not dressed for Mayfair and he was certainly not *well* dressed. He wore shapeless black trousers, black trainers, an open-necked shirt – *very* open-necked – and a thin blue jacket.

He was talking to a shop assistant. Greeting Reynolds with half a nod, he said, 'What's smoking well right now?' He had a Texas drawl, and a ponytail. The assistant showed Crawford some cigars, presumably suitably expensive, but he wasn't interested. 'Show me something vintage.'

The assistant was now delving down amongst wooden boxes to show Crawford some exceptionally long, thin cigars, while saying something about '1997 . . . a very refined smoke, sir.'

Crawford turned to Reynolds. 'You smoke a cigar?'

'At Christmas,' said Reynolds.

'It's Christmas now,' said Crawford, which was true enough. He was examining a cigar. It was about a foot long. 'Montecristo Number A,' said Crawford. 'Okay with you?'

'All right,' said Reynolds, 'thanks very much.'

This was not to be an interview under caution. He was allowed to accept a cigar. The three of them walked over to the till. Apparently it was perfectly legal to sample cigars on the premises with a view to purchase, although Reynolds knew in advance that he would not be purchasing any of these Montecristo Number A's since they were fifty pounds apiece. Crawford paid with a card while looking bored.

The smoking room was upstairs. As they entered, a young, upper-class English voice was saying, 'We did thirty thousand yesterday morn—' He stopped dead when he saw Eugene Crawford. Someone else in the room said, 'Good afternoon, Eugene.'

'Yeah,' said Crawford.

There were half a dozen in the room, four of them probably English, two probably not. Strong electrical fans were blowing; there was a coffee machine, and several coffee tables between leather chairs, with big ashtrays on them and matches that were more like firelighters. Reynolds and Crawford sat down. There was no question of any notebook being involved. It occurred to Reynolds that he couldn't have said, at that particular moment, where his detective's notebook actually was. Beyond the window, day had become night. As Reynolds and Crawford lit their cigars, one of the Englishmen was talking about the places offering the most 'interesting' skiing, as though skiing were an intellectual pursuit. But everything stopped again when Crawford said, 'You people think we killed this guy?'

'John-Paul Holden,' said Reynolds, treating the question as rhetorical. 'There are some aspects of his private and professional life that I'd like to ask you about.'

'Ah'll give you half an hour. Then ah have to go.'

'Where are you off to?' Reynolds enquired.

'Edinburgh,' Crawford said, somewhat unexpectedly. He called it 'Edin-burrow'.

'How are you getting there?'

He made a take-off gesture with his non-smoking hand. 'Sky rocket,' he said, which came out '*Skah* rocket'. If Reynolds wasn't careful he'd be hypnotised by the Texan accent.

Crawford reminded Reynolds that he'd already been interviewed by 'two previous guys from the London police'.

One of those would be Hussein; the other would be one of Hussein's DS's. The implication was that Crawford's patience had worn thin, and he was entitled to be jetting off to Edinburgh.

Reynolds said, 'Holden. What kind of . . . a man would you say he was?' The cigar was a pleasant surprise, milder than he'd envisaged.

'Ah would say he was a *boring* kind of man.'

'What makes you say that?'

'Ah personally have been bored by him.'

'In conversation?'

'Many a time and often.'

'What did he say that was so boring?'

'It was a question of what he didn't say. See, ah like a guy who's into some weird securities . . .' He tailed off, smoking.

'He wasn't bringing the necessary returns?'

Eugene Crawford pulled a face – could have meant anything.

'A guy works for me – he needs to generate a little mystique . . . Sorry about the change of arrangement, by the way. Over there,' he said, vaguely indicating the Duke's Hotel with his cigar, 'you can sample the James Bond Martini. You ever tried that, Mr Reynolds?'

Reynolds shook his head. You were supposed to go where the interviewee led, but Crawford appeared deranged.

'*Ah* have,' said Crawford. 'Ah was not shaken and ah was not stirred.'

Reynolds dragged Crawford back to the subject of John-Paul Holden. He was too unimaginative at work, apparently. What Crawford enjoyed – and what, it seemed, had made him rich – was short selling on complicated derivatives, and Holden did not do enough of that.

Reynolds said, 'He'd turned himself in for insider trading.'

'He did that to hurt us.'

'You mean he reported himself or did the trade to hurt you?'

'Ah guess . . . both.'

'He told the FCA that your compliance officer had told him to hush it up.'

'Not true. Rolling River would never do anything of the kind.' Crawford blew smoke. 'Not worth our while.'

'He was popular socially, I think. Would you say he was a sort of . . . people person?'

'What's a "people person"?'

It seemed he genuinely didn't know. Reynolds attempted an explanation, during which he heard from the room, 'We told the riff-raff from the RAC Club to get to their side of the garden.'

Having had the term 'people person' defined for him, Crawford just shrugged, saying, 'Ah never saw the point of the guy.'

'But you employed him.'

'Yeah. It was a mistake.'

Without pen and notebook, Reynolds was free to ask, 'Did he have a wife or partner or girlfriend, as far as you were aware?'

Eugene Crawford shrugged. 'Ah was not aware.'

'He didn't bring a woman to any company social events?'

'Ah really couldn't say. We do have dinners and so on but, see . . . ah don't go to them all that often.'

'Why not?'

'Mah managers lay them on to boost morale. But see . . . mah morale does not need boosting.'

'But presumably the idea is for you to boost *other people's* morale. As the top man, I mean?' The more he spoke, the more English Reynolds sounded in the presence of this man, who was now looking at the ceiling while blowing

184

smoke. After a while, Crawford asked, 'What was that you just said?'

Reynolds was back on St James's Street before the fifty-pound Montecristos were halfway down. All the Ferraris were going home. They would proceed in a series of darts. It was the low engine note that marked out the winners of the Mayfair world. All the other drivers . . . it was as if their voices hadn't broken. The beige Bentley remained outside Fox's tobacconist's, watched by the wooden Indian, somehow immune from parking tickets. It was a black four-by-four that had taken Crawford to the airport.

Reynolds had said he would get back to Hussein after speaking to Crawford. He could genuinely say that he had nothing to report. He began walking north, towards the Ritz. His phone rang; he answered. A quavering voice seemed to say, 'It's Quinn here.'

Reynolds stopped dead. He stood motionless at the junction of St James's Street and Jermyn Street until the man repeated himself.

'Quinn,' said the voice again. 'Charles Quinn – father of George. Am I speaking with Detective Inspector Raymond?'

Reynolds didn't correct the caller. He was practically gasping with the shock of that near miss. The voice was very patrician. More so than George Quinn's voice, from what he could recall of that.

'I'm so sorry to trouble you,' Charles Quinn continued. 'I called the Yard and they gave me Vicky's number at the unit – Victoria Clifford, I mean. She wasn't picking up, so I got back onto the Yard, and they gave me your number. Do you have a minute?'

28

In his workshop off Bond Street, Almond finished a phone call and lit a Silk Cut. It had been a very horrible conversation. The Arab had been talking about how he wanted a classic cut. 'Yes, Tiffany cut,' Almond had said. 'No, classic,' the Arab had shouted, 'like I told you before two weeks ago.' Two weeks ago he had said Tiffany, which was in any case the same as classic. The Arab had then proposed another meeting, but Almond did not want to see this man again. The Arab had suggested eleven o'clock on Thursday, so proving he was not a high-roller. Nobody in Mayfair got up before lunchtime; and he ought to be *sending* someone, not coming himself.

But then, if he'd been one of the High Net Worths he wouldn't have been calling Peter Almond, as Almond himself knew perfectly well.

The Arab had wanted 'a truly unique piece', and he did not believe Almond understood this. Almond assured him that he did, at which the Arab's agitation had increased. 'You are always contradict!'

Almond checked his messages. The copper had called again. He would be knocking on the door soon, with a search warrant in his back pocket. Almond was tired, and his wife's parents were coming round for dinner. He put his cigarette in the ashtray, leant forward on his high stool, folded his arms on the workbench and rested his head on his arms. Squinting along the top of the bench, he could see a page from one of the luxury magazines he was sent on an almost daily basis, never having asked for any of them. He read the headline, 'Where olden is golden . . .' Next to it was an Antwerp street guide, two platinum bands, a pair of pliers, and then, on white paper, a spread of small material: a little landscape of crystal. From his peculiar vantage point, Almond admired the way these shards handled the light from the lamp above – handled it collectively, a joint effort. Almond closed his eyes. The phone rang again. He was beginning to hate that phone. He sat up; picked up his cigarette, made sure it wasn't the copper again, and answered the call. He heard a man breathing, an unfit man by the sound of it. Then the voice: cockney with a hint of theatricality, the sound of a pub in the background.

'Peter?'

Not a copper, but Cooper. Ali Baba himself. It was the second time he'd called since their meeting of a week before.

'Peter? How are you?'

'Fine. And I haven't got long to talk, I'm afraid.'

'I'm fine as well thanks, Peter. Now this stone . . .'

'I've told you about that.'

'But the position has changed, Peter. I'm now willing to let you have it at a considerable discount. Say, thirty-three.'

'It's not my kind of goods. I've told you that.'

'But I fail to see why. It's a lovely stone, you told me that yourself. We both know it's really forty grand's worth.'

Almond said, 'As I explained, I want to draw a line under that whole business. It's a certificated stone. You'll have no trouble realising a decent price.'

'The same would go for you, wouldn't it? In actual fact, Peter?'

Almond's head was crowded with things he couldn't say: the killing of the boy Holden had rattled him badly, and he imagined it must be playing a part in Cooper's jumpiness. Almond would be re-cutting the stone that had been his own in-kind wages, but Cooper did not have that option, and he had to realise the value quickly. Almond had to get rid of Cooper, but then again he didn't want Cooper to turn threatening. Cooper had enough on Almond to see him put away for many years. Trying for something conciliatory, he said, 'Where are you keeping the stone?' But that was wrong. He had only kindled false hope in Cooper.

'I have it on me right now. You gave me the sling, remember. I have it on me at all times. I can bring it round straight away. Be there in an hour, if you like.'

'No. You mustn't do that, but a word of advice: get yourself a deposit box in a bank, and put it in there. I have to go now. Goodbye, Cooper.'

He hung up. He would have liked to have heard a civilised 'Good evening' from the other end, but there had been nothing. His advice about the stone had been genuine. Cooper did not have the physical authority to walk around with it on him. Almond would be willing to bet he wasn't above taking it out in a public place to examine it, half hoping to be noticed in possession of such a valuable item. From what he knew of the man he didn't have a great deal else to show for his undoubted skill at . . . what was it called? *Léger de main.*

29

Reynolds and Clifford were on the train north, and sitting in standard class, which meant earplugs were required. The youth on the opposite side of the aisle had just eaten a bag of crisps. When he was about halfway through the bag, Clifford had given him a look, and he had then tried to eat them more quietly, which only resulted in his eating them more loudly. He had now embarked on his second bag of crisps. It was 11.15 a.m., for heaven's sake. Reynolds, sitting opposite, was reading *Dead Souls* by Gogol. *Re*-reading it, he said. He was doing his homework. He was the kind of man, like Quinn, who took refuge in work from personal troubles. A murder detective was lucky in that way: whatever personal matter he neglected was less important than the professional matter in hand. She believed there must be something wrong with Reynolds' 'relationship', otherwise how would he be able to head out of London at such short notice? She watched him read until he looked up at her and frowned; he then smiled. Well, better late than never.

'Where are we?' she said, looking out at the wide, frosted fields that seemed to have been accompanying them since London.

'About ten minutes from Peterborough,' he said. He was presumably an expert on this line, since it connected London with his birthplace. He went back to his book. His skin stood up well to the low winter sun that was flashing through the windows, his hair not quite so well.

Reynolds was coming close to dangerous information, and it was all her own fault. She thought back to last evening. She had just got in from Down Street, poured herself a glass of the discounted Cava, admitted the cat, and logged on to her emails. There had been another from Dorothy Carter who was now, in effect, hitting Victoria over the head with olive branches. She hadn't dropped the pub quiz idea . . . and she and the Spouse Mouse would be spending Christmas in London with her mother in Islington, so perhaps they could get together, after which proposition there were three question marks where none was required.

The next one was from Rachel Reade. A long screed about some promising car-boot sale that would involve getting up at dawn and travelling to somewhere near Saffron Walden. She had immediately clicked the email shut; and at that moment the one from Charles Quinn had arrived.

Darling Vicky,

I do hope you are well, and keeping safe, because, as you know, I think you may be in danger from the same lunatic who took a shot at my boy. I've been on to the hospital again and could get nothing coherent from them. Fobbed off with, 'No news is good news, Mr Quinn,' or some such banality. Vicky darling, I called you at the Yard, who gave me the number of the Unit. No reply. Went back to the Yard and they gave me the number of your new colleague in the Unit, Rawlins (is it?). Got through to him anyhow, said he was in Jermyn Street (a man after George's heart!) and we had a quick word. Or not so quick. I had a lot of questions, and so did he, and the upshot was that this fellow Rawlins invited himself up here, in a roundabout, gauche sort of way. He suggested this weekend. That is, tomorrow. He certainly doesn't seem over-burdened with social obligations, but then nor am I, and I thought: why not? But when I'd put the phone down I wondered what I was letting myself in for. You'll have guessed what I'm coming to: do you want to come up with this chap? Do say yes. I suppose he'll be asking you the same question. Said he would be doing anyway. Let me know by phone. Land line! Since I turn this bloody thing off after 8 p.m. and go and sit next to the fire (and the drinks cabinet).

All love,
Charlie

She had walked through to the kitchen in a fury. She had poured more Cava and regretted that it was too late not to admit the cat, which was slinking about her ankles in one of its rare ingratiating moods.

She pieced together the fatal sequence. She had left the office early, having despatched Reynolds to see Eugene Crawford. She had then taken the Tube home. She had checked for missed calls when she came out, and found one: from Croft, saying he ought to be able to arrange what she had asked; and she had taken that to be the only one. As she looked resentfully at her phone, it had rung again, and that had been Reynolds, dutifully asking if she would like to accompany him north. At least he *had* asked her, but even so, he'd stolen a march. And since she couldn't stop him going, she would have to go herself, because he must not have a free hand up there. She had extracted a small revenge by asking him to go immediately to Berry Brothers in order to buy two bottles of their Extraordinary Claret and a bottle of champagne. It was unthinkable to turn up on Quinn senior's doorstep without claret, and the champagne could be his birthday present. He would be ninety, she recalled, on Christmas Eve.

Clifford looked at her reflection in the carriage window. She wore what she considered her country clothes: tweeds – longish skirt and short, trim jacket. Charlie Quinn didn't approve of a woman in trousers: not that this would have stopped him jumping on a woman in trousers any time up to fifteen years ago. She liked the flare of the jacket, and was proud that it still fitted after all these years. She eyed Reynolds, wondering how best to divert him. They'd already discussed Eugene Crawford, so . . .

'What's the plot of *Dead Souls*?' she asked.

He immediately put down the book, which suggested he was glad of the distraction.

'A serf, in mid-nineteenth-century Russia, was called a soul—'

'If he was dead,' Clifford put in.

'If he was dead *or* alive. The landowners had to pay a tax for every serf. When a serf did die, the landlord still had to pay the tax on him—'

'Sounds mad.'

'Until the next census, when the number of the landlord's serfs was counted again.'

'I see.'

'The main character,' said Reynolds, 'is called Chichikov, which is a funny name if you know Russian. He's a sort of Everyman of the Russian middle class, and goes round buying the title, the nominal ownership, of hundreds of dead peasants. They're worthless to the real owners, and Chichikov will have to pay the tax on them.'

'So why does he do it?'

'I haven't got that far in the book.'

'Well you'd better get on with it then, hadn't you?'

'But I've read about it on the internet. He does it so he can mortgage the dead souls, raise money against them, because by owning all those souls, he looks like a big landowner. He buys the souls off a variety of eccentric land-lords, including a miser, a sort of ingratiating creep, and a bully. The miser's called Plyushkin.'

'He's the one with the garden?'

'Correct. That's a famous passage – the description of this wild garden – do you want me to read you a bit?'

She thought about this for a moment. 'No,' she said. Then she asked, '*Dead Souls* is very important to Andrei Samarin?'

'Anna says he reads it over and over again.' Clifford noted the familiarity in that use of the girl's first name. 'She told me there's a quality of innocence about Chichikov that he likes.'

'But he's a conman, isn't he?'

'I suppose so. But a fairly harmless one.'

Reynolds now stood, reached into the luggage rack. He brought down . . . now that was a better bag. Her waves of mental hatred directed towards the old bag must have re-gistered.

Reynolds was taking out papers. Had he brought his en-tire Samarin file? But wait, he'd brought the floppy book. How on earth had he smuggled that out of the office? She was staring at it, so he said, 'I thought we'd show it to

Quinn's dad. See what he makes of it.'

She thought it best to say nothing.

Reynolds was scrutinising the floppy book for the hundredth time. He was so damned dogged.

Peterborough station came and went: a revolting building. York station was better: airy and gracious, with a big Christmas tree in what she supposed was called the concourse. She stood around for about five minutes watching Reynolds' bag whilst he decided another train would be better than the bus.

The little train to Malton was a nasty, hot, bus-like thing, full of people who seemed to be competing to sound as northern and lugubrious as possible. First class didn't seem to be available. She paid careful attention to her fellow passengers, as she had done on the big train.

Reynolds said, 'What's he like, Charles Quinn?'

'A sexist snob.'

'I thought you liked him.'

'Did I say I didn't?'

'He was in the City, wasn't he?'

She nodded. 'He owned a small bank.'

They looked out of the window, at horse riders emerging from some woods, steam coming from all their mouths. They looked as if they'd been up to no good.

Reynolds said, 'He'll probably ask me if I'm related to the Reynolds of Helmsley Castle.'

'And are you?'

'That's just a for-instance.'

He explained about what he called the County Set. He said, 'Some of the least northern people of all live in the north, you know.'

Clifford then decided to phone Charles Quinn, telling him they'd be at his place soon, in a taxi from the station. But when he picked up, he wasn't having that. He said, 'Darling, I'll come and collect you,' which she took to mean that he himself would take a taxi to the station and accompany them back in it, chivalrously and pointlessly incurring two fares where only one needed to be paid.

But when they got to Malton station – which reminded her of a ruined monastery – he had the Alpine, or whatever it was called, in the short-stay car park. He had actually driven it himself to the station – at the age of eighty-nine. The introductions were now taking place all around the pretty, green car.

'You must call me Charlie,' the old man instructed Reynolds, who had limply come back with, 'Yes, and please call me Blake.' The old man had kissed Victoria on both cheeks twice, and then held her out for inspection, as it were. 'You're looking so pretty, darling.' He then had the incredible gall to refer the matter to Reynolds: 'Isn't she, Blake?' Reynolds of course just went red.

The old man was very stylish, in an unfathomable sort of way: fawn tweed coat, and narrow, deliberately too-short black velvet trousers with elastic-sided suede boots. Yes, suede boots at his age. He was like one of those cooks who just throw some leftovers together. They might dust with flour; old man Quinn dusted with fag ash. Well, the fag ash was only implied now, since his heart scare. This was his true talent, the gift bestowed by Eton and Oxford: the ability to dress. He'd been pretty useless at everything else.

Reynolds, Clifford noticed, kept giving worried glances at the car, then back at Quinn, trying to work out how the one could have arrived with the other. It wasn't that the car was new; it was old, like old man Quinn, dating, Clifford thought, from the seventies. But that had been an irresponsible decade and the car could still presumably go like a rocket.

Reynolds was now putting the bags in the boot, shyly indicating the bottles: 'These are for you.' She had hoped that would be done on entering the house, giving her time to slip away. She would be slipping away in any case. The men seemed to want her to sit in the front, but that, she thought, would be the old lady role. She would be perfectly happy on the little back seat, and it really was little, almost residual.

Charlie Quinn seemed to drive perfectly well through the centre of the town, but when he rested his hand for any length of time on the gear lever, his hand trembled. He was asking about the case his son had been working on. He said, 'I only hope you haven't been followed because the house is very remote.' Clifford observed Reynolds looking at the passing streets, noting, she supposed, the absence of the super-rich, and signs in the window such as 'Two for One', or (even with Christmas coming on) 'Sale'.

They came onto an 'A' road. At 2.30 p.m. the day was closing down, and light rain had started. Dark hills came into view. 'The Howardian Hills,' Reynolds explained, turning round to her. 'The Moors are just to the north.' He was proud of his own county. She could tell he was also worried about the old man's driving. They were doing seventy now, and the old man had stopped talking; he was concentrating harder than ought to have been necessary. What was he trying to prove? Perhaps his own vigour, as contrasted with his debilitated, bisexual son.

'When did you last see George, Mr Quinn?' Reynolds asked.

Perhaps he thought that questions would keep the old man alert, as opposed to distracting him from the task in hand. At length, the old man answered, 'He came up quite a bit in November. Every weekend but one, I think.'

Clifford knew for certain he'd been up on *one* weekend in November, and that was the significant one, to her mind.

They were behind a big lorry. It was decorated to look like a giant Kit-Kat bar. Reverting to his tour-guide role, Reynolds turned around and said, 'They make Kit-Kats in York.' She did hope the old man would not try to overtake it. Reynolds said to the old man, 'I believe George was looking out for another sports car.' He didn't say how he knew. He couldn't let on to the father that he'd been given sight of the son's emails, even if by process of law. Whilst concentrating hard on the road, the old man said, 'I know nothing about that. I thought he'd put all his efforts into making this one roadworthy.'

Let's hope he succeeded, thought Victoria.

Much to her relief, they now rattled off the 'A' road. The old man would have to slow down now, but he didn't; and the rain was becoming heavier, the sky darker . . . and she'd reckoned without the bends in the road. It was with incredulity that Victoria now watched the old man turn very deliberately towards Reynolds in order to say, 'I don't think the brakes are quite right, you know.'

Reynolds flashed a look back at Victoria. He said, 'Would you like me to drive, Mr Quinn? I'm fully comp.'

All senior detectives were fully comp.

They were running alongside a verge with a white fence

197

on the boundary of a prosperous-looking farm or estate. The fence posts seemed to glow against the blue-black sky. The posts began to curve to the left. The road followed the curve, and the Alpine followed the road. It was leaning in order to do so . . . and then it was leaning more. The old man ought to slow down just a fraction, then they'd be fine. Reynolds moved his hand towards the old man, who nodded once, apparently to himself. She saw him making a pushing motion with one of his legs; he seemed to be practising braking but of course he was doing the actual thing and it was having no effect on the Sunbeam's desire to fly off to the right. He pushed his leg again. This time he said, 'No, you see,' and the Howardian Hills were shooting across the sky, and they were racing over the grass. The car gave a great bounce – it was trying to jump the fence – but it *hit* the fence and they stopped. Reynolds had taken the car out of gear, and put out his hand to steer, so in the end they'd crashed obliquely rather than head-on. He turned around first to Victoria.

'You all right?'

Sexism. But his performance otherwise had been faultless, and it was a shame she was going to have to be pulling the wool over his eyes when they got to the house.

She was pleased to get out the word 'Perfectly'. She was breathing fast, though. The old man was sitting thoughtfully at the wheel nodding to himself as if a point had been satisfactorily proved.

30

Quinn had the number of a breakdown service. It wasn't
the AA or the RAC, but the owner of a local garage. The
breakdown man was called Lowther and his lorry incorp-
orated a ramp for the carrying of broken cars, and a big
cab with one long seat, on which the four of them were
now sitting, absurdly, like people on a park bench. It was
fascinating to watch the way the two windscreen wipers en-
compassed almost the whole of the very wide windscreen,
onto which rain was now lashing. She and Reynolds had
their bags on their knees. Any less upper-class person in
the old man's position would have fallen into a shamed
silence, but Quinn's confidence carried him through. The
main thing was they were all right and they all jolly well
deserved a hot bath and a drink. Admittedly, he did not
seem willing to say much about the accident *per se*. This
had been analysed intensively by Reynolds (still operating in full northern-sensible mode) and the man Lowther.
Their verdict – both having crawled under the car with
torches to conduct a horizontal conference – was that there
were a couple of little holes in the 'brake line' from which
brake fluid had been gradually seeping. They might have
been made by sharp stones flying up, or they might have
been made deliberately, and this – the latter – Clifford
could not believe. But she tentatively suggested that the
brakes might have been tampered with as a warning that
had been prepared some time ago for Quinn the younger

– analogous to the more direct warning issued to Reynolds in the Mayfair back street.

Lowther, who had no imagination, explained that he had seen the action of sharp stones on innumerable other brake lines, especially those of old cars driven along rough country roads. Old man Quinn, who had seemed keen to talk up the danger she and Reynolds might be facing, now retreated from any suggestion of sabotage. When Reynolds asked, 'Are you aware of any Russians working in the area?' he said, 'Russians? Nowadays your average British workman is a Russian, isn't he? But I tell you for a fact there've been none on the property.'

They had now come to the property. There was no sign, just a gate. Reynolds opened it. They began driving along an unmade road. 'Sharp stones here,' suggested Reynolds, and Lowther said that a car couldn't work up any speed on this road, and speed was needed for the stones to fly and cut. The road twisted and turned past glum country features: a field of soil, a field of . . . something green, a pond with reeds in it, a pond without reeds, a small wood, a bigger wood, all under the heavy rain. The real countryside was in the hills beyond. But before the hills there was 'The House' that comprised the prestige part of 'the property': Queen Anne, therefore highly elegant. It was occupied now by an estate agent who had made his money selling much meaner properties. Quinn had grown up in The House, which the Old Man had had to sell, about twenty years ago. He now lived in 'The Farmhouse', the junior partner to the main property. They were bouncing their way up to the fork in the track that led to either one. Apart from the old man telling Lowther which track to take, the painful junction was passed in silence apart from the pounding of the rain, and beating of the dogged wipers. Victoria had briefed Reynolds about the two houses – told him to avoid the subject.

A little way beyond the fork was another copse, this one with a recess, a roughly paved space on which stood a leaning barn-like building with a canopy leaning at the same angle. The old man asked Lowther to insert the broken car under this canopy. After they had passed a further series of copses, they came to the farmhouse, and Victoria could see Reynolds monitoring the track and thinking that it would be perfectly possible to meddle with the car without the occupant of the farmhouse knowing. Or – under cover of darkness – to drive the car away entirely and bring it back.

Lowther parked his lorry in front of the farmhouse. Clifford climbed down, saying she needed the loo and could she have the key to the door because it was rather pressing? Reynolds was watching her. The old man indicated that the door was not locked. She walked over the cracked stone of what had once been a farmyard, and she was into the house which smelt of a dying coal fire. To the left was the living room, a jumble of predominantly red rugs and velvet chairs and predominantly green paintings: conservative Yorkshire landscapes. She climbed the narrow stairs, looked back. The men remained outside, talking in the rain. She turned left, went along the narrow corridor, bare boards with rugs like stepping stones. The white door of George's bedroom. The key was in the lock, but the door was *not* locked. The Quinn smell: cigarettes and sandalwood. She saw the single bed with, instead of Quinn, one of Quinn's country suits stretched out on top of it. She closed the door behind her. By the bed, a folder of papers, a copy of *Vanity Fair*, a novel, *The Line of Beauty* by Alan Hollinghurst, an un-opened packet of Capstan's . . . and a green floppy book. 'Wine Notes', she read on the cover. It was unused, every page blank, thank God. There was really only one hiding place. She stood in front of the wardrobe. Apparently nothing in it but suits and a very good, but broken, umbrella. She listened. Was that somebody climbing the stairs? Too fast for the old man. Must be Reynolds. She put her hand through the curtain of suits and there was a small painting – or an item shaped like a framed painting – wrapped in newspaper. She closed the wardrobe door. She moved towards the door of the room, and opened it. Reynolds stood there with a look on his face that she could not read. She took Quinn's dressing gown off the back of the door. 'You're soaked,' she said, 'Get this on. I'll run you a bath.' She leant forward and kissed him on the cheek. 'I believe you saved our lives.' In the motion of the kiss she had also pushed him out of the room, and stepped out of it herself. She closed the door behind them. When Reynolds was out of sight – and he had lingered for a while, disorientated, as she had hoped, by the kiss – she locked the door, and removed the key. She put it in her pocket.

Five minutes later she was unpacking in her own room. She would be dressing down for dinner. She put out her jeans and her lovely, loose merino sweater. After his performance in the car, the old man had forfeited the privilege of not seeing women in trousers. She could still taste the horrible train coffee; she knew she should have brought her flask. She took out her soap bag. She removed her tooth-brush and toothpaste; she did not remove the Glock pistol. Her accommodation featured what George Quinn had never been able to bring himself to call an *en suite* bathroom. She walked through to it now, in order to brush her teeth, but no sooner had she started brushing than she stopped. She was above the kitchen, where Reynolds had already collared Quinn about the floppy book he'd brought along. He was questioning the old man closely about the word 'Carlton'. 'Well, there are several Carltons in Yorkshire,' the old man was saying. 'There's one up on the Moors.'

'Is that the nearest?' Reynolds asked.

It was.

Victoria Clifford genuinely believed that 'Carlton' must refer to Carlton House Terrace in London, since it was so near to where Quinn had been shot, and it accounted for the 'HT'. She had told Reynolds that. She had told him almost everything she knew about the floppy book. Downstairs, the old man was, so to speak, putting up his hands in surrender. 'I really have no idea about these notes. He's my own son, but I didn't *understand* him, you know,' at which poor Reynolds immediately turned to lighter matters: 'Not to worry, and sorry to trouble you about it, Mr Quinn. What a lovely place you have here,' etc.

31

The fire, greyish when they had arrived, was now bright red. The old man wore entirely different clothes with exactly the same net effect as his previous ones. Reynolds looked fetching, Victoria thought, in Quinn's dressing gown, a rather regimental item, which he wore tightly belted over Quinn's pair of silk pyjamas. The room reminded her of one of those in Mark's Club, the cosiest of the London clubs, with its overflowing braziers. The second bottle of claret was nearly finished, mainly thanks to the efforts of the old man. In anticipation of their arrival, he had embarked on a primitive Irish stew (as he called it). Victoria had taken it over. He was very grateful, but she was in truth little better at cooking than the old man.

They had given him some further details – the details they jointly agreed were relevant, so to speak – of the investigation Quinn had been conducting. Quinn senior was now talking about his time in the City. 'In my day,' he reflected roguishly, '*all* trading was insider trading. The City was a village. Everyone knew everyone.' His eyes wandered over the mantelpiece, and its display of Christmas cards, every single one – Clifford had checked – sent by people who'd written their greetings in fountain pen not biro. 'Come Christmas time,' the old man said, 'the partners would buy turkeys for all the staff.' Then tea ladies had become coffee machines; dealing rooms became trading floors. His merchant bank was now part of an American investment bank.

He had first implied that he'd more or less had to sell up as a result of the Big Bang in 1983. But now, with the claret at a lower level, he reflected, 'We were greedy you know. Took the first offer that came along, which in retrospect was not nearly enough.'

That was graceful of him, Clifford thought, and he was quite mild about the new class of the super-rich, the avowed targets of his son's investigations. Regarding the Russians, his line was, 'We preached capitalism at the Commies for heaven knows how many years. We can hardly complain that they've turned out to be rather good at it.' His main regret about selling was that, if he'd kept the bank, 'the boy' might have gone into the business instead of making the eccentric decision to join the police.

He showed Reynolds some of the photographs of George Quinn the beautiful boy, standing close to the beautiful and long-deceased mother. The only one of Quinn in adulthood was taken in the uneasy light of dawn outside Annabel's nightclub. It was about 1985, and father and son were arm in arm. Victoria knew the story. The pair had dined at Green's restaurant off Jermyn Street, and had a fearful row. But somehow they'd resolved to go together to Annabel's, of which both were members. It had been one of those nights at Annabel's when everyone in the club had danced, and lift-off had been achieved. Against all expectations, it had been a magical evening. Quinn had introduced his current boyfriend – an Italian whose name Victoria had not retained – to the old man, who had *not* been so old back then, and who had been friendly to the Italian, almost seeming to have come to terms with his son's inclinations. Victoria supposed it was the Italian who had taken the picture. The old man was telling Clifford all about the evening, leaving out all the salient details. Victoria closed her eyes. She knew those evenings at Annabel's, the extraordinary displays of mass affection that could occur on the dance floor.

It's a love train, get on board.

Reynolds was looking rather left out. Clifford found herself feeling sorry for him. 'Blake is from York,' she said, which made the old man look at Reynolds.

'Lovely place. Were you at school there?'

A bloody silly question. Reynolds obviously wasn't part of the being-sent-away-to-school classes.

'George's first prep school was in York,' the old man was saying. 'He went on to Sedburgh, then of course Harrow. His grandfather on his mother's side insisted on that.'

'Was he the baronet?' asked Reynolds.

'That's right,' said the old man, half proud.

'It's an inherited title?'

'Right again.'

'Do you mind my asking what his ancestor had done to earn the title?'

A whiff of revolution in the air! And then Clifford saw the way this was going, and she didn't like it.

'Made a lot of money, I suppose,' said the old man, 'which they spent as fast as they earned. They liked to say it came from agriculture. In fact, it was from iron-making – in Middlesbrough.'

The old man distributed the rest of the wine. Clifford knew he was going to say more about money, and couldn't think of a way of stopping him. 'Of course the title, and such money as is left, goes down the male line, to George's uncle . . .' He indicated one of the photographs. The picture had

206

been taken, judging by the young man's preposterous hair, in the sixties. 'Still going strong,' the old man said, rather sadly. 'He has four children.'

Victoria watched Reynolds draw the necessary conclusion.

Silence in the room.

'Do you shoot?' the old man suddenly asked Reynolds, who flashed Victoria a panicked glance. But he rallied well.

'No,' he said, '. . . but I've been shot *at*.'

'Tell us about some of your murderers,' Victoria prompted, and she watched him go red. After a few false starts ('Oh, that was just a category C domestic'), she got him onto the Turks and the villain called Ender. Reynolds was a genuinely modest man, but with a genuine appreciation of his own worth, and he enjoyed telling the tale once he'd got going.

'So this chap actually was what you might call a *hitman*?' the old man suggested.

'Yes,' said Reynolds, 'but he *missed* me.'

That business had culminated in the arrest of the top Turkish gangster in London, which, Victoria recalled from her conversations with Quinn, had involved an impressive 'dart' on Reynolds' part. She asked him to remind her.

'The big boss was called Attila,' said Reynolds.

'Dear God!' said the old man.

'One of the few things we knew about him was that he wore a wig. Now what can you say about a man who wears a wig?'

'Fellow's losing his hair!' the old man said, stupidly.

'He's *vain*,' said Reynolds.

Clifford remembered now. They'd staked out all the top

Turkish tailors in London and found him that way. She didn't need to listen to the rest. She thought instead about the parcel in Quinn's room. Ought she to go in and peel back the newspaper a little way? She couldn't bear to do it.

They ate the primitive stew in the living room, which was the only heated room. The old man opened another bottle of wine, and the effect of consuming it was to make him seem his age. At one point he said, apropos of nothing, 'Some baronets are actually rather vulgar, you know.' Victoria was tired, but she couldn't leave the room before Reynolds. She believed he was angling for time alone with the old man, but at nearly midnight he gave up, and said goodnight. Once Reynolds had gone she kept looking for an opportunity to leave the old man, or to usher him up to his bed, but it was hard to stop the lachrymose flow. Of Reynolds, he said, 'I didn't hear the accent at first, but it's awfully strong, isn't it?' Then there came the usual, wistful, 'If only you and George had . . . But you've heard it all before.' She certainly had.

Like most British upper-class males, Charlie Quinn was essentially six years old, and she finally levered him into his bedroom with the promise of a cup of cocoa.

When she brought it up to him, he said, 'I'll do the washing up in the morning.' That meant: 'You do it.'

She made a start on the washing up.

32

Reynolds had spent much of Sunday morning lying under the Alpine. He now seemed sure there had been no tampering, but that the car had certainly been driven over rough roads. He then had a long bath.

All this time, the old man had been reading the Sunday papers. As for as Clifford could see, he took all of them – just as though it were necessary for him to keep his finger on the pulse of the world. He also took the local papers during the week. They were delivered by a man in a small van, an emissary of the local supermarket, and very much in the mould of Lowther, the mechanic of the previous day. Throughout all this, the key to George's bedroom remained in her pocket, and nobody asked after it. At 2.30, the old man summoned a taxi. From her bedroom window, Victoria watched Reynolds climb into it beneath a black sky. She put the key back in the door, descended the stairs and joined Reynolds in the taxi, which *was* driven by an East European. (A Pole, going by the flag sticker on his dashboard.) The old man stood at the doorway to see them off, waving like a six-year-old. The taxi turned around on the cracked stones of the farmyard, then Reynolds said, 'Hold on, I've forgotten my toothbrush.'

Clifford said, 'It's not worth going back in for it, buy another.'

But Reynolds went back into the house – and stayed in it for a good while.

'How many places can a toothbrush be?' she demanded of the driver, but she required no answer, as the Pole seemed to instinctively know. When Reynolds re-emerged, he was carrying the green floppy book that had been in Quinn's room. As the taxi drove towards the gate of the property, Reynolds stowed the floppy book in his bag. Victoria considered saying, 'I think you'll find that's completely blank,' but that might connect her with the locking of the room – if Reynolds was aware that it had ever been locked. Instead, she said, 'That's one of George's floppies.'

'I know,' said Reynolds. 'As I was coming out of the bathroom, the old man was at one of the doors in the corridor. He had it open. He said, he thought he'd lost the key or something, but now the key was in the door.'

Reynolds was eyeing Clifford.

She said, 'Is this leading anywhere?'

'I asked if I could take a quick look around.'

'And what did you see?'

'Nothing much, except the notebook – the Smythson floppy book or whatever it's called. He said I could take it away.'

Had Reynolds seen what was in the wardrobe? She couldn't ask.

On the train they paid the upgrade for first class. Clifford insisted.

She said, 'Let's see the floppy book, then.'

Reynolds produced it from his bag. 'At first sight, it seemed blank,' he said.

It proved to be blank at second sight as well.

'Oh well,' said Clifford, but then Reynolds produced a slip of paper from his pocket: a cutting from a newspaper.

'Found this in one of the novels by the bed,' he said. 'I think it's from the *Yorkshire Evening Press*,' he mused infuriatingly as he read it over, apparently for the very first time. Then he said, 'If I'd known about this, I'd have asked the taxi to drive over there.'

At this, she snatched the cutting from his hand.

It was dated Friday 21 November:

The sister of Joseph Caldwell has thanked the police for their 'relentless efforts' to find the missing pensioner. Mrs Betty Caldwell said the most likely scenario was that Mr Caldwell, 87, had slipped into a gulley while walking on the Moors, or fallen into the swollen river Riccal. 'That was Joe. He was so fit for his age, and he would go wandering off onto the Moors.'

Mr Caldwell, a lifelong Quaker and peace campaigner, who lives alone at Carlton High Top, near Helmsley, was last seen by neighbours on the morning of Saturday 15 November. Mrs Caldwell also wished to thank 'the many well-wishers who have been in touch with all their kind thoughts and prayers'.

'I remember now from a hiking trip with school,' said Reynolds. 'There's Carlton, then there's Carlton High Top a little way off. *Carlton HT.* It's too small to come up on Google.'

Victoria handed the cutting back. She had been wrong about the meaning of 'Carlton HT'. She said so. Reynolds' phone chimed, indicating receipt of a text. He read the text, in the same infuriating way as he'd read the cutting.

'Anna Samarina,' he said eventually. 'She and her father have invited me round to her house for drinks.'

'When?'

'Tomorrow.'

'She's sorry for the short notice, I hope.'

'If she is,' said Reynolds, re-pocketing his phone, 'she doesn't say so.'

The disappearance of a man called Caldwell was an utter mystery, but this invitation . . . It was about right, thought Victoria, which was to say that it was something she had envisaged. She turned to look through the window. There was nothing to see in the rolling darkness.

'The Fens,' explained Reynolds, after a while.

It was an intermediate space between the seemingly opposite poles of Mayfair millionaires and an elderly, northern Quaker who loved the Moors.

33

Cooper came out of The Whistling Man at a fair old lick. He'd had a few; it was half past ten, and he wanted to be in time for a curry at the Calcutta Star, which stopped taking orders at eleven on a Sunday. The lamb rogan josh, he'd go for. That was the speciality of the house. It was a shame that his *Good Food Guide* was more or less surplus to requirements in his own locality, but the Star, was, he believed, among the top ten Indian restaurants in East London, and the house white was a tolerable drop. They knew him there, and they had a photograph of him doing his routine with the steel rings. 'You see any holes or gaps in that ring?' he'd ask. 'Well, what about the one in the middle?' That could make him laugh even now, even after forty years. It was like the egg in the bag. 'Can you feel the egg in the bag? No? Not feeling well, then?'

Cooper had good reason to believe it was Mission Accomplished. He'd found a buyer for the stone. He'd only be getting twenty but he'd be getting it in cash. The buyer was called Mark. He was a scruffy bloke, but quite well spoken; definitely a university product. Well, everyone was a university product these days. Put it like this: he'd seemed to know what he was looking at when he looked at the stone. And what he was looking at was forty grand's worth, so Cooper did not believe the deal would fall through. Mark needed a few days to raise the cash, and he'd be calling before the end of the week. It had been the landlord,

Benson, who had made the introductions. Benson was dodgy. He'd run the Whistler as a lock-in for years, and he had strippers on the weekends. Cooper didn't like the place, but it had become the nearest pub to his house, since the Hope had become flats and the Oak had become a William Hill's. Benson, Cooper thought, could learn a few things from a walk around Mayfair. It wasn't all about money. Not having three giant TVs blaring out football or pop music – that was just a question of taste.

But Benson had his uses, and Cooper had asked him at the bar if he knew anyone who might be interested in buying an item of jewellery, and he'd simply pointed at Mark, who'd been sitting with a good-looking woman. Cooper had been about to go straight over, but Benson had said, 'Let me have a word first.' He'd come back to the bar and said, 'He's all yours.' Mark had introduced the woman – Yvonne – and they'd all shaken hands, very formal. Mark had said, 'Apparently you're a magician.' Cooper had produced his pack of cards and showed them some things. 'That's very nice,' Mark had said. Then they'd talked about websites. When Cooper said he didn't have one, Mark had shaken his head for a long time. He could put him in touch with someone who'd set him up with a very professional site for a couple of hundred quid. Then Mark had gone off to the gents, and the woman, Yvonne, had said, 'Can you make *him* disappear?' which Cooper had found a bit alarming, but then she'd said, 'I'm only kidding. Do you want a drink?' It went against the grain to let a woman he'd only just met buy him a drink, so Cooper had bought her one: white wine spritzer, and a pint of Guinness for Mark.

Mark had certainly been a bit different when he'd come

back from the gents. More businesslike, let's put it like that. The two of them had gone into the backyard but there'd been a couple of smokers there, so they'd gone out into the dark back street. They'd stood next to a garage that had said, 'Keep Clear. Garage in Constant Use.' But of course there hadn't been a soul about, and there was still undisturbed snow in the street. Cooper had shown him the stone, breathing fast and not really able to speak. 'It's all right, man, relax,' Mark had said. And he had inspected the stone. That was the moment of maximum danger, because he could have done a runner with it there and then, but he'd handed it back, saying, 'I'm not going to ask where you got it from. I suppose you want cash.' They'd agreed on twenty-five and gone back inside.

Cooper had then carried on drinking with Mark and Yvonne, and it had all been pretty convivial. Cooper had told them about his time on the cruise ships, and they'd talked about poker, which Mark seemed to play a lot of. After an hour or so of this, Mark asked Cooper to come outside again. He wanted to look at the stone again. This time Cooper hadn't been so keen. Mark had said, 'You're going to have to trust me, man.' This time, Cooper focused on another sign, in the yard next to the garages: 'No Ball Games'. When did all dustbins become big green plastic things? He was from the era of metal dustbins, when the Argos on the High Street was Woolworths; when the big Wetherspoon's pub was the Gaiety, where he'd performed a few times. Early doors in its last days. Average house about six. As he handed the stone back after this second inspection, Mark said, 'I'm sorry, man, but I can only give you twenty.'

In view of the fact that this stone was probably tangled up with a murder, Cooper had agreed. This Mark chap had had two opportunities to make off with the stone, and he'd played the white man each time. They'd gone back inside for one more drink. Mark and Yvonne had then left the pub, after handshakes all round.

If he cut down the side of Matalan he'd be at the Star for quarter to eleven. Cooper heard the word 'cunt' and he was on the ground. He couldn't assess what had happened, but he knew he couldn't get up. And then he had an image in his mind of one of the liners he'd worked on; the entire district of Mayfair was on top of the ship, which was sailing away fast over a dark sea; and then he didn't know anything at all.

34

Reynolds was glad to be back in Mayfair. He thought of it as an excitingly decadent medieval village, with the Ritz Hotel as the castle on the fringe. His whole life seemed to have moved to Mayfair, now that Caroline had vacated the flat, having taken half the furniture. She'd moved in with her sister, as a staging post on the way to Bob Ballantyne. Above the Ritz and its Union Flags – which indicated, not quite correctly, that this was a *British* village – the sky was dark blue and streaked with black. Afternoon and evening were fighting it out up there.

Victoria Clifford had discovered from a contact in the London Fire Brigade that the fire in which Max Aktin had been killed in 2001 had occurred in a street called Conduit Gardens, which was near Paddington Station. She had gone off to Paddington Library, confident that the coroner's inquest would have been written up in a local paper. At least, that's where she said she'd gone. Her last word had been to tell him to nip over to Jermyn Street and buy a new shirt before he went to see the Samarins, and he had taken the point and done so.

He had returned to Down Street, made a couple of calls, put on the blue suit and Quinn's Crombie. He had walked up and down Bond Street, and then – since he couldn't help noticing he was getting some appreciative glances from women – he'd walked up and down it again. He then headed west. In Berkeley Square he looked at some hundred-and-fifty-grand Bentleys in the car showroom. He would need one of these, and commensurate property, to follow through with any of the women who'd been eyeing him. A good suit was not enough.

He'd quit the Square to approach the Samarin house. But he had been asked for half past five, and he was ten minutes early. The Aston was parked outside as before, and had recovered its composure after his assault upon it. Reynolds knew now that this model was called a DB5. The copy of the *Northumberland Guardian* had gone from the car. Well, it had been cluttering up the pristine interior. That must mean Porter was in town. The door of the Samarin house opened behind him, and a mellow light spilled out. A tall, red-faced man emerged. He was broad but not fat: like a jump jockey. His face was long, and rather horse-like, with a lantern jaw. His hair, driven back, was light grey, as though burnt to ash by the redness of his face. He wore a tweed suit, well pressed but dead-looking. He suddenly unleashed something from his tweed pocket: a tweed cap. He put it on his head, setting it just right with two quick gestures.

Reynolds watched the man, as he moved towards the Aston. The man was staring back at Reynolds in the rear-view as he put the Aston in gear. He pulled away, then he abruptly stopped the car, blocking the road and continuing to eye Reynolds in the rear-view. He had resented Reynolds looking at him. An Audi came up behind the Aston, and its bulk severed the eye contact between Reynolds and Porter, if that's who it was. The Audi gave a blast on its horn, then a second blast, this one continuous. The door of the Aston opened, and Porter climbed out. He then stood next to his car, and resumed his staring at Reynolds. He

218

took out his phone and proceeded, apparently, to check his text messages. The door of the Audi opened, and a woman began shouting abuse at Porter in heavily accented English. Eventually he jerked his head in the direction of the woman, and said, 'I would advise you to reverse and turn around.' He had a very upper-class delivery. He returned to checking his messages as the woman continued to shout. Eventually she did climb back into her car and performed a furious three-point turn. With no further glance towards Reynolds, Porter then pocketed his phone, climbed back into the Aston, and roared off towards Berkeley Square.

Reynolds turned towards the Samarin house. The door opened the moment he stood on the doorstep. It was a smiling, middle-aged woman who admitted him. He noticed that she wore a walkie-talkie on her hip. 'Detective Inspector Reynolds? Please come in.' She seemed to be French, and incredibly calm. Reynolds entered a wide marble hall. There was a tall Christmas tree, and a fireplace whose creamy stone mantle was decorated with dancing urchins and naked women. The woman took his coat and put it in a room off the hall.

She and Reynolds climbed a gracious staircase, looking down on the Christmas tree, which was decorated with Victorian-looking toys: miniature rocking horses ascended and descended. On the landing, Reynolds was aware of quiet Russian speech from a room out of sight. The woman opened double doors, and there – in what Reynolds supposed was the drawing room – stood Andrei Samarin. The room was huge, with floor-to-ceiling sash windows. It might have been an art gallery, right down to chairs that looked not meant for sitting on, and paintings at regular intervals:

mainly geometric, foreign-looking modern art, but also some English-looking landscapes. The furniture, too, was a harmonious combination of eighteenth-century and modern, or that's how it struck Reynolds: a theme of yellow, white and gold; couches rather than sofas, a soft, golden light from a modern chandelier, a fire burning in the marble fireplace.

On a gilded and ornate table sat an Apple laptop with the screen lifted up. It was showing cricket. Must be on iPlayer, thought Reynolds. England were playing in Australia but it was too early in the day for live action. Samarin was shaking Reynolds' hand. His shoes, Reynolds noticed, were like – or actually were – black velvet slippers. He wore rather narrow green trousers, a pink shirt and a light-brown tweed jacket. His watch was a gold antique. Andrei Samarin was a slight, dapper man. He might have been a retired dancer. Seeing that Reynolds was looking at the laptop, Samarin said, 'The wicket's flat, you know. It is not doing anything.'

The probable French woman had departed, but another, younger woman was in the room. She was closing the shutters, and the light of the room was becoming softer, possibly as a result of something she had done a moment before.

'You like cricket, Mr Samarin?' Reynolds asked.

'Please call me Andrei. I don't know. I'm trying to familiarise myself with it; then I will decide.' A silence fell. Eventually, Samarin said, 'A man was here earlier. He was trying to interest me in some cigars. As you can see, he succeeded.' He indicated a wooden box of cigars, open on another table. 'Would you like one?'

Reynolds thought of the Gifts and Hospitality Register. That couldn't be shrugged off as easily as his detective's

220

notebook. He'd accepted a cigar on Friday; it mustn't look as though a cigar was his Achilles heel. 'I won't, thank you very much.'

Samarin seemed to be relieved. His left hand could remain in the pocket of his jacket, where it had been more or less since Reynolds' arrival.

As a sort of test, to see whether the name of Porter would be divulged, Reynolds asked, 'Was it the man who just left?' Samarin frowned. 'A man in an Aston Martin,' said Reynolds. 'I was wondering if he'd brought the cigars.'

Samarin shook his head. 'He is nothing to do with cigars.'

Another silence.

'To speak frankly,' said Samarin, 'Anna is in the bath. She will be here shortly. What will you have to drink?'

Reynolds realised the woman who'd been shutting the blinds was also waiting for his response. 'Anything that's going,' said Reynolds, and Samarin looked at him in a way he could not fathom. Reynolds found himself feeling lonely in the company of this man.

'Wine?' said Samarin, after a while.

'A glass of white wine then, please, thank you.'

Samarin spoke Russian to the woman in the corner. He turned back to Reynolds. He said, 'Please – sit.' Reynolds sat down on a white couch. A book lay on the couch, an antique in itself, but there was a bookmark in it. The book was in Russian, with only lettering on the cover. Samarin remained standing. Reynolds was picturing Anna Samarina in the bath.

'Hiatus,' said Samarin, and smiled. He seemed to play with the English language like a new toy. He would glance occasionally at the Apple screen. Reynolds didn't believe he really wanted to watch the cricket; he just didn't know what else to do. 'Somebody's trying to whip something away on the on-side,' Samarin said, then the young woman re-entered, carrying a wide silver tray. It held a bottle of white wine in an ice bucket, three wine glasses. Again, thought Reynolds: elegant but sparse. No peanuts, for example. The wine was poured; the label was very French. The woman departed.

Anna Samarina entered: she wore jeans and what appeared to be a man's blue shirt. Her feet were bare and brown. She looked American. She kissed Reynolds on the cheek, and poured herself a glass of wine. The wine was delicious. They all seemed to agree on that.

'At least Papochka gave you something nice to drink,' said Anna. She looked across the room, studying her father with great objectivity, but also affection. A mobile phone rang, becoming visible in the process. It lay on a bureau by the window.

'Please excuse me,' said Samarin, and he picked it up and made towards the door by which the maid had left. There appeared to be few formalities to the conversation, because Reynolds heard Samarin saying, 'But you understand thirty per cent?'

Anna Samarina said, 'That is Rostov. His partner. Everything must be explained to Rostov.'

'Is he the man with the Aston Martin?' Another test.

'I don't think Rostov has an Aston,' she said. She was examining her bare feet. Reynolds thought: she's trying to decide whether to say who owns the Aston. 'That was Major Porter. The car is called a DB5. He has a thing about them.'

'Who's he?'

'Security. I'm so sorry, by the way, about last week. Eva wanted me all to herself in order to moan, moan, moan.'

'Moan about what?'

'Work.'

'What does she do?'

'Nothing of course. But she might have to.'

'Who is she, exactly?'

'My friend – she thinks. She is from Petersburg. We were at the same school for about two days in Switzerland. She was a runner-up in Miss USSR UK in about 2006. She has a white Ferrari and a flat overlooking Harrods. It has strange windows: triple, or maybe quadruple glazing; bulletproof, because her papochka thinks she is a target, and quite soundproof too. The ambulances go screaming along Knightsbridge in total silence, and when it rains . . . Harrods goes blurred. Now she has a boyfriend who thinks she should be working.'

'What does *he* do?'

'He plays tennis. I mean he is a professional tennis player. Right now, he's in Abu Dhabi for an exhibition match; he is always somewhere for an exhibition match, and . . . are you interested?'

It seemed superfluous to mention that this was a lovely room, but Reynolds heard himself doing so. He also mentioned the paintings.

'That is a Gainsborough,' Anna Samarina said. 'And some others you wouldn't have heard of.' She stood up and poured more wine. 'I'm sorry. I mean, I have not heard of them either. They are mostly Papochka's Russian avant-gardists. Or sometimes French.'

Her father re-entered.

'That was quick,' said Anna. 'How is his new place?'

She turned to Reynolds. 'Rostov has bought a house in – which one is near the sea? Suffolk or Sussex?'

'Both.'

'But I think Sussex. No, Surrey, and it is not near the sea. He was considering many places. He has another house in Hampstead. You have probably looked him up, seen a photograph. He is a very badly dressed man. He has many T-shirts with—', and for once she was lost for the English word, but she soon found it. 'Slogans. They say things like "Size matters". Can you believe it? I am not joking!'

'Now darling . . .' said Samarin, who had been looking rather sadly at his daughter.

'"All this and brains too". Now he is going to have terrible fights over the house.'

'Fights?' asked Reynolds, 'With whom?'

Samarin turned his pale-blue eyes towards Reynolds, but it was his daughter who answered. 'The English Heritage . . . He has a sunken garden, which he has filled in. He has a maze, but he got lost in it, so he is going to have his revenge by tearing it down if he has not already. He calls the place his dacha. But a real dacha would have a pump and no running water.' She poured more wine for herself and Reynolds. 'Not fifteen bathrooms. I think Papochka will have to mediate. The English Heritage love *him*,' she indicated her father. 'Whenever he wants to make a change here, he calls around a lady called Grace, and she says, "No, it's impossible," and he says, "Thank you very much," and doesn't do it. But Rostov *will* do it. You know, he bought the house off-plan. He viewed it from his helicopter on his way to somewhere else. He wants it for his new art collection.' She looked for quite a long time at her father. '*I luff art*,' she said, evidently quoting the man Rostov. 'I seem to be speaking continuously, shall I stop?'

'It is very entertaining, darling,' said her father, 'if a little fantastical.'

'Papochka would probably like to go out for a walk,' she said. 'This is his hobby. Walking in Mayfair, alone. No motorcade! He looks at the architecture. It makes him very angry.'

'No dear, Mayfair is beautiful. But some of it has been spoiled irretrievably.'

'Such as?' asked Reynolds.

'Most of the squares. Park Lane.'

'He walks along Park Lane, seething.'

'I sometimes stroll about, looking with the eyes of the past. Park Lane was once beautiful art nouveau. All white, and no motorway along the front of course.'

He took a sip of wine. He nursed the glass, which involved use of his left hand. Reynolds thought: when he is happy he forgets about the missing finger.

Samarin said, 'Do you know The Only Running Footman, Blake? It is a public house near here, very curiously named.'

Reynolds nodded. It was quite a famous pub.

'In my mind,' said Samarin, smiling sadly, 'it still has a mansard roof.'

His daughter said, 'Papochka wants to recreate an old Mayfair mansion: Devonshire House.'

'And not forgetting the Devonshire House ball,' Samarin added, still smiling. This was some in-joke between father and daughter.

225

Anna said, 'He thinks if he arranges a ball grand enough, I will find a husband there.' Reynolds eyed her, thinking of her late fiancé, John-Paul Holden. 'Meanwhile Papochka is putting up flats along the river. He stops Rostov from making them too ghastly.'

'We are quite proud of our developments,' Samarin said to no one in particular.

'I thought there was a property bubble in London,' said Reynolds. Again the cool eyes of Samarin fell on him. 'Or that's the way it's going – from what I read.'

'Well then,' said Samarin, 'we will all climb into the bubble bath. Please tell me, because I am very curious to know: what are your current investigations?'

Reynolds tried to decide whether this could be considered a normal social question. But the tone was not light enough for that to be the case.

'The main thing we have on right now is the shooting of George Quinn.'

'Yes,' said Samarin, 'and now two further questions. Is he making any progress: and are you?'

'It's no to both really, I'm afraid.'

'Do you enjoy the work?'

Anna Samarina pressed something that looked like a TV remote. But it was *not* a TV remote. Reynolds nodded at Samarin's previous question, but that had already been forgotten. The maid reappeared. Anna Samarina indicated the wine bottle and she departed. Anna Samarina said, 'Papochka has a proposal to make.'

'I was hoping to interest you in a change of tack – change of career, in fact.'

Reynolds said, 'In terms of . . . ?'

'A consultancy role,' said Samarin, 'with ourselves.'

Anna Samarina poured wine for Reynolds. She smelt very nice; therefore she must have come closer than the previous time she had poured wine.

Andrei Samarin said, 'Today is Monday. Are you available on Wednesday? I would like you to come to the south of France to discuss this further.'

Reynolds smiled; he very nearly laughed. But Samarin was doing neither.

'Why the south of France?' said Reynolds.

'The relevant people will be there.'

'A fellow called Russell Page,' said Anna Samarina. 'Papochka's PR man. You'll like him very much. He loves cricket,' she said, indicating the Apple Mac, 'he is extremely English, and he has a medal for charity work.' She laughed. 'Papochka, what did Rostov say when you told him about Page?' She imitated a gruff Russian voice: '"This charity medal – is guarantee he is criminal!"'

'I don't see what use I can be to you,' said Reynolds. 'Unless you were thinking about security.'

'No, no, we have Porter,' said Anna, 'and he does a very good job, doesn't he, Papochka?'

'Well,' said Samarin, embarrassed, as Reynolds believed his daughter had intended, 'we are all still alive.'

'Or maybe we have all died,' said Anna, smiling at Reynolds, 'and gone to heaven.'

'Take some leave,' Samarin suggested, 'two days only.'

It seemed to cause him great stress to force the matter like this. What did he believe his daughter guilty of? Jewellery theft? Murder? Did he know of the engagement to Holden? Or was he trying to divert Reynolds from his own crimes, and specifically the shooting of Quinn?

Samarin was writing on a slip of paper. He handed the slip to Reynolds, who couldn't read it. Anna Samarina took it. 'Northolt – is lovely private airport,' she said, lapsing for some reason into her parody Russian voice. 'Reception B. Midday on Wednesday. You fly to Nice. Then drive to Hotel des Etrangers. *Is very nice.* For dinner. You will stay at the hotel – or Vallauris?' This last word – Reynolds *thought* he had caught it correctly – was added as a question directed at her father. He nodded. Anna handed the paper to Reynolds: 'Think about it and let me know by text,' she said, standing up. Samarin also stood. Reynolds was escorted towards the front door by the calm servant. The door swung open to reveal a badly dressed, burly man on the other side of the road.

Barney Barnes, late of the Yard.

Reynolds crossed the road, as the door of the Samarin house closed quietly behind him.

'Hello Barney.'

Barnes nodded.

'Andrei Samarin lives there,' said Reynolds, gesturing over his shoulder. 'He's a Russian oligarch.'

'Yeah,' said Barnes. 'Aren't they all?'

'He's a person of interest. I think I mentioned that.'

'I don't recall,' said Barnes, and Reynolds wasn't at all sure that he *had* mentioned Samarin.

'What are you doing here, Barney?'

'This and that. Walking about.' He half turned as a black Ferrari went past. 'None of your business really, is it? To be fair?' The Ferrari had been good enough to pause at the junction with Berkeley Square. It looked like the Batmobile. Then it roared into the square.

'You've got me interested in these super-rich, you have,' Barnes said.

'Thanks for giving me the tip about that jeweller. I haven't got hold of him yet. You want a drink, Barney?'

'No thanks.'

'I'll be off then.'

Reynolds began walking towards Berkeley Square. After a few seconds, he turned and saw Barnes moving off the other way.

Reynolds made a circuit of Berkeley Square, thinking hard about Barnes and the Samarins. Regarding Barnes . . . he regretted having gone to see him. Why had he done it? Because Barnes had been contacted by Quinn. About what? The elusive jeweller.

Once again, Reynolds had that lonely feeling, accentuated by the fact that Berkeley Square was full of beautiful women. Most were talking on their phones. In fact, Reynolds seemed to be the only person in Berkeley Square not engaged in a telephone conversation. He felt adrift. He'd abandoned his notebook, but he wasn't going to head off to the Côte d'Azur with some Russian billionaires on a strictly unofficial basis. He needed a line manager to talk to. In the absence of a current line manager, he decided to call his previous one. Flanagan picked up straight away, but he was obviously embroiled in many other matters, so it took Reynolds a while to get across who he was; and then Flanagan was in some doubt about whether he had a minute to speak.

'Right, so what's the trouble?' he said, emerging eventually from whatever chaos surrounded him.

Reynolds decided he'd better start on Flanagan's home turf. He said, 'Has Lilley got anywhere with the Quinn shooting?'

'Not to my knowledge, he hasn't.'

Reynolds had drifted over to the Rolls-Royce showroom window. He looked at the spec, displayed in the window, of the Phantom Saloon. He said, 'I've just been invited to the south of France by a Russian oligarch.'

The Phantom saloon cost £359,760 and no pence. That was including VAT.

Flanagan said, 'You've landed on your feet in this new unit, haven't you?'

Without VAT the Phantom Saloon was only £299,800.

Reynolds asked, 'Do you think I should go?'

'Why come to me about it?' said Flanagan. 'Is there a policing reason to go?'

'I think so.'

'Then you make the case to your man Croft. Ask him to minute the conversation and you've covered your back.'

'I haven't spoken to Croft about anything so far.'

'Well, you know what he's like. The Undercroft.'

'He's a very low-key operator.'

'He is and all.'

Amongst the extras you got with the Phantom Saloon were a lambswool travelling rug and 'courtesy umbrellas in rear door'.

Reynolds said, 'Do you remember Barney Barnes, sir? Ex of the Sweeney.'

'Christ, man, you're jumping about all over the place. I remember Barnes.'

'Do you know if he did the basic shot course at Bisley?'

'Now how the hell would I know a thing like that?'

Reynolds thanked his old boss, and hung up. He then called Victoria Clifford, explaining what had happened and saying he needed to speak to Croft as soon as possible. She asked why he didn't simply call Croft himself, and he replied that he didn't have his number, as he believed Clifford knew perfectly well, having gone to some trouble to keep it from him. She said she'd text him the number, but that it was the Commissioner's Christmas dinner, so there was no point ringing him until about ten. She hung up.

Reynolds wondered where Clifford was. He thought he heard foreign voices in the background; she'd obviously wanted to get rid of him as quickly as possible, and he believed she'd only accepted his call by mistake. But he'd thought it beneath his dignity to ask.

It was 7.15 but the Rolls-Royce showroom was still open for Christmas shopping. A Japanese family were being shown around the Phantom Saloon. It was very bright in the showroom, and increasingly dark in Berkeley Square. But Reynolds didn't want to go back to the empty flat in Palmers Green.

Then he remembered what he'd been meaning to do all day. He walked back to Down Street, climbed the dark stairs and admitted himself to the office. He took the two floppy books out of his desk drawer – the blank and the almost blank. He began counting the pages.

35

Clifford's taxi was proceeding fast through the Christmas town. She thought of the young Russians in London: all on a crash course in westernisation. There were many fine students among them and she envied them all. At home, one third of a bottle of Cava awaited her, and a probable electronic onslaught from Dorothy Carter, plus a slightly more seemly one from Rachel Reade. But none of that was important; she had brought matters to the tipping point in a very big game, and it was really quite sexy in the sense not only of excitement but also mutuality – because this would be the moment of truth for her every bit as much as for Reynolds. He had been in a bit of a state when he'd called. He apparently had to speak to Croft because he was in danger of 'knackering the case'. It wasn't like him to swear, if that counted as swearing.

He would be going to France, of course. She had made sure of that with Croft, who really had been at the Commissioner's dinner, and whose phone really had been turned off. But Reynolds had got on to his personal assistant, Celia Walsh, and Celia had gone to the restaurant – Langan's Brasserie, quaintly enough – in person and dug him out. So she would be sending Celia Walsh a bottle of Berry Brothers claret. The 'ordinary' would do.

Reynolds had been keen to find out where she was, but his pride stopped him from asking. Reynolds *was* proud, also rather vain. She kept noticing that the little mirror on the mantelpiece at Down Street had been moved. The trouble was that he didn't accept these as facets of his character, whereas Quinn had regarded fancying himself as not being any sort of problem at all. It was vital that Reynolds should not know where she'd been. Nothing must deflect him from following the path he was on. In any case her endeavours might not come to anything . . .

She had in fact spent the past two hours on the borders of Paddington and the West End; on the borders of London and the rest of the world, in other words. International London. There'd been little evidence of Christmas in those streets, but they were *always* Christmassy in their own way: brightly lit all-night pharmacies; Turkish delight in snowy piles in shop windows; teapots shaped like Aladdin's lamps; tea drunk in glasses in decorative silver holders; muffled-up men sitting outside cafés smoking those . . . she wanted to call them hubble-bubbles . . . sending clouds of white smoke flowing through the cold, dark-blue air. Arabs predominated on those streets; but the big synagogue was there too, and all sorts lived in the mysterious, half-smart mansion flats of the district.

Her contact had been Russian, and confined to a wheelchair. A silent helper had waited outside the café, which had been Mitteleuropean, with gloomy wood panelling, and many cakes laid out on a long, white-cloth-covered table, like the food at a funeral. The other customers had been vampiric, elderly Mitteleuropeans, with a couple of fat Mitteleuropean grandchildren. The former used knives and forks to eat their cakes, the latter their fingers. It had been tremendously hot; the till, and the girl who worked the till, were genteelly concealed behind a red velvet curtain.

Sombre classical music was emanating from the background – a sort of massed, buried choir. Her contact had selected a strawberry square. That had been at 7.30 p.m., an odd time to be eating a strawberry square, Clifford had thought. Then again, she herself had been tempted by the coffee éclairs, but she had come directly from Claridge's, where she had eaten a bowl full of crisps, so she just had a coffee. Then the envelopes had been exchanged. Hers had been Smythson, of course. Watermarked cream wove. The other envelope had just been any old scruffy brown thing.

36

Viewed from Port Hercule, Monaco resembled an amphi-
theatre, with the apartment blocks banked up on the hills
in place of the seats. As always when he brought *Queen
for a Day* into Monaco, Captain Grant Williams felt she
was the star of the show. All morning, tourists had been
lingering and taking photographs beyond the gangplank security gate. On the gate, the sign said 'Private Vessel, No
Boarding' in English and French. Samarin had paid ten million for a twenty-year lease on the berth. The *Queen* was at
the very limit of what was allowed in the port. Three metres
longer, and she would have been required to moor at a buoy
a quarter-mile out with the crass cruise ships, and be reli-
ant on the tender for coming and going.

It was the afternoon of Tuesday 16 December and the
day was overcast. The tops of the hills were lost in tumbling
clouds. Sometimes, depending on his mood, these clouds
reminded Captain Williams of steam rising off a dunghill in
some grubby farmyard. He ought to have been in St Barth's
by now, getting some rays. He stood on the aft-deck, and
watched a young woman swabbing the decks of the next
vessel along, a ninety-metre-long motor cruiser called *WTF.*
You didn't have to be an old-school sailor to disapprove
of that name. The sound of dance music, turned low, was
coming from the wheelhouse. Before long, Williams
believed, the music would be turned up. A party seemed to
be brewing up on *WTF*, and a little van had just pulled up at

its gate. *'Service Froid Monégasque'*: a delivery of ice. Two young guys came out of the wheelhouse to receive it. The Veuve Clicquot was already aboard.

In spite of the cold, the deckhand, who was quite gorgeous, wore hotpants. As the ice came aboard, she was engaged in bending low to fix a new chamois to the mop head. Women always bent from the waist rather than bending their knees. Captain Williams didn't understand why but he was glad they did, and he wondered whether this one was laying on a show for his benefit. That was quite possible, since she had glanced sidelong at him as she resumed her swabbing. She wasn't very vigorous about it, but then she wouldn't be used to manual labour: probably some trustafarian on a gap year. She was now hitching up her hotpants, as if they weren't short enough, and, yes, another glance. At this rate he wouldn't need to crash the party; he'd be invited. He could do with a few drinks after the morning he'd had.

Any other port in the world, and Williams himself would have been displaying his own, somewhat more scarred knees, shorts and flip-flops being his usual work attire. But in Monaco he always had to be smart-casual. That was specified in his contract. The specification came from the agency, he believed, rather than from Samarin himself, who was pretty laid-back on matters of dress whilst always being beautifully turned out himself.

There'd been a meeting of the big three that morning: Samarin, Rostov and Porter. Rostov had pulled up dockside in a black Mercedes with one of his security guys; then Porter, overall head of security, had turned up in what Williams believed to be one of the half-dozen Aston Martins he kept in various parts of the world. Samarin, who'd pitched up the night before, had received them in the library. All crew except Williams himself had been ordered on shore for the next two days with accommodation allowances. They'd all cleared off to Nice, where the allowances went that much further.

Williams knew to keep out of the way of the meeting, but he'd heard shouting from the library. That was mainly Rostov. There also came the occasional, soft mutterings of Samarin, and interjections from Porter in his staccato, incredibly upper-class accent. Porter had been in the Queen's Guards, or something. From the few snatches Williams could make out, the question was who would be going up to 'the hotel'. That would have meant either the Hotel Metropole Monte Carlo, or possibly the Hermitage. Or maybe the Hotel des Etrangers west of Nice, where Rostov in particular hung out a good deal of the time.

The meeting had ended at midday. Towards the end of it, Williams had distinctly heard Porter say, 'These are the ramifications. I give you them quite squarely.' That sounded pretty heavy, but everything Porter said sounded heavy. Samarin had stayed in the library after the conflab. Rostov and his security man had departed in the Merc, and Porter had gone to the aft-deck, where he'd sat on the stretched canvas cushion of the long bench under the aft awning and made a number of phone calls. Williams, who was always curious about Porter, had gone aft himself.

'Yes,' Porter was saying into his phone. 'No. That has not been established. No. The matter is under discussion. Be so good as to call me back as soon as you know.'

He terminated the call without bothering to say goodbye or anything like that. He examined the phone for a minute, then he pitched it over the railing of the stern and into the choppy, dark-blue water. Williams found it quite difficult to believe what he'd just seen. Porter noticed that he was being looked at; he went a deeper red.

'Can I be of any assistance to you?' he said.

'Do you want a coffee, or anything, Major Porter?'

'No. I do not.'

Probably just as well. Last summer, Williams had heard Porter ask Jones the cook to go ashore and get him an ice cream. 'What flavour?' Jones had asked.

'Raspberry ripple.'

'What if they don't have raspberry ripple, Major Porter?'

'I will tolerate any close approximation thereto.'

Well, that was big of him.

'Tell me,' Porter now asked Williams, 'how many of you does it take to sail this boat?'

Williams did not like the word 'boat'. He replied, 'Any fewer than eight would be a stretch.'

'But would you be kind enough to answer the question?'

'It would be possible with eight.'

'How much notice would you need to sail?'

'It would depend on where we were going.'

Porter turned his head quickly aside, as though in distaste.

Williams had then said, admittedly with a touch of sarcasm, 'Any more questions, Major Porter?'

'No. Since you don't seem disposed to *answer* my questions.'

He'd then waved Williams away, and Williams had had no choice but to leave, unless he wanted to be sacked, because he was sure that Porter had the *power* to sack him, even though he was merely the owner's chief heavy.

37

The Hotel des Etrangers was about ten miles west of Nice. It took the form of a white mansion on a headland. Reynolds sat in a white-and-gold lounge that gave a panorama of the sea. It was called the Observation Lounge. The sky was dark grey, the sea dark blue. The colours complimented the appearance of an old-fashioned blue-and-brown steamship that appeared to have moored so as to be perfectly framed by the wide windows of the lounge. It flew a red flag from the stern, with a Union Jack in the corner, like a stamp on a letter. Reynolds was glad to see that Union Jack, even if it didn't occupy the whole of the flag. If the worst came to the worst, he could swim out to that ship with Russian bullets landing in the sea all around him.

Reynolds knew he was out of his depth, chiefly financially. He had felt slightly ill from the speed at which Samarin's private jet had taken off – you were more aware of the speed of a small plane – and the rocket-like angle at which it had ascended. There had been ten cream-coloured leather armchairs in the jet. Two of these faced each other with a low table in between. Reynolds had sat at one of these. The Russian called Nicky, whom he'd last seen at the wheel of the four-by-four on the way between the London Library and the Orangery, sat in the other. Nicky would point at the various canapés that a member of the crew kept bringing from the back of the plane, repeatedly saying, 'Pliss'. Reynolds had eaten food to a total, he decided, of twenty pounds: not a lot of food, but some of it involving caviar. He had drunk a glass of champagne which he costed at six pounds. These were the figures that would be going in the hospitality register.

Driving was Nicky's speciality, not hospitality, and he had seemed more relaxed when ferrying Reynolds from Nice airport in a black Mercedes. He had said, 'This very good road!' and looked at Reynolds for a response. Reynolds had said, 'You mean it's empty?'

'Empty! Always!'

At the hotel, Nicky had deposited Reynolds in his current location, and told him, 'Wait pliss. One hour maximum.' That had been nearly an hour ago.

The Observation Lounge featured a well-proportioned Christmas tree, with a perfect helter-skelter of white lights. They raised the dreamy question of whether the lights were ascending or descending the tree. Reynolds was hypnotised by it. There had been no mention of a booked room. When Reynolds asked whether he was to stay at the hotel, Nicky had said, 'Of course, of course,' but Reynolds had not quite believed him.

For purposes of 'fitting in', Reynolds had ordered a white wine, which he had offered to pay for, and it had been with mixed feelings that he had received the news that it was taken care of. Looking at the wine list, he couldn't find the price of wines by the glass. A Carlsberg was fourteen Euros. So that was twelve pounds for a cheap beer, so to speak. The cheapest *bottle* of wine appeared to cost fifty-five Euros. He would put down ten Euros for the glass. Pretty soon, he would start refusing things, however much the 'offence or damage to working relationships'.

The waiter who'd brought the wine returned and asked, 'Will you be dining with us tonight, sir?' Reynolds believed he would be; otherwise why was he *at* the hotel? So a waiter gave him a preview of the menu. Reading it, Reynolds felt that what he was really seeing was a copy of the Bribery Act 2010, with its specification of 'conduct leading to improper performance'. But was a police officer guilty of bribery if he didn't know what he was being bribed about? Probably. Croft, when Reynolds had finally got him on the phone, had drawled, 'Stay on the right side of bribery.' He'd seemed a remarkably ordinary and laid-back person for someone so elusive. Then again he was *Under*croft. When he'd tried to go over the whole case, Croft had said, 'Yes, yes, Victoria's put me pretty well in the picture, I think.' It appeared that she'd spoken to Croft immediately before Reynolds.

Reynolds no longer trusted Clifford. She'd been up to something in the country, trying to keep him out of Quinn's room. She was playing some sort of double game. On Monday night, he had counted up the pages of the two floppy books. Quinn's from the farmhouse had 110 pages. The one from Argrove that Clifford had given him had 108. One leaf – two sides of possible writing – had been neatly sliced out. Reynolds had been alerted by a stray sliver of paper in the binding.

When, the next morning, Clifford had pitched up – rather late – at Down Street, Reynolds had asked her, 'Did you cut a page out of Quinn's floppy book?'

'Why on earth would I do that?'

'Well, a page is missing.'

'The obvious conclusion', she'd said, fluffing up her hair (she'd arrived in a kind of crocheted cap), 'is that Quinn cut it out.' Reynolds had watched her sit down and click open her emails. She began to read them: 'Trevor Kennedy says you're to try to avoid using the minibar at the hotel. Honestly, that man.'

As she'd begun typing something very fast, and presumably rude, in reply, Reynolds said, 'I expect you could spend several thousand pounds in the minibar at the Hotel des Etrangers.'

'Well *don't*. Likelihood of rain on the Riviera. You'll take the Aquascutum, and the blue suit of course. If I were you, I'd also buy a new white shirt.'

She'd then begun printing something out on the old printer. Clifford eyed Reynolds as the thing juddered away. She said, 'I've half a mind to buy a top-of-the-range printer right now. See how Trevor Kennedy likes that. Does he think there's a cheaper OCU in London?' She'd handed Reynolds the printed result. 'Contact details for the Chief of Police in Nice. The hotel comes under him. The Euros are coming at three.'

'In a security van, would that be?'

'On a bike. From Baxter in the Finance Group. He had to go through Foreign Office liaison if you can believe that.'

'Are you going to give me a pen that turns into a small-calibre pistol?'

'What?'

'And a grooming kit that assembles as a nuclear bomb?'

'Oh. Like Q, you mean? Are you implying that you're James Bond?'

He had told her something about the meeting with Samarin, and the sudden appearance of Barney Barnes. She said, 'Barnes is a nut, with too much time on his hands,' but by then she was into a phone call to the Royal College of Surgeons. She was trying to get a second opinion on Quinn's condition, with the ultimate aim of getting the original anaesthetist replaced.

Reynolds had left the office before Clifford. As he walked towards Piccadilly, he had looked back and seen her at the high, illuminated window, watching him depart with, as it had seemed to him, great anxiety.

The chairs in the Observation Lounge were covered in white canvas, and the staff wore white. The place suggested a luxurious asylum for rich lunatics. The idea seemed to be to put everyone into a languorous dream. A waiter would periodically trundle a heavy, wooden trolley laden with cocktails to some new table, and he might have been a nurse with the evening medicine. Gentle jazz played. Beyond the side windows, the empty swimming pool, set into an outcrop of white rocks, was illuminated in such a way as to make the water turquoise. Wind from the dark sea ruffled the water. A worried-looking man in black paced next to it, talking into a mobile.

It was winter outside, but the women in the Lounge wore skimpy clothes – almost as much in the way of jewellery as clothes. Reynolds was reminded of slaves of ancient Rome, in togas and chains. The men had not made such an effort. Some wore suits, like Reynolds himself, others chinos and polo shirts with cashmere sweaters over their shoulders. They had perhaps been playing golf, or tennis on the orange cinder courts that were surrounded by trees, as though the tennis courts themselves were a natural feature.

Then Reynolds saw three men approaching him: all wore suits.

38

It was possible to have an expensive dinner in the Observation Lounge. But it was possible to have even more expensive dinners elsewhere in the Hotel des Etrangers, and Reynolds now sat in a smaller room, with medieval-looking tapestries on the wall, and still the sea beyond the window, although now it was difficult to tell sea and sky apart.

The three men were Samarin, his partner, Viktor Rostov, and Russell Page. Rostov had a big, red face and wild – yet not enough – hair of a suspect, russet colour. He wore a crumpled black linen suit and a shirt that might as well have been untucked but in fact was not. He also had on Chelsea boots that would have suited a thinner man. Russell Page's suit jacket and spectacles were so old-fashioned as to be ultra-modern: very wide lapels on the jacket, tortoiseshell for the glasses. He was the youngest of the four men: perhaps forty; quite fat and smooth-skinned. He looked like a sort of junior grandee, Reynolds thought. He and Rostov had their phones on the table. Page had introduced himself by handing Reynolds a card that Reynolds couldn't read, the writing being tiny for reasons of style. He explained, 'We supply public relations and marketing services to many of Mr Samarin's and Mr Rostov's companies.'

At this, Rostov, whose English wasn't as good as Samarin's, grunted, 'Not really marketing. Publicity, yes.'

But Russell Page was not fazed: 'We are in a range of

deployments across the communications spectrum.'

They were all looking at the menus. Reynolds would go for the cheapest option. Melon and Parma ham: thirty Euros. Then sea-bass fillet, tomato confit, fresh basil: forty Euros. Russell Page was reading the menu very intently, flicking the pages back and forth, cross-referring. Rostov was reading the wine list. He called a waiter over, asking Reynolds, 'You like white wine, my friend? You do, I think.' He indicated something on the wine list to the waiter. 'This,' he said, '*two.*' He turned to Reynolds, saying, 'Thank you that you agree to meet.'

Then his phone went, and he began speaking Russian into it. The wine came, and he tasted it while talking into the phone. Russell Page said, 'Since we're on the Montrachet, I'm going for the scallops.'

Samarin gave a half smile to Reynolds. 'The flight was painless, I hope?'

Reynolds nodded. 'My first time in a private plane.'

Samarin nodded. 'It is an indulgence – more or less un-forgiveable.'

Without looking up from the menu, Russell Page said, 'As one of Britain's top ten philanthropists I think you are allowed a few indulgences.'

Samarin didn't seem so sure of that.

Reynolds said, 'Could I ask? Will I be staying at the hotel tonight?'

Page said, 'Were you not sent a personal storyboard? You will be staying at Mr Samarin's chateau.'

Reynolds said, 'Are we all staying there?'

'I'm not, worst luck, and I think Andrei's heading back to his boat in Monaco. Not sure about Viktor. Andrei's very tied up tomorrow, but we're hoping to get you over to the boat for a follow-up meeting.'

Rostov had finished his call. He was pointing an accusing finger at Page. 'What is your *"storyboard"*? Like waterboard, no? I hope not!'

Page said, 'It simply means an itinerary, Viktor.'

'Yes. Then you say what you *mean*, my friend.'

Rostov drank a glass of wine very quickly, and seemed to become immediately drunk. 'We like England and we want quiet life, no trouble,' he said, addressing Reynolds. 'In Russia – is impossible. You are police detective. You investigate the rich in London? There is rich and not so rich. Mr Abramovich. He is rich guy, different level. But nothing to investigate. If we make mistake, you find anything, you tell us. Is accident; we will compensate.'

'But Viktor,' Samarin gently protested, 'that's not—'

'One minute my friend,' said Rostov, and he turned back to Reynolds. 'We had very difficult time in Russia,' he continued. 'Before we start business, and before *that*. You cannot imagine how cheaper was the life I lived, and this gentleman, my friend – out in cold when he was little boy. He lose finger. Frostbite, and . . .'

A beautiful woman was crossing the room. Rostov followed her with his eyes and Reynolds' eyes had wandered that way too.

'You very impressed!' Rostov said to Reynolds. 'And I too!'

That seemed to be the end of Rostov's speech.

Now Samarin spoke up: 'Of course, we have not asked you here in your role as a police officer. It is a separate matter we wish to discuss.' He indicated Russell Page.

Page said, 'What I think Viktor has reminded us of in his remarks, is simply this. These two gentlemen really are on the most epic journey, and we as an organisation are very proud to be on that ride with them.'

'Yes,' said Rostov. 'Get on.'

The food came, and Page continued his speech in between mouthfuls of scallops and sips of wine. He seemed keener on the food and drink than on the speech he had to make, especially since Rostov, in spite of his relatively poor knowledge of the language, obviously had a keen ear for English bullshit.

Page told how Andrei Samarin's daughter, Anna, had developed a very exciting plan for a series of nightclubs in the West End of London. Her father was committed to making this vision a reality. The clubs would be high-end of course, impeccably conceived and managed. A range of property acquisitions and licensing applications would be necessary. Reynolds was a former Metropolitan Police 'club scout' (these were Page's words; he knew they were wrong, but he was not deflected by Reynolds' frown). It was obvious he had the relevant experience to assist with such applications and this would lead to a wider role in the running of the establishments.

Rostov came in again: 'You have been into the English education, my friend. First class. You have good leadership skills. Now. You talk and we listen.'

This clubs scheme struck Reynolds as owing something to Samarin's desire to see his daughter engaged in some constructive activity. Running clubs rather than going to them. But it was chiefly a transparent and desperate attempt to buy him off. As such, it was proof that they suspected him of knowing as much as, or more than, he did.

But how to answer?

Drops of rain had begun to hit the dark-blue window. How dangerous would it be to give a straight refusal? Reynolds couldn't believe violence would be used in the vicinity of the hotel, or in the vicinity of Page. He took comfort from Page's Britishness. In a few years' time he'd be Mr Toad. He was like the Union Jack in the corner of that red flag. As to the other diners in the room – they were French or Americans: *étrangers* but strategic allies, surely. The danger lay in the night in the chateau.

'Before we discuss further,' Reynolds said, 'I have to go to the gents.'

Rostov nodded, disappointed.

As Reynolds left the room, he heard a mobile phone ring. Samarin's, and he was answering. Then Reynolds was descending marble stairs indicated to him by a functionary of the hotel in an oriental-looking blue suit. He was passing black-and-white pictures of the famous who had stayed at the hotel: Groucho Marx (possibly) in swimming trunks; Mick Jagger in a bathrobe, reading a book on a sun lounger. Glass cases were set into the wall. They held Swiss watches, or Cartier handbags. They reminded him of relics displayed in a church. But if he accepted the Russian offer, he could reach in and take. He stopped on the staircase. He would – whatever happened – be rich; and he might have Anna Samarina into the bargain. He saw himself walking next to her through the streets of Mayfair, not arm in arm, but companionably close and relaxed, in much the same way he had walked with Caroline. A wave of love for Caroline came over him. He saw her playing her cello in the streets of Hampstead: an outdoor Christmas concert. She had been playing beautifully, as far as he could tell, and looking at the music only occasionally. How could she harbour all that secret knowledge? She was too artistic for him, and a couple of notches higher socially. In a way, he would have liked her to be able to express her superiority, but the two of them were buried in London suburbia. They had found themselves camping, so to speak, on the margins of London as the time ticked by, working long hours with no house, no child, increasingly little in common. It was very simple really: there had been a chronic lack of glamour in their lives. He felt he owed it to Caroline to accept the Russian offer: to show her what could be done, even if they were no longer together.

Reynolds continued down the stairs, imagining himself a rich man.

He thought he had the wide, marble gentlemen's to himself, but halfway through peeing, he saw another functionary waiting by the sinks, with towels, creams and soaps ready. He was French in some way. 'Good evening, sir,' he said, turning on a tap. 'Rain is coming, I think.'

Well, it wouldn't be coming down here. Unlike Reynolds, this man was in no immediate danger of anything untoward. On stepping out of the gents, Reynolds saw an antique cabinet that had been placed before a gilded mirror. He had noticed this on the way in, thinking the table was nothing more than a decorative companion to the mirror, but he now saw a display of magazines on the table. In fact, there was only one magazine twenty times over. The mainly black cover showed diamonds floating like planets in a starlit sky. The magazine was called *Charisma*. Reynolds picked it up and flicked through articles about either luxury in the south of France, or luxury in what appeared to be the West Indies. The attendant now stood in the doorway of the gents.

'That is a new magazine for us,' he said. 'It is very good.'

Reynolds said, 'What was the old one called?'

'Easy to see,' said the attendant, and he walked over and opened the doors of the cabinet. He pulled out a magazine whose cover was mainly white instead of mainly black; it showed a Fabergé egg instead of diamonds, and it was called *Allure* rather than *Charisma*. It was the magazine that Reynolds had seen in Quinn's flat.

'This was the one before,' said the attendant. 'It is also very good, but we have a new publisher now.'

Reynolds asked, 'Are these magazines available any-where else but this hotel?'

'Two places only,' the attendant said proudly. 'Here, and in our sister hotel in the Bahamas.'

'How often does the magazine change?'

The attendant did not understand this, and Reynolds couldn't blame him. Eventually he *made* himself under-stood, and he was told the magazine was bi-monthly. This Fabergé egg edition had been around from mid-November to last week.

On the face of it, then, George Quinn had been to one of the two hotels since mid-November, and Reynolds' money was on Quinn having been at *this* hotel. He had not declared any such visit on the hospitality register, and if Clifford knew of the visit, she had failed to inform Reynolds.

When Reynolds entered the dining room again, Rostov was speaking fast Russian to Samarin, who looked miserable. The main courses had arrived, and Page had taken refuge in his food. Before Reynolds could sit down, Rostov said, 'Shake hands now, is done. Hundred per cent.'

Surely, thought Reynolds, they can't expect me to decide just like that.

'What would be the salary?' he said, sitting down.

Page looked up from his food. 'It's too early to define the specifics.' He took a sip of wine. 'But Mr Samarin is an excellent employer.'

Rostov eyed Reynolds. 'What you like,' he said. It was not a question.

Reynolds thought of Caroline and of Bob Ballantyne, and how he would eclipse their joint salary. He would sail past them on the voyage to all their dream homes. He imagined himself – what was the word? – gazumping them. No, because he wouldn't want whatever property they wanted.

'This is best alternative for you,' said Rostov.

It was the nearest thing to a threat so far.

'It's a generous offer,' said Reynolds. 'I'll think it over and let you know.'

'Yes,' said Rostov. 'When?'

'Could I have three days?'

This did not go down well, and the meal was concluded in near silence. There was no question of coffee. Samarin paid the bill. Reynolds collected his coat. Then they were out onto an illuminated gravel forecourt that Reynolds didn't recall seeing when he'd arrived at the hotel. The wind blew the palm trees and the sea, and it was difficult to tell the one sound from the other. Salutations were perfunctory. Rostov said, 'Yes, good night,' and Reynolds believed he then turned towards Samarin and said in English something like, 'I'm tired of this shit.' This was as the first car drove up – the one for Reynolds. Nicky was at the wheel, and it was the same black Merc as before, making Reynolds think that the partners were running low on funds, or energy.

'Dinner was good, boss?' Nicky asked, because Nicky now called Reynolds boss. As they approached the gates of the hotel grounds, they passed a gravelled bay in which some cars were parked under gentle illumination. One of the cars was a vintage Aston Martin. It was hard to make out the colour, and this hotel was presumably a magnet for Astons, but Reynolds had never had any doubt that Porter would be somewhere in attendance.

Nicky drove fast along winding roads made white by moonlight, past high gates signifying ranch-like houses. For all their twisting and turning, they were heading relentlessly towards a district of blueish, dangerous-looking wooded hills.

39

They had reached the wooded hills, and penetrated to a dark valley in the heart of them. Reynolds thought of Plyushkin's Garden. It was not a big chateau, but evidently very old – and as perfectly symmetrical as a carriage clock. A woman of about sixty opened the door as Nicky turned and drove away. The first thing Reynolds saw in the hallway behind her were paintings propped against a wall, with white sheets draped over. So Reynolds thought of her as a sort of Russian Miss Havisham, living a forgotten life alone in this mansion. But of course she was only the housekeeper, and when she showed Reynolds into a room off the hall, Anna Samarina stood there.

On the face of it, she was the second part of the bribe. But their greeting was so confused, so inept on his part and hers, with a sort of missed kiss, that he wondered whether she might genuinely like him. It was not impossible. She had seemed to like him in the clubs; and she had seemed to like him, in a sad sort of way, on the Thursday of parties, and on the following Monday at her London house.

The room they were in might have been classed as a study, with tall bookshelves half full of books, but some stacked on the floor; and there was a new-looking couch entirely given over to books. There was a high stone fireplace, in which a futuristic wood burner had been lit. The walls were papered with white and yellow stripes. The floor was some sort of beautiful wood, and there were rugs, one with the label still attached. For all the expense involved, there was something improvised about the room. It was as if the stylist – or some such functionary – had not turned up. Anna Samarina was leaning against the mantel, and kicking her left heel with her right heel much as she had done in the CCTV footage of the diamond theft, and this expressed her trademark frustration and restlessness, which no amount of money could correct.

In the flurry of greeting, Reynolds could not find the appropriate remark, so he said what was on his mind: 'Will I be sleeping here?'

She laughed, and said, 'I see. Small talk.'

'It's not that small,' he said. 'I've had a long day.'

'How did you like the dinner?' she said. 'Did Rostov have two puddings? His record is four; his personal best. They were going to take you on a Mediterranean cruise.'

'That sounds like a euphemism.'

'No. A cruise. The boat on the sea, and you on the boat.'

But probably not for long, Reynolds thought. The cruise might have been the option if he'd refused them point-blank. Instead they had decided on a more literal seduction than a good dinner. Perhaps Anna Samarina had intervened to spare him from the cruise. Had she been the one calling her father when he'd left to visit the gentlemen's?

She said she would show him his room, and this became a tour of the house, carried on with glasses of the very good red wine she had been drinking. They walked side by side up the baronial staircase. She wore thin jeans, a rather tatty pair of what looked like white ballet shoes with pink ribbons by way of afterthoughts; on top, a white T-shirt and a short jacket of some yellow feathery man-made fibre. It was the kind of thing you might wear if you were dressing up as a chicken. It was impossible to say how much thought had gone into this outfit, but of course it looked great.

She gestured along the long gloomy landing. Reynolds said, 'Is there a light?'

'Actually yes.'

She turned on the lights – you actually had to switch them on in this house – and some chandeliers came to life, but most of the gloom remained. There were boxes and crates, and sometimes the contents had spilled out: vases, books, paintings, lamps. You imagined there must be dust, but of course that was *not* compatible with super-wealth. So it was a clean sort of neglect; a mansion kept ticking over, biding its time. 'The old servants' rooms are . . . still the servants' rooms,' Anna Samarina said, laughing. But the house seemed empty of staff except for the housekeeper. Reynolds suggested as much. 'Yes, they have all gone away,' she said.

'Why?'

'Christmas,' she said, and then, as if that wasn't a good enough answer – which it wasn't really – she added, 'I sent them.'

Reynolds presumed that many of the paintings, whether leaning or hung on the walls, were Samarin's Russian *avant-gardistes*. One showed a sort of bus queue of people going up into the sky. There were multi-colours, and the persistent effect of the shattered prism; but as before, there were also older, and more relaxing landscapes. The window shutters were sometimes shut and sometimes open, in which case Reynolds saw the silhouettes of French trees.

'This is my father's house,' she said. 'He hates it.'

'Is that why he's gone back to his boat?'

'Yes. Partly.'

'How did he come by it?'

'He bought it. Anyway, what do you mean? When we left Russia we came to France first. To here.'

'Then you'd think he'd like the house. It would be associated with escape from a place he *didn't* like.'

'Who says he didn't like Russia? He had to leave; his life was in danger. My mother had just died. I was eighteen months old, not very well, in and out of hospital.'

'With what?'

'Intestines. It was probably quite disgusting, but not very serious. But he was very worried about me. It was all in the balance with his business. He was taking some very big risks. And he was not well himself. He has never been well. As a boy, as a young man. You know, he was drafted out of the army after only four weeks because of it. It's easy to be excused military service if you pay, but not so easy for illness.'

'Had he teamed up with Rostov by then?'

'Yes. They came here together.'

'What do you think of Rostov?'

'I think he should get his hair dyed professionally. It's not as if he doesn't have the money.'

They wandered into a certain room that contained little more than a fireplace and some big vases. 'He should wear a blue Italian suit. Not a tracksuit. Last year he was turned away from some club for wearing jeans, but he was pleased about it.'

'Why?'

'Because a big star – Bruce Willis – was also turned away from the same club for wearing jeans.'

'He was wearing a black suit this evening.'

'Really?' But she didn't want to talk about this evening. 'His wife is very nice – a sort of *jolie laide*. And you know he has personally contributed a hundred million pounds' tax to the British Treasury in the past five years.'

'Here is your room,' she said. 'It is the best one.'

It was a big room, illuminated by a single bedside light with a green shade. Wooden beams were very much in evidence. There was a double bed, covered with a gauze curtain, and Reynolds thought of Miss Havisham again, but it was a mosquito net, left over from summer. There were some novels by the bed: Nabokov, Elizabeth Jane Howard, Hilary Mantel, Colette. Back in the study, with another bottle of wine between them, and Anna Samarina smoking a cigarette (which Reynolds had never seen her do before), he asked, 'Do you know who shot Quinn?'

'So we have finished with small talk. The answer is no.'

'What about John-Paul Holden. Do you know who stabbed him?'

'I have an idea,' she said, after a pause.

'Who?'

'I am not telling you.'

'That could make you an accessory.'

'Only if I was involved in it, and I was not.'

'But you knew him.'

'Who?'

'Holden.'

'A bit. I knew him and his lifestyle. You should think about that.'

'*Tatler* magazine said you were engaged to him.'

'*Tatler!*'

'So to sum up: you haven't killed anyone.'

'Not so far, Mr Blake Reynolds.'

If that was true, then it was just as well, in view of the fact he would be spending the night in the same house as her.

'And what about theft?' said Reynolds. 'Because I know you have committed a theft.'

'I see,' she said, perfectly coolly opening the door of the glass stove and throwing her cigarette in. 'So – theft,' she said, sitting back down. 'What is the definition of it?'

'The appropriation of property belonging to another with the intention to permanently deprive.'

'Very good. I did not steal anything.'

Reynolds eyed her. He said, 'Do you remember Russia?'

'How could I? I was not even two when I left. Well. Maybe. I have some pictures in my mind. One is a machine in the kind of foyer of a kino. You know, a cinema. There is a red carpet, red curtains and this machine, like it was on a stage: a Super Mario . . . and my father showing me. It was like a symbol of everything that would be coming in the future.'

'Where was that?'

'It might have been Novosibirsk. But I don't think . . . I also remember a car going through forests. I will tell you something about that car. Not just front seats and back seats, but three rows of seats, and so it was a very long thin road through the trees, and a long thin car, like an arrow. I think that was Russia, but it might have been here.'

'Do you remember your mother?'

'Wait,' she said, and she left the room. When she came back she was holding a photograph: half a dozen young women sitting at a table in a restaurant or a club. It was perhaps a fish restaurant because there seemed to be yellow porcelain fish flying up the wall. It wasn't particularly smart: the overhead lighting was fluorescent. All the women were good-looking, one especially so. 'My mother,' Anna said. There was a resemblance. She and her mother were both small, fairylike people, but with determination somehow indicated. The photograph was possibly over-exposed. It was tinged with orange and yellow, and the stone – quite small – in the necklace of the woman indicated was the yellowest of all. 'But I do not remember her, no,' Anna Samarina continued, setting the photograph carefully on the mantelpiece. 'I was looked after by a lot of babushkas, all very kind, so they are like one person. Nannies, you know.'

Reynolds believed she'd just told him, in a roundabout way, that she'd stolen the yellow diamond, and had every right to do so.

Reynolds said, 'Your father was orphaned.'

'Yes. Lived with his father's sister: his aunt, in fact. His mother died of cancer, father in a work accident.'

'What did he do?'

'What *could* he do? He was like five years old.'

'I mean his father.'

'Railway worker. He was doing some separation between two trains. Sorry, two carriages. Well, maybe it *was* two trains. They came together and he was crushed to death by the . . .'

She looked at Reynolds until he said, 'Buffers.'

'Buffers. You are obviously an expert. It was very late at night, and very cold. It was always dark and cold in that place. Why not work for Papochka? Even if it's all a disaster you will come out with a lot of money.'

She then insisted on his speaking about his own early years. When he said his own mother had died when he was young, she said, 'That is obvious.' But he thought it was just his downbeat northern-ness she had detected, not the true melancholia of her own character. She brought another bottle of wine and he told her the story of the Turks, which, he guiltily reflected, he had worked up to a fine polish.

He went up to bed at one o'clock in the morning, folding back the gauze curtain to climb into the bed. He fell asleep immediately and he dreamt of Quinn, who was walking about London W1, which had become something between a Monopoly board and a model village. After a while, he sat down on the Ritz Hotel and lit one of his strong cigarettes. Reynolds too was there, also giant-sized. Quinn had been about to give Reynolds something: another floppy book perhaps. But it was not forthcoming; he was withholding it.

Reynolds turned over in bed. There was somebody in the room. This person was moving fast towards him. *She* was in the room. She wore a white T-shirt, nothing else. She climbed under the duvet, and lay down with her back to him.

She said, 'This is my bed, you know.'

'Then I'd better get out of it.'

She turned around to face him. She sat up and took her T-shirt off.

'Goodbye then,' she said.

She lay down again, closer than before.

'I don't think you really want to be doing this,' he said.

'Well,' she said. 'It is very easy for you to find out.'

He was in range of the heat of her body. He simply had

260

to turn towards her. It would be worth any amount of trouble
. . . Any amount of trouble. It was natural to go towards her,
just as it is natural to recline rather than to stand or sit upright. The magnetic force was irresistible.

He rolled away through the gap in the gauze curtain,
moved towards the chair on which he'd draped his clothes
– it was necessary to make a certain adjustment on the way,
at which she laughed – and then he was stepping into his
trousers. It was like a bedroom farce, only sadder.

'Where are you going?' she said.

'I don't know. Nice. I'll get a flight from there.'

'Not until six o'clock, you won't.'

'Is there a car here that can take me?'

'I can order you a car. A taxi. Then I think you should
take a train to Paris.'

'Why?'

'He won't be expecting you to take a train, since you
came by plane.'

'Porter. In effect, you're doing this to save him. Because
he's the bad man, right?'

'Doing what? I'm lying here in my bed.'

Maybe she was only trying to save *herself*. But no: there
was something more at stake. Reynolds believed that she
wouldn't be close to tears over just herself; and she did
seem to be close to tears.

40

Reynolds departed from the airport anyway. He couldn't afford to spend a whole day on a train, and there was no
sign of Porter. He thought himself both risible and honourable for having refused what had been offered in the
chateau. Risible/honourable. The coin kept spinning in the
air for as long as the aeroplane – easyJet – was itself aloft.
Mainly, his thoughts were unworthy. He thought especially
of Anna Samarina's naked body . . . and he had only *just*
been honourable. The case might well have been ruined by
such intimacy as had occurred. He kept thinking of Miss
Havisham's possible testimony, or then again: had there
been a camera in the room?

He'd had the option of flights to London or Manchester.
He bought a ticket for Manchester, since that was closer
to the Carltons by two hundred miles. From the departure
lounge, he called the Duty Desk of North Yorkshire Police.
When he said he was calling about the disappearance of
Joseph Caldwell, he was put through to a Detective Sergeant
Eddie Ibbotson. Reynolds had expected to be put through to
a more senior man. Ibbotson, whom Reynolds had possibly
woken up, said, 'It's been snowing here for two weeks. The
bloke's got to be dead, it's just a matter of finding the body.'
Reynolds said there might be a tie-in with a case he was
working on. Ibbotson was very interested in this, although
he was sure the likely death of Caldwell would turn out to
be a 'natural'. Reynolds assumed he'd have no objection to

his going up there to ask a few questions. Ibbotson did not – in fact could not – object. Would Reynolds mind if he came along? Reynolds said he wanted to keep it as low-key as possible, in other words 'no'. Ibbotson said the man Reynolds needed to get hold of in the village was a neighbour called Morley. It seemed he was the world's leading expert on the disappeared man.

It wasn't until he was sitting on the plane that Reynolds assembled the letters in his head: Detective Sergeant Eddie Ibbotson might be reduced to 'SERG E I', and he believed it had been so reduced in Quinn's floppy book. He tried to call Ibbotson again, to ask whether Quinn had been in touch, but this time he got voicemail just as a stewardess instructed him to turn off his phone. In any case, Ibbotson would surely have mentioned any earlier contact from the Met.

After passport control at Manchester, Reynolds walked up to the police desk and flashed his warrant card. Half an hour later he was driving an unmarked Saab from the police pool at ninety miles an hour along the M62, which made a black ribbon over the snowy wastes of the Pennines. The sky seemed made of clouds of snow. As he drove, he experienced intermittent waves of love for Anna, followed by waves of love for Caroline. In between, he was thinking about Quinn: the flat in Argrove, the art collection, the Mayfair lifestyle, the membership of Annabel's; then the undisclosed trip to the Riviera. George Quinn had been on the take, and Victoria Clifford could not have been unaware of the fact. It was a conclusion that answered a lot of questions even if it begged many others.

He approached Carlton over the snowy North Yorkshire Moors. Occasionally a house – or something resembling a cross between a stone barn and a house – would be indicated by a sign dangling from a gibbet-like post. All trees had been banished to the horizon, like an army in retreat. Occasionally, Reynolds would see a man standing on the hills, usually with a jeep nearby. On one horizon, he saw two men in combat jackets walking with guns. The snow was dirty snow, having lain for some time. It was the same colour as the sheep. He passed a couple of yellow police signs: 'Appeal for Information' – that was Ibbotson, asking after Joseph Caldwell. Some signs, indicating roads apparently leading nowhere, read 'Except for access'. So they must have led somewhere. Apart from a couple of motorbikes exceeding the speed limit, Reynolds had this road to himself. He kept thinking it would eventually be blocked by some rock fall from a ravine, or a flood of the secretive, black river that came and went beyond the verges. But as long as he kept driving, the road was there. Reynolds felt that he was continually calling its bluff.

Carlton was on the edge of the moor, and preceded by a forest of pines. As the road twisted and turned, the headlights of the car picked out rocky tracks leading into the trees. The 'Carlton' nameplate was set on an old millstone. A stoical horse in a blanket stood nearby. It looked as though it was on sentry duty. There were only about a dozen houses in the village, and no people. Two of the houses had farms attached. Not being able to figure out where Carlton ended and Carlton High Top began, Reynolds drove into one of the farmyards and knocked on the door. A dog began barking but not from within the house. A smiling young woman answered. He said he was looking for a Mr Morley. She said, 'Oh, Anthony,' and pointed into the darkness.

Reynolds drove in the direction indicated, which took him through some further trees and towards another half-dozen stone houses. Morley apparently lived in the first of these. Reynolds knocked. A deep voice came from within. 'Who is it?' Reynolds shouted 'Police!' which made him feel rather thuggish. The door was unlatched. Anthony Morley was about seventy: a wiry, bald, grave man. He stared for a long time at Reynolds, as Reynolds held up his warrant card.

Morley ushered Reynolds into his house, but only as far as the hall. Reynolds explained that the missing man's name had come up peripherally in a cold case that might need to be revived. He was not in any way a suspect, and it was unlikely the matter was connected to the disappearance, but it was better if he didn't go into too much detail. He would simply like to find out a bit more about the man. Morley eyed Reynolds; he nodded. He left Reynolds in the hall, while he went into another room to make a phone call.

Morley returned wearing a duffel coat, and carrying a file of papers and a torch. Families of silent sheep watched from the verges as they progressed towards the house of the missing man. If Carlton High Top was a satellite of Carlton, then the house of Joe or – as Morley called him – Joseph Caldwell was another satellite again. And a church stood a little way beyond it, at a diagonal distance of about fifty yards. Caldwell, as a Quaker, had had nothing to do with that church, which was C. of E. Quakers did not attend church services: in their plain and spartan way, they attended 'meetings', which largely consisted of sitting in silence with their fellow Quakers, or 'Friends'. Morley explained that people could speak out at any time, 'providing they felt moved by God to do so'. *With that small proviso*, thought Reynolds. Morley pointed beyond the church to a grassy hummock where once had stood the Carlton Meeting House, the centre of Quakerism in the locality from 1650 until 1936, when it was pulled down, a new meeting house having been built in the nearby town of Helmsley.

Morley admitted Reynolds to the house of Joseph Caldwell. He turned on the lights and Reynolds saw a room with not much in it but a circle of plastic chairs. They walked through to the kitchen. The room was dominated by the clicking – not exactly ticking – of an electrical wall clock of seventies vintage. It was ten to five. The cooker was old enough to have legs. Reynolds could not immediately see any fridge. Morley went upstairs and came down with a file of papers. Reynolds heard a car pull up, and two women came into the house. Morley introduced them as the missing man's two sisters, Betty and Helen. Betty had been quoted in the newspaper report that Quinn had read. They were nut-brown women in their seventies, both dressed, it seemed to Reynolds, for hiking, and with snow on their boots. As Reynolds explained himself, Betty made tea, which involved the lighting of gas under a blackened kettle, and the filling of a giant earthenware pot with loose leaves. There was no milk, but there were biscuits: broken digestives in a battered tin.

'If you're lucky,' said Betty, 'there might be a couple of chocolate ones left.'

Reynolds got the idea that the occasional chocolate biscuit was as near as Joe Caldwell – the sisters had reinstated Joe – ever came to self-indulgence. They decided to speak in the living room, where the circle of chairs stood.

'Let's have the fire on, Anthony,' said Helen, and Anthony Morley switched on a two-bar electrical fire. Reynolds watched one bar begin to glow red; he would wait in vain for the other bar to come on. Reynolds and the two women sat on adjacent chairs. Anthony Morley – who had declined tea – sat two or three chairs away, with arms folded and the papers he'd brought on his knee. There were posters, tacked straight to the walls. One showed a dove flying towards a rainbow above the words 'Peace Museum'. Another showed a dove sitting on a pound sign, and the slogan, 'Taxes for Peace Not War'.

'Now, love,' said Betty when they'd all sat down. 'How can we help?'

Reynolds asked first for a potted biography of the missing man.

'In his working life he was a schoolteacher,' said Betty. 'Taught history and R.I.'

'It's not called that now, dear,' said Helen.

'She means Religious Instruction,' said Morley. 'Which is now Religious *Education*. He also taught English. He retired in 1987, when he was deputy head of Helmsley Secondary Modern.'

Morley was like the umpire of the conversation. He would intervene to make factual clarifications.

Caldwell had lived in Carlton all his life. He was, according to Betty, 'a lovely, lovely man', always keen to see the best in people.

'To find "that of God" in people,' Morley interjected.

Reynolds wondered whether they were all Quakers.

'Oh yes,' said Helen, delightedly.

'We generally say "Friends",' said Morley.

267

'But you can call us what you want,' said Betty.

Caldwell was an elder of the church, whereas the others were only members. There were no vicars in Quakerism, but Caldwell was as near as they came. His lifelong aim had been to raise the funds for rebuilding the old Meeting House. Meanwhile he had been involved in running two other meeting houses in the locality, and latterly he had been holding meetings in the room in which they presently sat. According to Betty he'd had authorisation from a body called Monthly Meeting to do this.

'Not that authorisation was needed,' said Morley, and it seemed that Quakers could meet anywhere at any time. Caldwell had devoted much of his spare time to a Quaker-affiliated body that Betty called the Committee for International Peace and Reconciliation, and as she said this, Anthony Morley looked up slightly startled, and said to Reynolds, 'Yes. She has the name right.'

Reynolds asked, 'Did that bring him into contact with Russia?'

'The Soviet Union, as was,' said Morley.

It appeared that Caldwell had been in regular contact with the Soviet Union as was, both directly and through the embassy in London. This was all in the seventies, when he would quite frequently travel down to London to stay at what Helen called 'a lovely little sort of Quaker guest house, right in the very centre'.

'The Pen Club,' said Morley, 'off Russell Square.'

His main activity had been to promote British–Soviet student exchanges, as a means of fostering cultural understanding.

'They were quite controversial at the time,' said Helen.

At this, Anthony Morley moved into the seat next to Reynolds.

'You may find these of interest,' he said. He began passing selected papers to Reynolds. Some were old photocopies, all from the same source. 'They're from *The Quaker*,' said Morley, 'the principal Quaker journal.' Certain items were high-lighted. Reynolds read things like, 'The Committee decided to seek a meeting with the Indian High Commissioner and send a letter to the British government on the question of recent nuclear tests'; 'The appeal for funds to establish a Chair of Peace Studies at the University of Bradford was launched at a press conference at Friends Meeting House, London on Wednesday 22 March.' Reynolds looked up; he thought he could hear a car approaching the village. He looked down again, reading, 'The banner of the International Committee for Peace and Reconciliation will again be carried at the Aldermaston march this year.'

Reynolds could no longer hear the car. He asked, 'Is there anything on the exchange visits, Mr Morley?'

Morley flipped over some pages. He pointed to a para-graph beginning, 'Four young people from the USSR have recently returned home after a summer exchange visit under the auspices of the Committee for International Peace and Reconciliation, the World Churches Peace Committee and the Soviet Embassy. This is the third such exchange in as many years. Joseph Caldwell, secretary to the Committee for International Peace and Reconciliation described the ex-change as "a great success, which we hope to repeat next year".'

The sheet was marked in a handwritten note, 'Sept. 1974'.

Reynolds asked, 'Is there any more on these exchanges?'

Morley said, 'You have everything that's in the house,' and he remained silent as Reynolds continued to flip through the papers. Reynolds believed that Morley was hiding some further revelation.

After another twenty minutes of desultory discussion, the women left the house – Helen saying of their brother, 'He's in God's hands.' For the next five minutes, neither Reynolds nor Morley spoke. But Reynolds hoped an invisible third party *was* speaking.

Morley rose to his feet. 'Would you follow me?'

Reynolds couldn't help congratulating himself. In not speaking, he had made a silent leap. What was Clifford's word? A dart.

As before, Morley held his torch. They were heading towards the grey hulk of the church; then they were crunching over snow-covered grass beyond the church.

Reynolds asked, 'Mr Morley, what do you think happened to Caldwell?'

'It's more than likely that he fell while walking on the hills.'

'Then why hasn't his body been found?'

'I believe it will be.'

After a while, Morley said, 'We are on the burial ground of the Meeting House.' Reynolds could see no gravestones in the roving torch beam, only a couple of stunted trees with sheep beneath them. Morley said, 'There were forty-two interments between 1867 and 1903.' There was no moon; and now there were snowflakes in the soft grey mist. Some appeared to be descending, others floating gently *upwards* in a somehow dizzying way. Reynolds heard movement in the heather: the sound of sheep departing. Morley's torch showed that the stone borders of the building were still visible. He moved one of the stones with his boot, and there was gravel beneath. He scooped out four handfuls of gravel and produced a package made of several twisted carrier bags. They were Sainsbury's carrier bags, but the old sort: mainly white instead of mainly orange.

They returned to Caldwell's house. Inside the plastic bags was an A4 padded envelope. It contained bank notes: perhaps two hundred fifty-pound notes and a hundred twenties. They looked wrong somehow, like they'd run in the wash, or were forgeries. But they were not forgeries, just old. Not *that* old, however. 'That's Christopher Wren,' said Morley, 'on the back of the fifties. They were issued in 1981, withdrawn in 1996. On the twenties, it's Michael Faraday. They were issued in 1991, withdrawn in 2001.'

'What have we got here? About twelve thousand pounds?'

'Thirteen thousand and sixty,' said Morley.

There were also further documents with the notes. They related to the British–Soviet student exchange of 1971. A black-and-white photograph showed three young Russians – two male, one female – standing shyly in what might have been a public park. They had longish hair and big collars. They might have been sixteen or seventeen. Morley said, 'They were all top students at their schools in Russia, and they'd all done well in an essay competition. That's why they qualified for the exchange.' One of the three held a guitar; the other two might have been singing. The caption read: 'Andrei Samarin attempts to spread a little love (and music). Also pictured are Dina Alkaev and Vitaly Utkin.'

Morley was saying, 'The essay was on the theme: "How to make war an anachronism."'

Reynolds asked, 'And how would, say, Andrei Samarin have done that?'

Morley said, 'I'm afraid the essays have long since been lost.'

Reynolds was studying the photograph of Samarin. He was in the act of strumming the guitar with his right hand. He did this with a plectrum, gripped between his thumb and forefinger. The other fingers were splayed.

Reynolds said, 'Most of his little finger is missing.'

'Yes,' said Morley.

'But on the right hand.'

'Why do you say "but"?'

The little finger on the left hand was present and correct. Reynolds could tell from the way the boy held down a chord on the fretboard. He was a good-looking, thin boy with regular features. He *could* have been the young Andrei Samarin. But only if the older one had grown another left little finger.

Reynolds asked Morley, 'Do you know anything about this boy?'

'I never met him myself. Joseph told me he was very shy, although he doesn't look it here because of the guitar. He was from Siberia. Both his parents had died, and he'd been brought up by an aunt. He'd got frostbite at one point and the finger had to be amputated.'

'Is that all you know about him?'

'I know he's now one of those oligarchs,' said Morley.

'And did Joe Caldwell know that?'

Morley nodded. 'Samarin keeps a low profile, but Joseph

heard he was living in London, and he wrote him a letter. It was in about 1995.'

'Why did he write?'

'To say hello; congratulate him on his great success.'

'Perhaps to ask for a donation.'

Morley frowned. 'A donation for what?'

'Help rebuild the meeting house.'

'From what we knew, Samarin has made his money from fossil fuels. Joseph wouldn't have accepted a donation from such a source.'

'Do we have the letter?'

'No, but we have the reply.'

Morley fished into the bundle. Reynolds read a typed note on unheaded paper. It began with a spelling mistake:

Dear Mr Calderwell,

Thank you for your recent letter. I'm afraid it comes at a time of many difficulties in my life, all in connection to my departing Russia and the difficult political situation. At the present time there may in actuality be physical danger for anyone connected to me or even with knowledge about me, or speaking about me. And so it is I prefer to live as quietly as possible, leaving myself to myself.

I am hoping very much that you will understand.

Yours,

A

Morley said, 'The money came with the letter. Tax is not payable on a cash gift, so Joseph was not obliged to declare it.'

Given the choice between ignoring Caldwell's own letter and trying to buy his silence, the writer had opted for the latter, which was possibly unnecessary, since a man like Caldwell would surely not have harassed anyone. But it was clearly essential that Caldwell should not pursue the connection between the guitar-playing young Samarin, and the billionaire of that name. In particular, Caldwell must not meet the oligarch called Samarin, because then he might realise about the missing fingers. In other words, he might realise they were not the same man. Surely the writer ought to have said, 'You have the wrong man. Yours must be a different Samarin. I never came to the UK on any exchange.' But that could be dangerous because the two Samarins were presumably supposed to be the same for the wider deception . . . and Caldwell had accidentally obtained proof that they were not. The fashionable words 'identity theft' came to Reynolds, and then the words of Chamberlain, spoken outside Argrove: 'The biggest money crime you could imagine . . . and murders as well . . . murders, plural.' He said none of this to Morley.

Instead, Reynolds asked, 'How did he react to this – well, it's a snub, isn't it?'

'Joseph wouldn't have seen it like that. He had no right to the man's time and attention. I believe he understood that Samarin was in some distress when he wrote that letter. He didn't want to cause further trouble for him.'

A car headlight swerved over the peace posters. At the uncurtained window, Reynolds could see faster and denser snowfall, luminous in the darkness.

Reynolds continued to leaf through the papers. The young man called Samarin had apparently been playing guitar as part of something called a 'Peace Caravan' that had visited London and a number of northern cities, and into which the exchange students had been recruited. It had been organised by Caldwell. There was no further detail about Samarin or the other exchange students. Reynolds mentioned this to Morley, who said, 'Joseph thought that one of them was dead. In a road accident in Moscow. I don't know the details.'

It appeared that after Caldwell had taken his friend Morley into his confidence about the arrival of the cash, they had sought God's 'clearness' on what to do about it.

Reynolds asked, 'Why didn't you just throw it away?'

Morley almost laughed at this. 'I don't know,' he said. 'I suppose it would have seemed wasteful.'

Over the years, Caldwell had become silent about the Samarin question, and the pair had ceased to talk about it.

'What would Caldwell have told me if *I'd* asked him about Samarin?'

'He'd have politely changed the subject.'

'Even if I said I was a policeman?'

'Probably. Joseph was answerable only to his own conscience. He was very determined and very strong.'

Reynolds was now flicking through the original bundle, the one Morley had brought from his house. There was a letter he had missed before. It had been published in *The Quaker* in March 1972, and outlined in biro.

Dear Sir,

It has come to my attention that Quaker groups in Britain have been involved in organising student exchanges with the Soviet Union. As a recent emigrant from that country, and the sometime inhabitant of one of its notorious labour camps, I find these exchanges a matter of concern. British Quakers ought to be aware that such exchanges are a considerable propaganda asset to Moscow, helping to legitimise a repressive and criminal regime. I do not doubt the honourable motives of Mr Caldwell and his Peace Committee, but I suggest that the thinking behind these exchanges is naïve to say the least.

Yours sincerely.

Max Aktin

There was the connection. Quinn had known something about Aktin; he had known something about Caldwell. He had probably suspected that the present-day Samarin was an imposter. How had Quinn used that information?

Reynolds asked, 'How did Caldwell react to this letter?'

'I think he tried to get into contact with this . . . Max Aktin. I think there was some correspondence between them. I think Aktin is long dead.'

Aktin's concern in 1972 was the relationship between British Quakers and the Soviets. It must be that later on, when Samarin emerged in London as an oligarch, Aktin connected him with the exchange.

Reynolds asked, 'Did Caldwell think the original Samarin had been replaced by another?'

'Another what?'

'Another man.'

'What an extraordinary idea. No, I don't believe for a minute that he thought that. But he knew something was amiss.'

A perfect silence – of a kind entirely unavailable in London – had descended on the room. Reynolds again realised the importance of not speaking. Eventually, Morley said, 'Joseph was last seen on the morning of Saturday 15 November. On the previous Saturday, I saw him speaking to a man where the road goes through the woods here. The man was standing next to a parked car, and I assumed he was asking directions. I saw this from the window of the bus that goes to Helmsley. I only thought of it after Joseph disappeared.'

'What sort of car did the man have?'

'I know nothing about cars. A *fast* car, I would say. A sports car.'

'Colour?'

'Green, possibly.'

'Did Caldwell seem scared afterwards?'

Morley looked rather hostilely at Reynolds. 'He was never scared. What would be the worst that could happen to him?'

'He could be killed for what he knew.'

'What he *knew* was that whatever followed after death would be good.'

'And what *would* follow?'

'Love.'

'What did the man look like?'

'Handsome, I suppose. Well-dressed. He looked a bit like you, only twenty years older. He wore a coat exactly like yours.'

41

While approaching the M1 after taking his leave of Morley, Reynolds had turned on his phone. It had been off ever since the flight. There was one message: from Detective Sergeant Ibbotson. How had it gone in Carlton? A regular Yorkshire terrier, this bloke. There was nothing from Clifford. Reynolds called Ibbotson, told him as little as possible; verified that Quinn had never been in touch. ('Hold on, wasn't he the guy who got shot?' Ibbotson had said, and it had then been very difficult to get him off the phone.)

Reynolds put his phone on the passenger seat of the Saab, together with the bundle in the Sainsbury's bags. He'd had to practically prise them out of Morley's hands. Reynolds had suggested to Morley that he and the sisters of Caldwell might like to leave Carlton for a few days, but Morley was having none of that.

An hour later, Reynolds was doing ninety southbound on the fast lane of the M1 when a little grey Porsche appeared to drop from the sky into the space immediately behind him. Reynolds braked hard, veered into the middle lane, putting himself two feet behind a white van marked 'The Complete Building Service'. But the Porsche was now alongside him, and the window was coming down. It was Porter at the wheel. His head flicked towards Reynolds, as Reynolds veered left again, into the slow lane, where an exit was immediately available, the first of two that were coming up. Reynolds took the exit, noticing the word 'Worksop' on the sign and 'South . . .' somewhere. He was coming up to a roundabout. He took an exit at random to 'Market . . .' somewhere, and he accelerated again. He was apparently on the A614. No sign of the Porsche. Here was another roundabout. He took the first left. He was on a smaller road, with occasional houses, a 50 mph sign. He slowed to sixty, and an alarm sounded. He was low on petrol. He glanced from the gauge to the rear-view: the Porsche was fifty yards behind, the low-slung lights hoovering up the road. He accelerated to a hundred. Another roundabout was approaching. How had he been followed? He glanced down at his phone, reached out and turned it off while accelerating to a hundred and twenty. The road was about to fork, but he had to give way whichever fork he took. He took the left fork without giving way and was quite surprised to find himself still alive. He was doing a hundred alongside a football pitch. No sign of the Porsche. Two turns later and he was very near Mansfield. He rejoined the M1 somewhere near Nottingham. No sign of the Porsche. He had failed to get the registration.

42

After escaping the Porsche, and Porter, Reynolds pulled into what might have been Beeston services and bought a pay-as-you-go mobile. He saved his contacts to the SIM on his smartphone and put the SIM into the new phone. That required turning on the smartphone but only for a second. He then called Ibbotson, who'd been on the point of going to bed. But he was immediately galvanised by what Reynolds had to say. Reynolds had asked Ibbotson to send a patrol car up to Carlton High Top. A bad man might be heading up there.

If Porter had been tracking Reynolds by his phone he wouldn't know for sure that Reynolds had been at Carlton; Porter would only have picked him up southbound on the M1, when he'd switched the phone on, but Porter might guess where he'd been. Reynolds assumed Porter was operating from his house in Northumberland, which was after all the county immediately north of North Yorkshire. It was import-ant to find out whether he'd gone back there, or continued south to London. Reynolds ought to go to the Missing and Wanted at the Yard, who'd then put Porter on the National Police Database. There might be reasonable suspicion enough for an arrest – but then again for what? Certainly there wasn't the evidence for a charge, and Porter would probably flee the country after being released. Reynolds mentioned something of this to Ibbotson, and it seemed Ib-botson could help. North Yorkshire was always doing joint ops with Northumberland. He'd get onto one of his mates up there, and he'd find out whether the bad man was at home, but for that he'd need a name. So Reynolds gave the name.

Reynolds continued south in the Saab. He replayed the moment that Porter had turned his long, red, horse-like head towards him as they'd raced side by side. Porter's face had betrayed intense concentration amounting to enjoyment. He must be the man who'd shot Quinn. He had the nerve, the weapons training . . . and why else would he be so well paid? The estate in Northumberland, and every new car that he produced, was further evidence of his guilt. Reynolds was now very far out on a limb indeed. He didn't know what Porter had meant to do had he caught up with him, but he was undoubtedly now in danger. If he went to Croft about it, he'd be taken off the case, such as it was. Any substantive conversation with Croft would surely have to result in the arrest of Anna Samarina, for the theft of the diamond at least. It would also have to include his discoveries about the suspicious movements of Quinn, and the likely complicity of Clifford.

Reynolds was at his flat by 3 a.m.

There was no Porsche outside the door, but Caroline had visited in his absence and removed further items of furniture and all the wine. So Reynolds drank two glasses of Marsala, which they'd bought to make an ambitious stew about three months before, and went to sleep. At 10 a.m., it was Eddie Ibbotson's turn to wake Reynolds. Graham Porter was at home or, as Ibbotson put it, 'on his farm'. ('Can I speak to the owner of the property?' some Northumbrian constable had been sent to ask. He'd then handed Porter a leaflet warning of door-to-door conmen.) Reynolds imagined that Porter would have looked tired.

He himself was tired, and it turned out that Caroline had also taken all the coffee. When he stepped out of the front door, he saw the Saab. It was like a woman he'd spent the night with . . . but now the two had nothing to say to each other. He'd wait until Manchester came asking for it back.

At eleven o'clock Down Street was empty and dark under the rain, except for the glow of the Mini-Mart, where he bought a coffee and a bun. Emerging from the shop, he took out the cheap phone and called Anna Samarina. No answer. He looked up at the office window, and Clifford stood there, looking down at him. It was as though she hadn't moved since he'd left for France.

By the time he'd climbed the stairs she was sitting at her desk, arms already folded. It was as if she knew he was going to challenge her. He gave her the bare outline of his adventures in France and Yorkshire, and his discovery about the two Samarins. He had not so far mentioned the magazine at the Hotel des Etrangers, which proved that Quinn had been there, or his belief that Quinn had also been in Carlton High Top.

He now did so.

'Quinn was on the take,' he said.

Clifford unfolded her arms, only to refold them. She looked down at her lap, as if mustering her forces. She looked up.

'And what evidence do you have for that?'

'He never declared the trip to France in the hospitality register. Perhaps he told you, but you never told me. I think they made him an offer, and I think he accepted it. I believe you know this.'

'What do you think he accepted?'

'I don't know. Cash. Diamonds. He'd be perfectly capable of concealing whatever it was. He'd found out that Anna Samarina . . .'

'Whom I assume you slept with in the chateau, making yourself an unreliable witness.'

'I did not sleep with her. Quinn discovered that she'd stolen the yellow diamond, and that gave him leverage over some of the richest men in London. He wanted some of their money. Why wouldn't he? Look at his lifestyle. Membership of Annabel's, and God knows how many other clubs. He likes paintings, expensive food and drink, good clothes, vintage cars. He does everything in the most expensive possible way. He's not going to inherit anything from his father. The money on the mother's side has gone to a man with four children. You're not telling me Quinn wasn't thousands of pounds in debt?'

'If he was "on the take" as you put it, then it didn't do him much good, did it? Since he got shot.'

'He wasn't necessarily shot by the people who bribed him.'

'Then who did shoot him?'

'Perhaps it was Barney Barnes.'

She did not so much frown as scowl. 'Barnes? Why? There's a strong suspicion he was on the take himself, twenty-five years ago.'

'And look at all the grief he got for it.'

'So Barnes shot Quinn because he was jealous that Quinn had got away with being corrupt?'

'It's not impossible.'

'It's *nearly* impossible.'

After a while, Reynolds said, 'I agree, it's *more* likely

that Quinn was shot by someone acting for the Russians he was investigating.'

'By the girl, perhaps.'

Reynolds reminded her about the fashion show at Heathrow.

'Then by Porter, who came after you on the motorway. Or Rostov, or Samarin himself.' She stood and walked over to the window, looked down at the Mini-Mart. 'Do you want another coffee?'

'No,' said Reynolds. It was important she didn't have time to collect her thoughts. She'd do anything to protect Quinn, or to protect his reputation.

She said, 'You still haven't told me why they shot Quinn if he was on their side.'

'Maybe they recruited Quinn. They knew this Caldwell in Yorkshire had something on them. They asked Quinn if he would get rid of him. He was seen talking to Caldwell on the weekend before he disappeared, and he was in Yorkshire on the weekend he was last seen. I also think Quinn had been driving his car through those woods. That's how it got damaged. There might have been an element of blackmail. Perhaps Quinn had taken money off them already, or maybe he did it for an even bigger payday. Either way they'd want rid of him once he'd done what they wanted.'

Clifford walked back to her desk. 'And how do you think he killed this poor man in Carlton Old Place or whatever it's called?'

'He could get the old man's confidence, as a policeman. Maybe he was paid to find out what he knew; then he shot him when he was out on one of his walks.'

'Shot him with what?'

'The Glock that he'd booked out and never returned, and that you say can't be found. I don't know how much you know about all this, but you cut two pages out of his notebook, and you didn't want me to go into his bedroom in his father's house.'

Victoria Clifford reached into her handbag. 'I was lying about the Glock. Here it is.'

It was in her hand, with silencer attached.

Reynolds thought: *This is it. There's nothing to say that she was here, and she won't be in the frame, since any number of other people want me dead.*

She was fishing in her handbag with her left hand while holding the gun in her right. She produced a zippered pouch of good leather: her make-up bag. She turned towards Reynolds, walked towards him. She placed the pistol on his desk. She turned towards the little mirror on the mantelpiece and began applying her make-up.

'It's such a revolting day, I need cheering up. I'm off to lunch at Green's. Do you want to come? Bring the pistol if you like.'

43

Green's was only five minutes from Down Street. Clifford had walked under her umbrella, which – she prided herself – was a very good umbrella, the shift being made of a single piece of sycamore, and easily big enough to accommodate two. But Reynolds chose to walk outside it. So Reynolds got wet.

It was principally a fish restaurant, so Reynolds naturally ordered the sausages. It was all she could do to get that one word out of him. She herself had two starters: crab bisque and mackerel pâté. Reynolds refused a drink. She had a glass of Sauvignon – a big one.

Victoria Clifford had always liked the stately, calm, green-and-cream interior of Green's. She and Quinn used to go regularly in the early evening: not for dinner, but for the pre-dinner 'offer' of a glass of wine and three oysters for ten pounds. She mentioned this to Reynolds. 'Ten pounds,' she said. 'It's not completely unreasonable, is it?'

He muttered something sullenly.

'You see, Quinn's policy,' she continued, 'and *my* policy to some extent, was to enjoy the good things in life in a modest way. Before we died, you see. Neither of us has children; neither runs a car, at least not in London. We don't have mortgages. Mine's paid off and Quinn rents – and he's not paying much, as I told you. What's an occasional purchase of a good coat, or even a nice painting, compared to the thousands people lay out on mortgages and school fees?'

'Membership of Annabel's doesn't come cheap,' Reynolds said, in a truculent, northern way.

'You know nothing about it,' said Clifford. 'The sub stays at whatever rate you start out paying. Quinn joined in 1971 or so, when the sub was about fifty pounds. That's what he's been paying every year since. He thought in hundreds, not millions. It's the difference between old Mayfair and new.'

'Why did you cut the pages out of the notebook?'

'I did do that, yes.'

'I know you did.'

'He'd been invited to that same hotel in France by Samarin. Like you, they flew him from Northolt. I wasn't supposed to know, but I heard him take the call, and I saw him jot down the details on a page in the floppy. It was important you didn't know about it.'

'Why?'

'It would have put you off your stride. You'd have started investigating *Quinn*. He went on the weekend of the eighth and ninth of November. As I've told you, Quinn stopped talking to me about this case at the start of October. I thought they'd try the same with you as whatever they'd tried with him, and I wanted to know what that was. But I don't think they took him to the chateau. And of course, it would have been a long shot to offer him the girl. I think he stayed overnight at the hotel. It's possible they offered him the same job they offered you. He might have been rather better at it, with all due respect. He's not nearly as stupid as you . . . seem to think.'

But she was thinking of the painting: the bloody painting in the cupboard.

'Why did he go?' asked Reynolds.

'So as not to cause offence or damage working relation-ships. Unlike you he had the confidence to do it without asking permission.'

'Tell me what he knew.'

'Well . . .'

'With nothing missed out.'

'When I brought you into the unit, all *I* knew was that he'd figured out Samarin's daughter had stolen the diamond. He began investigating the Samarins and he came to be-lieve, or perhaps confirmed what he'd suspected for years: that Samarin was sitting on a big secret. I now see – from what you discovered in the London Library – that he knew a Russian journalist called Max Aktin had been on to it; and that he suspected the old man in Carlton knew about it as well.'

'He was seen talking to that old man on the weekend after he was in France. What do you think he was saying to him?'

'In light of what you've said, I think he was trying to find out what he knew; or was trying to warn him. And the man was refusing to say what he knew, and refusing to be warned. I don't think there was anything more Quinn could do.'

'He could have taken the whole thing to Croft; got a wit-ness protection order for Caldwell.'

'I don't think Caldwell wanted to be a witness. As for Croft, Quinn had to be careful what he told him. Anyone else brought into this would have started by charging Anna Samarina with murder over the killing of Holden.'

'Except me.'

Clifford said, 'It was necessary to bring in someone

who would proceed with sensitivity. That way there'd be a chance of getting at the big thing . . . Are you sure you won't have a glass of wine?'

A rather corny move, but he accepted.

Reynolds' new phone then gave its unfamiliar beep. He had a text message. After he'd read it, he said. 'Forensics. They found a tracking app in my other phone.'

'Did you leave it lying around in the presence of the Russians?'

'There were a few times they could have taken it out of my coat pocket. It only takes a second to put it in. You connect the phone to a laptop and press "send".'

'Pudding?' she said. He shook his head, and she called for the bill. 'The big secret,' she said. 'It all comes down to the missing little finger?'

Reynolds explained his theory, based on what he'd seen at Carlton. It took quite a while. When he'd finished, she said, 'I think that's probably about right. We'll know for sure very soon.'

He frowned at her. '*How* will we know for sure?'

But then his cheap phone spoke up again, and this time it was a call. At first, he obviously wasn't going to take it, but when he saw the number he murmured an apology and stepped outside.

44

Peter Almond had been smoking a cigarette in his work-shop while reading the *Evening Standard*. He had been smoking and reading the *Standard* for some time, never progressing beyond a single small news item. 'A murder enquiry was launched after a man was found dead in an east London street on Sunday . . . The victim has been named as Ronald Cooper, 65. It is believed that Mr Cooper was the victim of a violent robbery . . . A police spokesman said, "We would like to speak to anyone who has know-ledge of this incident . . . Anyone with information is urged to call *Crimestoppers* . . ."'

Cooper could cause no further trouble for Almond. But Almond was now more concerned about the people who'd caused trouble for *Cooper*. It looked as though the plan was to take out anyone who might know about the killing of the boy Holden. It seemed highly possible to Almond that he would be next, and maybe his family (whereas Cooper had had no family). He also had the police on his back. He couldn't keep dodging this Detective Inspector Blake Reynolds. He was in danger of looking like a party to these killings, whereas in fact his role in all this was utterly peripheral. What had he done when you came down to it? He'd made a copy of a stone. Almond lit another Silk Cut and dialled the number left by Reynolds. As soon as Reynolds picked up, he regretted calling, but by then it was too late.

'Hold on please,' Reynolds said. 'I'm in a restaurant. I'll step outside.' There was then some whispering to a woman. Almond couldn't help wondering whether this was all being subsidised by public money.

'You've been trying to get in touch with me,' said Almond, when he had Reynolds' full attention. 'Sorry about the delay in getting back to you but I've been away.'

'Thanks for calling,' said Reynolds.

Almond noticed that Reynolds then didn't say anything.

Almond said, 'What was it regarding?'

'The theft of a diamond, Mr Almond, in which a real stone was substituted for a fake. Your name was mentioned as someone who could produce good copies of stones.' Had Almond detected a professional compliment? 'This theft might be related to some more serious matters,' Reynolds continued, and Almond saw the first glimmerings of a deal. He could open up a little.

'A man was killed last Sunday in east London,' Almond said. 'Have you heard about this? His name was Ronald Cooper.'

No reply from Reynolds, so Almond continued:

'I thought I'd better call you because Cooper came to me with an unusual request back in September. He wanted me to make a duplicate of a diamond.'

'And you've called me now because this man is dead?'

'I'm calling because *you* called me, but this has come up in the mean time.'

Reynolds asked, 'Why did he commission the duplicate stone?'

'I don't know. People want stones duplicated all the time. So they can wear them quite casually in public, or so their wives can. Or maybe he wanted to use it in his act. He was a magician.'

'A magician.'

Clearly, this was all news to Reynolds, who was having to think on his feet. He said, 'I assume this Cooper owned the stone he wanted duplicated.'

'Well,' said Almond, 'I'm not sure.'

'But he must have brought it to you if he wanted it copied.'

'He brought me a photograph of it.'

Copying was often done from blown-up photographs, Almond reasoned, even when the original was right there on the workbench.

Reynolds said, 'So that was the first time you'd seen the stone? I want you to be sure about this.'

'Are you going to read me my rights?'

'This is an informal chat, not an interview under caution. You can tell me whatever you want, and you can deny it all later if you want.'

'You're not recording me?'

'I'd have told you if I was. Mr Almond, can you tell me anything about a young man called John-Paul Holden?'

Almond put out his cigarette. Lit another one. He said, 'Holden was a client of mine. I read about what happened. Appalling business.'

'A client. You sold him more than one stone?'

As a matter of fact, Almond had done: the two principals cut from the yellow rough. Why not admit it? That would muddy the waters. The rough was illegally traded, but it sounded as though Reynolds wouldn't be too concerned about that.

Almond said, 'I sold him various stones, yes. Thinking about it, there may have been a similarity between the duplicate that Cooper wanted, and one of those I sold to Holden.'

'How many stones did you sell to Holden?'

'I think – two.'

'What sort of stones?'

'Fancy yellows. Between two and two-and-a-half carat.'

'In other words two diamonds that could be used in engagement rings?'

'Yes. I set them myself.'

'Do you know what became of these stones?'

'No idea. But I began to wonder about Cooper. It's possible he was up to no good. In retrospect, I see that I shouldn't have got involved with him. I thought he was rather strange, something of a fantasist, and I wasn't sure about the company he kept . . . as far as I knew it.'

'Do you have anyone in particular in mind?'

'I would have to think very carefully. It wouldn't be right for me to start casting aspersions all over the place. It could be very dangerous for the people concerned, and for me.'

Reynolds said, 'Are you worried for your own safety, Mr Almond?'

'Well, I've done nothing to anyone.'

'Even so. I can send an officer round to talk to you about witness protection.'

Looking down at the *Standard* cutting, another thought occurred to Almond. Had Cooper simply been flashing the stone, and then been robbed of it by any common or garden thug? If anyone was destined to be mugged it was Cooper. Almond suddenly decided on a Christmas holiday. The kids were off school. His wife had been complaining about how they never went anywhere. Two weeks abroad. That would give him time to think, and a place of safety.

'I have a holiday booked,' said Almond, 'I'm going away tomorrow. Can we speak later?'

45

Reynolds walked back into Green's restaurant, where Victoria Clifford was looking thoughtful, and possibly worried. She'd made some sort of a case for the defence, but he still wasn't sure about her integrity or Quinn's. However, she did have a smartphone. Sitting back down at the table, Reynolds said, 'That was Almond, the jeweller Barnes told me about.' He then asked her to look up Ronald Cooper. As she did so, he said, 'Almond sold John-Paul Holden the engagement ring with the yellow diamond in it. He said a magician then came and asked him to duplicate that stone.'

It was beginning to sound like a fairy tale, he knew.

'A magician?' she said. 'Was he the one who did the switch?'

Half a minute later, Clifford looked up from her phone. 'A violent mugging, apparently. He doesn't appear to have a website, but there's an article about him.' She handed over the phone. The article was from some other magician's website. It was headed: 'Self-declared old dog learns new trick!' A photograph of a smiling bald man was captioned, 'Sleight of hand master, Ronald Cooper.'

'I told you it was a wig,' she said. 'Do you think he was killed by the Russians? Because he'd facilitated the robbery for the girl?'

Reynolds eyed her. He would not believe that Anna Samarina was a killer or had anything to do with killing. He asked Clifford to put the name Ronald Cooper into

Crimintel. This took a little longer, since she would have to log in. When she looked up again, she said, 'A man's been arrested for it. Drug and assault convictions. Shopped by his girlfriend.' And she read out the details. Reynolds was delighted to hear about this unpleasant-sounding pair – Mark and Yvonne by name – because they were extremely unlikely to be anything to do with the Russian milieu of Anna Samarina.

Reynolds then said, 'Almond also told me he sold *two* yellow diamonds to John-Paul Holden.'

'Yes,' said Clifford, who was paying the bill, 'I was beginning to think that might be the case.'

'What do you mean? And what did you mean when you said we'd soon find out for certain about the big secret?' Reynolds had the uneasy feeling that his own discoveries were lagging some way behind those of his personal assistant.

She said, 'We haven't had coffee. So let's go to Claridge's.'

They walked, sharing her umbrella. But she refused to speak on the way. It was preposterous but quite impressive. Her black boots, Reynolds noticed, were worn down at the heels. She wore what looked like a highwayman's coat, and she did look a little like . . . well, a highway *woman*, with her great confidence, her touching smallness and determined walk; and the tokenistic ponytail, Reynolds had just noticed, held by a funereal black ribbon.

In Claridge's, the lobby fire burned brightly, if too cleanly. It seemed to frolic in its pristine hearth, a fire kept as a pet. The Claridge's staff knew Victoria Clifford, and she was relieved of her umbrella as if it were a hospital patient in need of the tenderest and most urgent attention.

They were seated in the green-and-white lounge that Reynolds now learnt was called The Foyer. Everything shone with Christmas lustre. Clifford didn't bother with a menu but ordered two black teas rather than coffee.

'You don't want milk,' she informed Reynolds.

It was four-thirty. Some of the other tea-takers looked so sleek and refined they might have been part of a different species. Soon after their own tea arrived, Clifford touched Reynolds' arm. He looked up and saw an Indian woman of about twenty. Life must be strange for her, Reynolds thought. Her life must be inverted somehow, since she approximated so closely to the ideal of the opposite sex, except that she was a little too thin. At the moment she sat down, a long pink drink was brought for her, and Reynolds saw her for who she was: the girlfriend of Rakesh Dutta, the Indian hedge-funder who'd blamed the murder of Holden on Eugene Crawford.

'Not the girlfriend,' said Clifford. 'Sister. She's called Robin Dutta. Don't ask me how that came about. I think one of her parents is part-English.'

Robin Dutta took a sip of her pink lemonade, and half smiled at Reynolds. Every nuance of her face would have been a very good photograph. A second waiter was advancing towards her. 'Now this proves she actually eats,' Clifford was saying. 'She's having the apricot and caraway cake.'

After giving profuse thanks to the waiter, which must surely have set him up for the entire Christmas season, Robin Dutta ate a forkful of the cake with great grace but no false gentility.

'She's got a criminal record as long as your arm,' said Clifford.

'Come off it,' said Reynolds.

'All right. She's got one conviction. For assault – against a boyfriend. Can't remember the defence, but it kept her out of jail. Something psychiatric. I don't know whether she was engaged to Holden, but she was going out with him.'

'*How* do you know?'

'Asking around. Her brother's obviously very loyal. It's interesting that he tried to palm you off with Crawford rather than directing you towards Anna Samarina. But I suppose he wanted to avoid the whole question of Holden's love life.'

'One interview under caution ought to do it,' Clifford was saying. 'Oh, and look at her ring.'

46

They returned to the office at a quarter to six. At five past six, Clifford had received a delivery by motorcycle courier from forensics at the Yard. It contained two memory sticks. Both, Clifford explained, contained the same material: recovered and cleaned-up versions of data that had been in . . . not a floppy book, but a floppy *disk*, an almost equally ancient method of data storage. This, she continued, had been given to her at a sort of patisserie off Edgware Road on the day before Reynolds had left for France. One memory stick was for Reynolds, one for her. She proposed that they now read what was on them. But first, she gave him the background.

Using the files at Paddington Library, Clifford had tracked down the elderly common-law wife of the late Max Aktin. Since she did not have the same surname as Aktin, that had not been easy. Nor was the woman Russian, but Hungarian. She, like Aktin, had been a Jewish refugee from the Soviet bloc. It appeared that Quinn had also tracked her down, and the woman had been trying to decide whether to agree to his suggestion of a meeting. Clifford had talked her into a meeting with the promise of a nice cake and one thousand pounds in cash, the payment authorised by Croft. In return, the woman had given Clifford the floppy disk.

After an hour of work, Reynolds had formed his own digest of the material on the disk.

Max Aktin was anti-Russian, full stop. He had been

against the Soviets; later he was against the oligarchs, and he devoted his life to chronicling the iniquities of both. The file – written mainly in English – contained numerous references to a paper archive, the whereabouts of which was currently unknown, and which may have been destroyed in the fire that killed Aktin, and hospitalised his common-law wife.

Andrei Samarin was probably born in 1954, possibly on one of two islands in the Kara Sea. His mother died when he was very young, and he was brought up by his father, who was perhaps originally a fisherman. That job was incompatible with raising a son, so he moved to the mainland, to Tomsk. He worked – in fairly menial roles – on the railways: on a branch line of the Trans-Siberian. Sometimes his work took him further east along the railway, and his son would be educated in rather makeshift railway schools, but Andrei Samarin was a bright boy. It was at this time that he caught frostbite in his right little finger, which had to be amputated.

In his early teens, Samarin was sent to a boarding school for gifted children in Novosibirsk, and here he befriended a certain Pyotr Genkin, who looked similar. They shared a passion for literature and architecture. In 1971, when he was seventeen, Samarin won an essay prize and was selected to travel to the UK under the auspices of the Soviet Embassy and a peace campaign by British Quakers. Pyotr Genkin also did well in the essay competition but it was decided that only one student should be selected for the exchange from that particular school.

Genkin differed from the young Samarin in that he had a mother but not a father, the father having died of cancer. Genkin's mother was a scientist: a geologist at the university complex of Akademgorodok in Novosibirsk. Her work took her all over Siberia, and so the young Genkin, like the young Samarin, was seldom in the same place for long.

Preparation for the exchange trip brought Andrei Samarin and possibly also Genkin – even though he didn't ultimately travel – into contact with a KGB officer from Moscow called Viktor Rostov.

Max Aktin had discovered little about the next twenty years of Samarin's life. He was possibly a student of architecture and a teacher of English and French. He may have lived in France for a while, when rules on foreign travel were relaxed under Gorbachev. At the first opportunity, he went into business. It appeared that Samarin actually set up his frozen-food business a couple of years before Yeltsin's thoroughgoing economic liberalisation of the early nineties, and it was an immediate success. Samarin received protection against gangsters from Rostov, with whom he'd become re-acquainted.

In 1992 Samarin acquired a chateau west of Nice, and he lived there reclusively for much of the time while Rostov oversaw the business in Russia. By 1992, Samarin had also acquired a daughter. She was probably born in Russia, to a woman who may have died in childbirth. The two were never married. In 1993 – according to Aktin – Samarin and Rostov had an argument at the chateau. Having begun his move into coal, Samarin wanted to pay Rostov off, and make the new departure on his own. But Rostov wanted to continue as a business partner. Rostov killed Samarin, or arranged for him to be killed – and by now, a former Guards officer and amateur racing driver called Graham Porter was probably on the staff.

Shortly before his death, Samarin had made the fatal

mistake of resuming his acquaintance with his equally clever, equally shy, and very similar-looking friend, Pyotr Genkin. He had sought his assistance with a book about architecture. A suicide by drowning in the Ob river of Western Siberia was mocked up for Genkin, who was meanwhile smuggled to the Riviera, where he was substituted for Samarin, and given his name. There was a difference of appearance around the mouth, and Genkin – as Samarin – grew a light beard. There was the problem of the missing finger. Genkin agreed to undergo an amputation, and a French doctor called Ballard amputated the left finger instead of the right. At the centre of the whole conspiracy, a simple mistake over left and right.

There was also the problem of the daughter, which turned out *not* to be such a problem. As Aktin had written, 'Her father was changed.' She was simply transferred to the new man, who doted on her, presumably stricken by conscience. It was very likely – Aktin surmised – that the girl was too young to know.

Genkin was an excellent choice as stand-in for Samarin. He, like his predecessor, was intelligent, discreet and reclusive. But Genkin lacked Samarin's flare for business, and he and Rostov made their money from implementing the late Samarin's ideas with little further creativity of their own.

As Aktin had written (ascribing the phrase with some bitterness to Lenin), 'You can't make an omelette without breaking eggs.' Some people knew about the switch. Most were paid off. Samarin's aunt, who had largely raised him, became a very rich woman, and moved to Paris. Unfortunately a few people had to be killed. In 1999, the doctor called Ballard died in a suspicious car crash at a spot called Coudoux on Autoroute 8 in the south of France. One of the students who'd travelled on the exchange with Samarin died of an unfathomable wasting disease in Moscow in 1993. Aktin made the case for a couple of other killings in Russia.

Then Aktin himself had died in a fire occurring in the small hours at his flat in Conduit Gardens in 2001. Victoria Clifford had not yet unearthed the coroner's report but she had spoken to her contact in the London Fire Brigade. Evidently the coroner had recorded a verdict of death by misadventure, this largely on the basis of the LFB's own report, which had concluded that a bird had picked up a lighted cigarette from a patch of nearby grass – the actual dusty garden of Conduit Gardens – and dropped it down the chimney of the building. This had happened on one previous occasion, when a small and non-fatal fire had resulted. Clifford's LFB contact remembered the Conduit Gardens blaze. Aktin's roof was accessible from other, nearby roofs. He had told her, 'You wouldn't have to be Spiderman to get up there.'

And then there had been the 'new' killings, post-dating the ones Aktin had unearthed. First came the arranged 'disappearance' of Joseph Caldwell in the village of Carlton High Top, necessitated by the fact that Quinn had tracked him down. Then came the shooting of Quinn himself.

Reynolds looked across the office to where Clifford sat. She'd already finished reading her file. She smiled at him, and then his phone rang. When he saw the number, his heart beat fast: Anna Samarina. She wanted to meet him straight away. Somewhat amazingly, she suggested the barriers at Green Park Tube station, and Reynolds said he could be there in ten minutes. When he told Clifford what had occurred, she said quite casually, 'Are you going to take the Glock?'

47

As he approached Green Park station, Piccadilly seemed to become progressively brighter. It was like an *ascent* from dowdy Down Street: past the Park Lane Hotel, and then the side streets with the beautiful names: Clarges Street, Half Moon Street. He had not taken up Clifford's offer of the Glock pistol. He had broken free.

There was a festive crowd outside Green Park station, and a festive crowd inside. Reynolds approached the barriers. He could not see Samarina, but then she came up to him from behind. She touched his shoulder and they kissed. Only on the cheeks, but they hadn't needed to think about it. She wore her leather jacket. He said, 'I thought you were coming by Tube.'

She seemed puzzled. 'Oh yes, because this is a *Tube station*! I came by taxi. It's my favourite form of public transport.'

'Where do you want to go?' he asked.

'Doesn't matter.'

He believed she had decided to talk. Well, he had to believe it. Everything depended on her talking. Surely, she knew her father had been 'changed', that her father was not her father? Their physical similarities amounted to little more than the fact that they were both small, slight, good-looking and neat-faced people. He reasoned that she had already been trying to tell him what she knew. Andrei Samarin found the quality of 'innocence' in *Dead Souls*.

Well, Chichikov, the central character, had not been party to the deaths of the dead people he exploited. Reynolds had also . . . not actually read, but read *about*, the other work by Gogol that she had mentioned, *The Overcoat*. That might be a good place to start, he thought, as they climbed the steps of the station.

On Piccadilly, they turned left – east. They walked past some Russians who were climbing out of two white Rolls-Royces.

'Of course, the post-Soviet flashiness is over now,' Anna said, smiling.

Reynolds said, 'I was reading *The Overcoat*.'

'Not only reading but wearing,' she said, because he had on the Aquascutum. 'Is very nice,' she said, in her parody-Russian voice.

'Do you know why your father likes that story so much?'

'You tell me,' she said.

'Well, it's a dreamy story about a clerk called Akaky. He's a copyist. He never does any original work, but only makes very good copies. His coat is threadbare so he saves up for a new one.'

'As you have done,' she put in.

'He's robbed of the coat. He dies. His ghost returns to steal overcoats from men on the streets.'

'So far,' she said, 'you have got a B in your exam.'

'The overcoat made Akaky a different person, more dynamic. So there is the theme of the doppelganger, or double: "Dvoinik" in Russian. Of course there's a Dostoevsky novel all about that.'

'Of course,' she said. 'B plus.'

Reynolds wasn't sure where all that had got them. They

were crossing Piccadilly. They began walking down St James's Street, going south. This was quieter. They passed Fox's, the cigar place where he'd spoken to Eugene Crawford. It was closed. They stopped in front of Berry Brothers, the wine merchants. It resembled the Old Curiosity Shop. It too was closed, and all the wine had been taken out of the window. But they had stopped and were looking in. 'Yes,' said Anna, 'some very nice wooden boxes.'

They walked on, and she put her hand in his. Shortly afterwards she turned towards him with an expression of surprise – as though she hadn't quite realised what she'd done, but was glad about it anyway. Reynolds believed he had no choice but to utter the sentence that could end his career or gain everything he wanted.

'The jewel theft,' he said. 'I can make that go away. There was a more important switch that I want to know about.'

She said nothing. They simply carried on walking. There were no more than two or three other people in the street. On the right was Le Caprice, attended by expensive cars. But they proceeded beyond – towards St James's Palace, where they turned right, into quiet, courtly Cleveland Row: a collection of mansions and palaces, outposts of royalty and the Foreign Office. They approached two Georgian houses: one was absurdly pretty: lilac-coloured; its neighbour was traditional brick but equally handsome. They were like an elegant married couple.

Blake and Anna walked through the gap between the houses, and the night before them was now darker and wilder: gas lamps, and the wind moving giant chestnut trees. They were in Green Park, the one along from

St James's Park, where Quinn had been shot. They were both Royal Parks – no CCTV. I ought not to be here, thought Reynolds. They were on a wide and gracious path bordering the dark grass. They turned left, following the gaslights. It might have been the year 1870. But then a jogger went past, and Reynolds noticed CCTV cameras above the hedges and railings to his left. They protected the gardens of the mansions that overlooked Green Park. He made sure that he and Samarina turned that way.

One of the cameras moved as the two of them went past. She had removed her hand from his, and gone on a little way. She turned around holding the gun that had obviously been between them all along. *Of course* it had been there, and as for the CCTV, she hadn't bothered about that in the jewellery shop, and it wouldn't deter her now. Well, he had gambled and he had lost. He was perfectly calm about it. Reynolds saw from the corner of his eye that a man was approaching across the grass. Reynolds turned towards the man, and made a gesture, as though trying to push him away. Reynolds turned back towards the girl, and the pointed handgun. He embarked on some rapid statement about the man coming over the grass. He was then deafened and all the birds he'd never noticed were rising up from Green Park. Anna Samarina lay on the pathway. The man on the grass was putting a Metropolitan police baseball cap on his head; he held a monstrous rifle. Another man with another rifle was coming from a different direction. There was body armour beneath their coats. All the birds of the park, having massed in the sky directly above Reynolds and his dead companion, had come to an agreement: they wanted none of what was going on with the humans below, so they flew off to the south.

48

As they progressed along frosty Bond Street, Clifford was looking in the shop windows. Most had been cleared of their expensive trinkets. But it was something to do while Dorothy's so-called partner – the man whom Clifford always thought of as 'The Spouse Mouse', being unable to keep his actual name in her mind – held forth:

'Of *that* place,' he was saying, 'it really can be said, *"le patron mange ici."'*

If by 'that place' he had meant the restaurant in which they'd just eaten Christmas lunch, the remark might have been tolerable, but he had taken them all to some other French restaurant unpromisingly located near Tottenham Court Road, which, as he rightly said, had been 'deeply disappointing'. An apology might have been in order; instead he was claiming the credit for knowing about other, better places.

They were now, as he pompously had it, undergoing their 'post-prandial penance'. A walk. It was three-thirty, and they were heading north along Bond Street. Clifford had dragged them over this way. She would not have done so, had the Mouse not said, as they'd quit the restaurant, 'I suppose you'll want to avoid Mayfair, Vicky.'

He wasn't allowed to call her Vicky.

The Mouse had clearly been under orders from Dorothy to behave over lunch, and when he said, 'So it was effectively down to you – your phone call – that the armed response unit was sent?' Dorothy had been trying to signal him not to ask this.

'The decision was taken by an Assistant Commissioner,' said Clifford. 'But it was at my suggestion.'

The Mouse said, 'I'm not sure I could have made that suggestion, or taken that decision.'

Clifford was quite *sure* he couldn't have.

Dorothy said, 'Victoria knew the girl was dangerous, darling. She had to make that call.'

'No,' Clifford said. 'I didn't know she was dangerous. I couldn't decide about that. But she had one fixture in her life, and that was the man who masqueraded as her father.'

'It was, you know, *love*,' Rachel Reade put in, with a rather fetching sad smile.

Clifford said, 'It occurred to me that Reynolds was going to be undermining her . . .'

'*Profoundly*,' Dorothy put in.

Clifford wasn't sure whether she preferred her friends when they were being antagonistic as opposed to (as they would say) 'supportive'. But she supposed she ought to be grateful, particularly for the companionship of Rachel Reade, who had insisted on moving in with her, and cooking numerous casseroles, while the papers were full of the whole business – as indeed they still were.

'You see,' Rachel was explaining to Dorothy and the Mouse, 'Anna Samarina had attempted to find another anchor in her engagement to John-Paul Holden. But when that failed she was thrown back on her father.'

Clifford had suggested as much to her in the days after the shooting, but there was really no 'you see' about it, because the understanding of one human by another was surely a matter of the finest nuance. She believed that Reynolds overestimated the influence he was likely to have over the girl. Possibly he believed she loved him, and was therefore safe. This negative assessment of hers was influenced by the fact that Reynolds had been wrong about Quinn being 'on the take'. But he had been *nearly* right about that, and he had been absolutely right about a good deal else.

Part of Rachel Reade's programme of support had involved the two of them jointly trying to value Clifford's paintings, and Clifford hadn't minded looking at art now, having solved the problem of Quinn's small painting.

She had seen him carrying a wrapped-up painting when climbing into a taxi on Berkeley Square on the evening of Friday 14 November. She had seen him by accident. She thought he had already left for the north, but it seemed he had collected a painting on the way. Five days before, he had been the guest of the Russians in the south of France – the trip she was not supposed to know about. His one material aspiration was to own good art. It would have been pushing it – even for Quinn – to have accepted a painting temporarily 'to preserve good working relationships'; to have made a pretence of being corrupt. If he had tried that, he would have needed authorisation from Croft, and no such authorisation had been asked for or received. Her suspicion that he might have given way to temptation had been minute. But she hadn't dared ask him about the painting he'd been carrying because she might have provoked a lie. While Quinn had certainly withheld data from her, he had not – as far as she knew – lied to her. She believed she would have been able to tell if he ever *did* lie, and she couldn't bear the thought of it.

Even so, forty-eight hours after the shooting of Anna Samarina – it was the day on which they'd arrested Robin Dutta, who'd confessed to the killing of John-Paul Holden – Clifford had called Charlie Quinn. She'd told him about the painting in the cupboard, of which he'd been unaware. She asked him to tear back the paper, and it turned out he knew the painting. It was by the famous Victorian landscapist, Atkinson Grimshaw, a smaller version of a painting of Scarborough Harbour that was in the Scarborough Art Gallery. Charlie Quinn had been almost tearful when he unwrapped it. Here was a version of his favourite painting by his favourite artist. 'It must have been for my birthday,' he'd said gauchely, but probably correctly.

Victoria had then called Hugh Jenkins, ex of Art and Antiques. Had Quinn ever mentioned acquiring this work? With some reluctance – 'Because I still think George is going to wake up' – Jenkins explained that he had advised Quinn of the availability of the painting, and loaned him half the asking price of thirty thousand pounds. The old man would have it for his ninetieth birthday, and until he died. Jenkins would then pay Quinn fifteen thousand for full ownership of this work by an artist he, too, very much admired.

Bond Street was largely deserted. It was a cold day of white sky. They had stopped outside Tiffany's, whose window featured a display of miniature, chalet-like white houses draped in diamond necklaces. The backing to the display suggested it was night-time in the fantastical, alpine realm. The necklaces must be paste, Clifford reasoned. Too much risk of a burglary on Christmas Day.

311

Clifford led them west, via Grafton Street and Hay Hill, into Curzon Street, where she saw a foreign-looking gent affectionately watching the automatic closure of his Rolls-Royce's boot. He was communing with his car, as a better alternative to going into some big house for a lavish but perhaps boring family party. She thought of Quinn's car. A GPS tracker had been fixed into the wheel arch, so the Russians had known he'd been in Carlton. The damage to the underside of the car was still a mystery, but she believed he'd driven through the woods to look for Caldwell, or possibly for the body of Caldwell, which had still not been found.

Clifford had now brought them to the north end of Down Street.

'Oh, *Vicky* dear,' Rachel Reade said, in a disappointed tone, having seen the street sign.

Rachel Reade was allowed to call her Vicky.

Behind the two of them, Dorothy and the Mouse were going over what had been said at lunch. Dorothy was trying to answer his questions before he put them, in a possibly provocative way, to her fragile friend.

'So Samarin's in custody?' he was saying.

'In a secure psychiatric unit, yes. They found him on the Embankment, you know that.'

'He was about to jump into the river?'

'And he'd taken a lot of pills.'

Clifford looked along Down Street. The church showed no sign of having hosted a Christmas service. The tapas bar was closed. Nobody had parked on the few parking spaces. There were just the opposing cliff faces of cavernous but reserved mansion flats, largely unoccupied, since London wasn't the right place to be on Christmas Day. Not for the well-off.

. . . And there was the closed-down Tube station. A man stood outside it. He was therefore also outside the Mini-Mart, which was possibly open, because the man seemed illuminated, in the dying day, by a spilled light.

'And they still don't know who shot George Quinn?' the Mouse was asking.

'Weren't you listening at lunch?' Dorothy was saying. 'They're now almost certain it was the English security man, Porter, but Samarin had told the girl that he himself did it.'

'Why?'

'To stop her speaking out. She was probably on the point of doing that. But Samarin knew she wouldn't say anything if she thought he'd done it.'

'And how do they know this?'

'Oh God, Geoffrey—'

That was the Mouse's name.

'I'm sorry, I'm genuinely baffled.'

'Samarin's *told* them. He's co-operating.'

'He might just be *saying* that.'

'No. They believe him.'

How strange, Clifford thought, to be them, engaged in this perpetual conclave. The man outside the Mini-Mart had not moved; he was looking upwards.

Dorothy was correct in her explanation, as far as it went. What she'd missed out was that it was Reynolds who had made the crucial breakthrough in the questioning; the crucial *dart*. Samarin hadn't *volunteered* the information about what he'd told his supposed daughter. He had been totally silent, until Reynolds had put the suggestion to him. At this, the dam had burst, because Reynolds had been correct, and Samarin, something of an intellectual snob, had respected that.

313

Samarin was happy to admit a course of action that had – he said – been intended only to keep them together, for the sake of the girl's mental health. Another way of putting it would be to say he had exploited her love for him in order to buy her silence. At what point, he had told his daughter the lie . . . that was not clear. Probably very late on. It was also unclear at what point she had learned that Samarin was not her true father. Probably she had known, in some way, for years.

The girl had fired at Reynolds at the very moment she'd been shot. This was evident not only from the spent cartridge, but also the CCTV footage. The bullet that killed her had also deflected her aim, and this had taken some of the heat out of the public outrage. Reynolds apparently maintained that Samarina would not have fired had the armed officers not been present. So was Clifford wrong to have asked for SO19, the Firearms Command, to be sent? She did not believe so for a minute. She had not had the chance to put the case to Reynolds because he – knowing she was responsible for the intervention – had refused to speak to her since the shooting. Everything she knew of his subsequent role, she'd had from Croft, or other officers. (Croft had taken her out to dinner – rather daringly at HIX Mayfair this time – to congratulate her on her own 'dart', the one concerning Robin Dutta.) Reynolds was no longer a semi-flyer, he was airborne, albeit controversially. He had taken a risk in order to crack the case, and as far as he knew, he was risking himself rather than the girl. He had turned away from her pointed gun to warn off the Met men, and he had got points for that. Chivalry was not dead after all.

In the village of Carlton, Reynolds had discovered the

motive for the cover-up; he'd had the crucial insight into the behaviour of Samarin, and this had set the man talking – for a while. Samarin had offered some help before lapsing back into his monumental depression.

'. . . And the other Russian?' the Mouse was saying.

'Rostov,' said Dorothy. 'They can't find him. They think he's gone back to Russia.'

'And the security man is the one who they arrested in Marseille a few days ago?'

'Well done, Geoffrey. His name is Porter, and he shot his way out, killing four French policemen.'

Geoffrey had no French tag for that.

That Porter had been taken into custody was also down to Reynolds, and his mixture of flare and doggedness. Having learnt that Porter was an amateur motor racer, Reynolds had mentioned his name to the editors of some of London's more traditionalist motor-racing magazines (be-cause Reynolds had Porter down as a traditionalist). One of them – the editor of something called *Motor Sport World* – came back with a ten-year-old letter to the magazine com-plaining about excessive safety precautions at some racing event. It was signed 'G. B. R. Porter, Aix-en-Provence'. The copy of the original had been kept, and a fuller address appeared on that: the name of a small village outside Aix. This was, or had subsequently become, Porter's bolthole, and it was from there that he had been taken into custody at Marseille. It wasn't Reynolds' fault that Porter had then escaped.

49

The man who'd been standing outside the Mini-Mart was now approaching. When he saw Clifford his walk slowed; but he kept on coming, and he passed her by without a word. Rachel Reade said, 'Vicky, darling, wasn't that Blake Reynolds?'

But Victoria's phone was ringing. She answered it. A man said, 'Oh hello, it's Mr Henderson here, from St Michael's Hospital.'

Mr Henderson. Because she hadn't been able to get rid of him, and consultants were not called 'doctor'.

'I'm sorry to bother you on Christmas Day. I'm calling about George Quinn—'

As he spoke on, Clifford looked back down the street towards the retreating figure of Reynolds. It had meant something to her that Reynolds – evidently alone on this Christmas Day – had returned to commune with the scene of their exciting December. She was now further gratified that he was turning his head and looking back at her. His expression from this distance was quite unfathomable, but she would settle – at the moment – for that one backward glance.